DATED CHINESE ANTIQUITIES

Sheila Riddell

DATED CHINESE ANTIQUITIES

600–1650

FABER AND FABER

London   Boston

First published in 1979
by Faber and Faber Limited
3 Queen Square London WC1N 3AU
Printed in Great Britain by
BAS Printers Limited, Over Wallop, Hampshire
All rights reserved

British Library Cataloguing in Publication Data

Riddell, Sheila
   Dated Chinese antiquities, 600–1650.
   1. Art objects, Chinese
   I. Title
   730'.0951   NK1068

   ISBN 0–571–09753–7

In
memory
of

His Majesty King Gustaf VI Adolf of Sweden

1882–1973

Contents

9

Contents

V *Ivory and Horn*

Illustrations

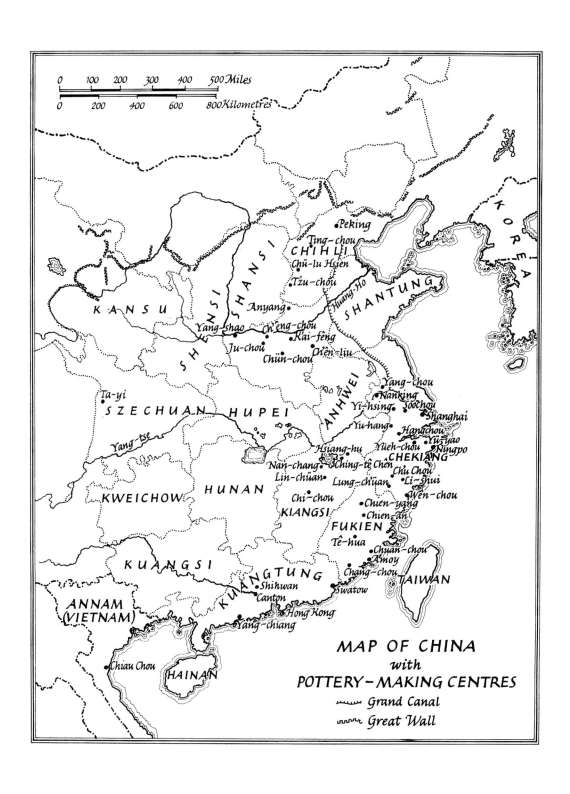

KOREA

Peking

Ting-chou

CHIHLI

Chü-lu Hsien

Tzu-chou

SHANSI

SHENSI

KANSU

Anyang

Huang-Ho

SHANTUNG

Yang-shao   Weng-chou

Ju-chou   Kai-fêng

Chün-chou   Chên-liu

Ta-yi

Yang-chou

SZECHUAN   HUPEI

ANHWEI   Nanking

Yi-hsing   Soochou

Yü-hang   Shanghai

Yang-tse

Hangchou

Hsiang-hu   Yüeh-chou   Yu-yao

Nan-chang   Ching-tê Chên   Ningpo

Lin-chüan   CHEKIANG

KWEICHOW   HUNAN   Lung-chüan   Chu Chou   Li-shui

Chi-chou   Wên-chou

KIANGSI   Chien-yang

Chien-an

FUKIEN

Tê-hua

KUANGSI   Chuan-chou   Amoy

KUANGTUNG   Chang-chou   TAIWAN

Shihwan   Swatow

Canton

ANNAM   Hong Kong

(VIETNAM)   Yang-chiang

Chiau Chou   HAINAN

MAP OF CHINA
with
POTTERY-MAKING CENTRES

〜〜〜 Grand Canal

〜〜〜 Great Wall

Introduction

China has for centuries suffered from the vicissitudes of war, invasion and internecine conflict. The resulting sense of insecurity gave rise long ago to the tradition of art-lovers acquiring objects of a portable size and cherishing them in secret. The evolution of Chinese art was widely influenced by this tradition. Artists and craftsmen cultivated their talents in the creation of small objects, easy of concealment. Hence it is that so many of the artistic treasures of China are diminutive in size though of great beauty and refinement, and that the true Chinese collector rarely shows his pieces. If they are shown at all, it is only to privileged and knowledgeable guests. The occasion is always one of ceremony. Each object is brought out from storage, carefully removed from its silk-lined box or wrapper, and passed round to the small admiring assembly of connoisseurs who handle it fondly and lovingly, and then as carefully and as lovingly it is put away before the next object is brought out. It is in fact impossible otherwise to appreciate to the full the rather precious atmosphere of these works of art, or the technical ingenuities which are concealed in their production.

The Chinese are essentially a literary nation, and literary traditions have played a predominant part in the development of Chinese art. Calligraphy itself is accounted a fine art; indeed it is the greatest of all the arts of China. To us in the West, writing is merely a convenience; to the Chinese, it is a religious cult. For them the old Western maxim, *littera scripta manet*, has a spiritual significance. The written work is esteemed in China for its permanency as well as for its inherent beauty and vitality. The great calligraphers of China were great men, great in statesmanship, in philosophy, in religion, in poetry, in scholarship. They were honoured above all others; their script was treasured and carefully imitated; their lines were remembered and repeated long after Imperial edicts were forgotten.

From the beginning of this century, the subject of Chinese antiquities has gradually emerged from relative obscurity to a role of such prominence that many diverse lines of inquiry have been assiduously developed. These have included the excavation of tombs and other sites, and have revealed a past more spectacular than the most imaginative historian could have envisaged. In many cases, the *terminus ad quem* for a tomb's entire contents has been established by the precise dating of the tomb itself.

Equally rewarding have been the technological discoveries, inspired by the quest for positive data and confirmed by scientific investigation. Careful excavation and scientific scrutiny are certainly important in determining a correct attribution and dating for a work of art, and equally so are its artistic qualities. Yet, in the final analysis, it is only the object with a contemporarily dated inscription that can be positively authenticated.

This naturally raises the question of how to establish the authenticity of an inscription. In the resolution of this all-important problem, the connoisseur must play a vital role, for without his specialized knowledge the inscribed object might well be accepted simply on its literary merits. Some methods of applying an inscription are more readily acceptable as being contemporary than others. In the case of porcelain, for instance, to be wholly convincing the characters should appear under the glaze, the alternative—though slightly less reliable—method being to inscribe the vessel in ink after firing: the potter wishing to record the appropriate reign-period—often of short duration—had on occasion to delay doing so until he was sure of his facts. That could apply equally to inscriptions incised on ivory, jade and wood. On some pieces fashioned from these delectable materials, however, the inscription appears in relief, being intended to form part of the decoration, and is thus acceptable as being contemporary with the object. This is a highly skilled technique which involves carving away the surrounding area so as to leave the decoration on a higher plane. A similar distinction is valid for lacquer. The inscription applied in colour-contrasting lacquer on a lacquered base is more acceptable than perhaps an incised mark would be. Although it is acknowledged that the method of applying an inscription is important, and that doubt is cast on some inscriptions added after objects were finished, they must certainly not be condemned on that score alone. There are extenuating circumstances, as I have said. It could possibly have happened sometimes that the craftsman who was primarily concerned with the decoration, only decided on contemplating his finished product to commemorate the event by recording the year, perhaps the month, and even the day on which his creation left his atelier. The inscriptions on some pieces are attempts to gild the lily and fail abysmally to the tutored eye, and this is why I have stressed the role that the connoisseur must play in determining the authenticity of an object. Without an inscription, certain stylistic and technical features would be the main grounds for dating a piece—to within a span of perhaps sixty years.

It is to an attempt to establish such criteria that the present volume is devoted, for it deals entirely with Chinese dated and datable art objects in all materials, and it covers the period from the seventh century to the end of the Ming Dynasty—that is, 1644. It is hoped that it may enable scholars, art historians and social scientists to assign to a specific period other works of art and artifacts, and even to date events which have so far been undatable and whose significance may not have been fully appreciated.

There have been books on related materials of contemporary date, books concerned with a single subject over its entire history, and many others that treat of a theme purely from the historian's point of view without consideration of aesthetics. But there has been no attempt to portray the art of a country over a single period of time in widely separated areas, using factual evidence supplied by contemporary inscriptions as a basis. It is just this that I hope to accomplish.

The importance of these inscribed pieces cannot be over-emphasized, for only by such records can one understand the art of China as a whole, and assess the respective merits of an object made to Imperial order and those of the work of an individual. It is for this second category that we are indebted to the Chinese scholar, who, with his somewhat unorthodox approach, has found original forms of expression. Because of his resourcefulness, we are able to appreciate the ingenuity with which an inscription can be recorded, and the imaginative use that can be made of selected materials.

The creation of art objects continued even during periods of political confusion, when life for the majority remained essentially undisturbed in spite of frequent upheavals. Those who had participated in artistic pursuits found they could still do so, and were little disorientated by events outside their own environment. It is not without interest, however, that their apparent quiescence seems to have manifested itself in the decorative motifs of ceramic wares whose inscriptions often refer to recurring conflicts between native Chinese and foreign invaders.

Such pieces give us an uncensored view of historical events and make an interesting comparison with other contemporary records. It is but one of the many revealing features of inscribed material; and it is indeed the unusual nature of the subject that has inspired Western scholars to follow the traditional approach to collecting of the Chinese antiquarian. It was such a view of the subject even more perhaps than the aesthetic appeal of the pieces that provided the creative mainspring of the collection formed by the late Sir Percival David. This he presented to the University of London, who, recognizing the tremendous academic importance of a collection which had been created for the promotion of the study and teaching of the art and culture of China, then proceeded to establish the Percival David Foundation of Chinese Art.

The collection occupies a unique place in the world of Chinese pottery and porcelain, for it combines artistic supremacy and precise documentation to an unrivalled degree. It has a higher proportion of marked and inscribed specimens than any other collection anywhere, including that of the National Palace Museum in Taiwan, the present home of the former Imperial Collection in Peking. Among the documented pieces in the Foundation are many with inscriptions contemporary with the date of their manufacture. These illustrate various interesting characteristics of the Chinese way of life at different times, and thus provide an original source of information for the history, philosophy, literature and traditions of the Chinese people, not for a remote and alien past but for the period from the early years of the

T'ang Dynasty up to the middle of the seventeenth century.

A great deal of the information contained in this volume is the result of extensive research into every aspect of the subject in which I was privileged to participate under the inspired guidance of Sir Percival David, both as his wife and as curator of his collection, during an association of some thirty years. No book, article, pamphlet or catalogue, in Chinese or a European language, did he consider too insignificant to be worthy of careful reading; for until all such works had been studied properly, it would not have been possible to assess their merits and record those which should be noted for future reference. Only by such a method of research can one elucidate the complex intricacies of this absorbing topic. I have made this point because it is desirable to establish sources for information which will not be found in the select bibliography or in any form available to the interested student.

The Chinese book I have frequently quoted from is the *Ko Ku Yao Lun (The Essential Criteria of Antiquities)*, and I have used two editions of this, the original edition of 1388 [O] (in three chapters) and an augmented edition of 1462 [A] (in thirteen chapters), both of them as translated by Sir Percival David. Unless otherwise indicated, the quotations are from the original. The author of the original edition was Ts'ao Chao and the book was written in the 'Studio of Precious Antiquities' on the fifteenth day of the third month of the twenty-first year—1388—of the Hung-wu reign-period. In his Preface, Ts'ao Chao writes: 'Whenever I came upon an object of interest, I would search through all the books and illustrated catalogues at my disposal in order to trace its origin, evaluate its quality, and determine its authenticity before I laid it aside.' This could equally well have been written by the translator of Ts'ao Chao's important work, so similar was his approach to the researching of an object of antiquity!

London, August 1978   SHEILA RIDDELL

I

Ceramics

I

YÜEH, JU AND CELADON

THE POWER OF THE FEUDAL STATES which had increased during the disintegration of the Chou Empire, reached its culmination in the Warring States period (481–221 B.C.). One of these states was Yüeh in Chekiang, with its capital at Yüeh-chou, modern Shao-hsing, where a type of proto-porcelain began to be made in the later years of the Warring States period, the manufacture of which continued indefinitely. By the Han Dynasty (206 B.C.–A.D. 220) the products had attained a notable degree of artistic competence and technical proficiency. Pottery vessels, it is well known, were the prototypes of bronze, just as these became in turn the prototypes of pottery. It is this second stage that we reach in the Han Dynasty, so that the most important of the pottery vessels made in that period copied the form and decoration of bronze ancestors. This ware was hardly surpassed by any of the later so-called 'classic' ceramic wares. Yüeh is high-fired and resonant; its body-clay is close-grained and varies from grey to greyish-white, while its glaze can be olive or pale blue-green, or any of the infinite number of shades in between. Two localities in the area of Shao-hsing have been found to have kilns, one being Shang-lin hu, the other Chiu-yen—or 'Nine Rocks' after its 'Nine Pierced' stone bridge—a small village lying between Hangchou and Shao-hsing. Chiu-yen ware is rather similar to that of Shang-lin hu, though the shapes of its vessels are different, for the Chiu-yen kilns antedate those at Shang-lin hu by some three or four centuries. These kilns appear to have been in operation from the first century of our era down to the sixth century when those of Shang-lin hu seem to have started to take their place. The Chiu-yen pieces have many links with the Han bronzes. A basin in the Percival David Foundation, of metal form, decorated outside with four monster masks and inside with two fish, came from this site. It is of interest because in the *Illustrated Catalogue of Antique Metal and Stone (Chin Shih So)*, published by the two Feng brothers in 1821, there appear several rubbings of this type of basin. Three of them are dated to the years 101, 132 and 194 of our era.

Yüeh ware developed over a period of about one thousand years, from the first to the tenth century. Fragments have been found in ninth-century sites from Brahminabad in India to Ctesiphon, Tarsus, Jerusalem and Cairo. It is the earliest ceramic ware to be inscribed and was but a poetic legend until some fifty years ago. It has, since the T'ang Dynasty, aroused the imagination of a succession of Chinese connoisseurs and antiquarians, and Hsu Yin, a celebrated poet of the period, expressed his regard for the ware by describing the vessels as being 'Like bright moons cunningly carved and dyed with spring water. Like curling discs of thinnest ice, filled with green clouds; like tender lotus leaves full of dewdrops floating on the riverside.' Lu Kuei-mêng, a ninth-century poet, showed equal admiration for Yüeh by writing of the ware in these romantic lines: 'Among the autumn winds and the dew, Yüeh is born, and lifted from a myriad peaks, its blue green colour comes.'

Yüeh ware continued to be eulogized in Chinese literature but was not positively identified in the West until 1929 when Sir Percival David described as 'prohibited colour ware'—the *pi sê yao* of Chinese literary fame—two gold-rimmed bowls, of which similar fragments have been found at Shang-lin hu in Yu-yao Hsien, some forty miles east of Shao-hsing and since identified as the location of the actual kiln site. One of the two bowls is in the Fogg Museum and the other in the Percival David Foundation. According to a native authority, the colour of this ware is a 'curious admixture of blue, green, and grey, like the tints of distant well-wooded mountains'. This description has been substantiated by a passage in another Chinese text reading: 'Wang, Prince of Shu, among the gifts which he sent to Chu of Liang, included some gold-rimmed bowls. These gold rims protect the glaze of the precious bowls; its secret colour brings out the tone of the green porcelain.' Now, Wang Chien, a native of Honan, was created Prince of Shu (Szechuan) in 891, and died in 918. Chu Wen, also of Honan, ascended the Imperial throne as first emperor of the Later Liang Dynasty (907–22). He reigned seven years and was murdered in 914. These gold-rimmed bowls must, therefore, have been presented between 907 and 914 by Wang Chien to his friend and fellow-countryman on the occasion of Chu Wen's investiture as emperor at the Liang capital of Loyang. This 'prohibited colour ware' became the prerogative of the ruling house of the state of Wu Yüeh, when the kilns are believed to have reached their apogee, and the precursor of celadon.

The importance of the manuscript and the printed book in recording historical facts is shared by two other media, the inscribed stele and the funerary tablet. On the latter is recorded the dead man's descriptive name, the details of his life, an epitaph and a eulogy. The two following items are well-documented examples. Since they can only be represented by rubbings, which do not lend themselves to reproduction, they are not illustrated here.

The first is a funerary tablet—*mu chih ming*—covered with a pale greenish-grey glaze, under which is a long inscription giving the actual name of the celebrated kiln, Shang-lin hu, in addition to the date of the 'Thirteenth year [778] of Ta-li' (Institute for Humanistic Studies, Kyoto University).

Some fifty years later and of comparable significance is a funerary tablet with the date of the 'Third year [823] of Ch'ang-ch'ing' (Institute for Humanistic Studies, Kyoto University).

The T'ang Dynasty (618–906) was a period of expansion, one might say even rejuvenation, for now the various states were united in a common cause: perpetuation of the empire. The expansion had led to an infiltration of foreign influence, both at court and in the constant stream of traders, travellers, and priests who brought numberless innovations to a progressive country receptive to new ideas.

As the dynasty progressed, the advanced technical skill of the potters enabled them to achieve products of great distinction. Under the Five Dynasties (907–60) which followed, these were to attain a degree of perfection almost without parallel, for it was at this time that Imperial patronage of the ceramic industry could be said to have begun, with one of the five 'classic' wares. This term as applied to Chinese ceramics is used in reference to those wares which the literati have always valued most highly. Such pieces won commendation throughout the country by reason of their reputation no less than their beauty. The earliest and most coveted is the legendary Ch'ai, still awaiting identification, the others being Ju, Kuan, Ko, and Ting. Ch'ai is reputed to have been made at Ch'êng-chou, Honan Province, for the exclusive use of the Imperial House of Ch'ai in the Hsien-tê period (954–9), when the Emperor Shih-tsung is reported to have said, 'Let its colour be the blue of the sky after rain, as it is seen between the rifts of the clouds.' The *Ko Ku Yao Lun* has this to say on the subject: 'Ch'ai Ware. According to tradition, this was made in the North, [at the command of] the Emperor, Ch'ai Shih-tsung, after whom [the ware was] named. It was azure in colour, fine and unctuous, with many small crackles. The foot [however] was rough [unglazed], to which yellow clay [adhered]. Ch'ai ware is seldom seen.'

Apart from the funerary tablets, the earliest precisely dated piece of Yüeh—a ware equally worthy of inclusion in the select 'classic' group—is of the Northern Sung period.

In 959, Chao K'uang-yin became regent because the deceased emperor's son was only six years old. He came from a noble family and had seen both civil and military service under the empire at Loyang. In 960, Chao seized absolute power, and by 979 he had crushed all the secessionist states, the penultimate to fall being Wu Yüeh, Chekiang Province, in 978. Fortunately, there are two precisely dated examples from this disastrous period in the history of the Kingdom of Wu Yüeh.

The large number of fragments dating from 978 may be explained by the fact that it was in that year that Ch'ien Shu, the ruler of the Wu Yüeh Kingdom, surrendered to the Sung forces. It has been suggested that he ordered his kilns to turn out large quantities of ceramics so that he could use them as gifts in connection with his political negotiations. At any rate, several fragments with the same date have been

27

excavated at the Yü-yao kiln site, and a shard in the Percival David Foundation is inscribed 'Sixth year [981] of the T'ai-ping period', just three years later.

1. **977** Shallow BOWL with straight sides and everted foot-rim. Surrounding the exterior is a whorl of carved lotus petals. On the base is an inscription reading: 'Made in the second year [977] of the T'ai-ping period'. Diameter 4.5 in (11.5 cm) *Carl Kempe Collection, Stockholm*

2. **978** Shallow BOWL with bulbous body, inturned mouth and low everted foot. Scrolling leaf ornament round the lip. On the base is an inscription reading: 'Made in the third year [978] of the T'ai-ping period.' Diameter 5.5 in (14 cm) *Museum of Fine Arts, Boston*

Incidentally, one of the earliest appointments of a superintendent of an Imperial porcelain manufactory was made in the T'ai-ping Hsing-kuo period (976–84). This honour was bestowed on Chao Jen-chi, a member of the Sung Imperial family, who was Attendant Han-lin at court and superintendent of the porcelain manufactory at Yüeh-chou.

In the case of Yüeh, it is not surprising that a ware which had reached its apogee in T'ang times should continue to be imperially patronized in the succeeding Sung Dynasty (960–1279). It only confirms the opinion of ancient and modern connoisseurs that it was throughout its long career one of the most beautiful and most sought after ceramic wares ever to have been made.

Just a hundred years later are two more precisely dated examples of the high quality we have come to expect of Yüeh, and a third piece which brings us to the first year of the twelfth century.

3. **1080** TEMPLE VASE with dome-shaped cover, ovoid body, tall contracted neck and spreading mouth. On the shoulders are two loop handles. The body is divided by incised lines into six compartments in each of which part of an inscription appears. This reads: 'On the fifteenth day of the intercalary ninth month of the third year [30 October 1080] of Yüan-fêng, I have baked this first-class urn, in the hope that it may hold fragrant wine for a myriad of years; that, after a hundred years, it may be handed down to my descendants; that I may have a thousand sons and ten thousand grandsons; that they may have wealth and occupy high positions in the government continually; that they may live long and enjoy good fortune and unlimited happiness; and that the world may be at peace.' Height 15 in (38 cm) *Percival David Foundation*

4. **1080** Five-spouted JAR decorated with horizontal rings above a long dedicatory inscription in vertical ines round the lower half of the body dating it to the 'Third year [1080] of the Yüan-fêng period.' Height 11 in (28 cm) *Yamato Bunkakan, Japan*

5. **1100** INK-STONE, rectangular in section; the flat unglazed top has a depression at one end, the sides cut in parallel grooves. The body and base are covered with a thin greenish-grey glaze, and under the latter is an inscription reading: 'Fine object made in the mid-autumn of the third year [1100] of Yüan-fu.' Length 6 in (15·5 cm) *Percival David Foundation*

The following year (1101), the great painter-emperor Hui-tsung, aged nineteen, succeeded to the throne on the premature death of his brother. He was as gifted as he was famous, as skilled in wielding the brush as in promoting the artistic potential of his contemporaries. At his enlightened court were received only those scholars whose talent for literary achievements and philosophical studies were on the same intellectual level as the revered members of the Academy of Painting. Before attaining this distinction the would-be candidate attended a palace school where he received tuition in the minutely detailed study of flowers and butterflies, birds and insects, fruiting trees and plants. All had to be accurately drawn in the slightly artificial manner decreed by the Imperial academicians. This was the style favoured by Hui-tsung himself, by whom several paintings, reliably attributed to him, have fortunately survived. Such an example is the signed painting *Dove on a Branch of Blossoming Peach* in a Japanese collection. There is little lineament used in the drawing of the dove, as it is built up almost entirely of colour in the so-called 'boneless manner', whereas the twigs and blossoms are delineated but with contours so fine as to be scarcely visible. It bears an inscription in Hui-tsung's elegant calligraphy and is dated to the year 1107.

It is in this year, too, that we have a precisely dated specimen of the second 'classic' ware, Ju, which establishes beyond doubt the date of the manufacture of perhaps the rarest and most beautiful of all Sung wares. It is a piece without parallel for it more than fulfils the minimum requirements needed to make a precisely dated object one of historical impact. This documentary inscription records not only the date of manufacture and the personnel concerned, but describes the type and colour of the material and the occasion for the making of the piece.

6. **1107** Test piece of Ju ware in the form of a RITUAL RING. Buff ware with closely crackled greyish-blue glaze. On the under-side are three elliptical spur-marks, and on the face is incised under the glaze an inscription reading: 'On the fifteenth day of the third moon of the first year [9 April 1107] of the Ta-kuan period, Hsiao Fu, Vice-Minister of the Imperial Household and Superintendent of the Imperial Porcelain Manufactory at Ju-chou supervised the mixing of this *ch'ing* glaze and the firing of this first test piece.' Diameter 3.5 in (8.9 cm) *Percival David Foundation*

The *Ko Ku Yao Lun* has this to say on the subject: 'Ju Ware. This was also made in

31

the North. That which was baked in the Sung Dynasty was of a pale *ch'ing* colour. Pieces with "crab's claw" markings *(hsieh chao wên)* are genuine, but those without such markings are especially good. Its paste is unctuous, and very thin. Pieces are also difficult to obtain.'

Many important Sung pieces from the former Imperial collection are now in the Foundation, some twenty inscribed with poems and other comments from the brush of Ch'ien-lung (1736–95), who was a dedicated patron of the arts. These Imperial inscriptions conclude with the terminal phrase 'Imperially Written' in a particular cyclical year, and are followed by one or more of the Emperor's seals. These have been delightfully rendered as 'Deriving refined pleasure', 'Refreshing the mind after affairs of state', or 'A measure of virtue'. With their recondite allusion to classical poems and historical references, the inscriptions give us a glimpse of the obscurity and affectation of the Chinese literary style during the eighteenth century. The titles of the poems are interesting, too, in that they reveal the critical abilities of the Imperial advisers of the day, whose opinions, in great part, have been substantiated by modern research. This is particularly true of the 'classic' Ju ware, identified and described by Ch'ien-lung as 'rare as stars at dawn'.

The kiln of this particularly rare type of celadon was established in the district of Ju-chou, not far from the capital Pien-ching—modern K'ai-fêng—in northern Honan. In Sung times, Ju-chou formed part of the wide-spreading metropolitan area of the capital. Considering that the prefectural town of Ju-chou lay some ninety miles from the centre of Pien-ching, the fact that it was then included in that area, points to the vast proportions to which the capital city had by then grown. This small factory obviously supplied part of the ceramic requirements of the palace, for which its output is said to have been reserved. The Ju glaze is usually of a light bluish-green *(ch'ing)* tint, and has been compared with the colour of a duck's egg, although sometimes it appears to be suffused with a soft lavender tinge. Unfortunately no contemporary textual authority has been found, but it is unlikely that such a factory would have continued to operate after 1127. It was in that year that, the Sung armies having been routed by the invading Chin Tartars, and Hui-tsung with thousands of his loyal subjects having been taken into captivity, Pien-ching finally fell to the rapacious robbers. A young prince and the remaining officials fled south across the Yangtze to Hangchou. Here they established a temporary capital, and their royal charge, Kao-tsung, became the first emperor of the Southern Sung Dynasty (1127–1279) (see page 34).

When we recall that not a single specimen from Hui-tsung's famous collection of bronzes seems to have survived and probably very few paintings, not many specimens, we may be sure, remain of the ceramic collections of the old palaces of Pien-ching. In any case, with its bare twenty years of manufacture, Ju ware has always been elusive, and so the importance of this precisely dated piece cannot be exaggerated.

The appeal of Ju ware is readily apparent in the simplicity of form and in the subtle texture of the lustrous glaze, undecorated except for its crackled surface, either faint and stained violet blue, or resembling broken ice in structure. An unusual dish in the Percival David Foundation introduces an additional feature, for in the interior of the piece is a skilfully concealed design of two sesamum flowers. This technique of incised decoration is clearly a precursor of that of the *an-hua* designs which became so popular a feature of Ching-tê-chên wares of the Ming Dynasty, when the method was exploited to its full artistic limits.

From the same region comes a similar class of ware—Chün—although its centre of production was located at Yu-hsien, towards the eastern boundary of Honan Province. Like Ju ware, the vessels observe purity of form, although now they are usually covered with a thick opalescent glaze, the palette ranging from bluish-green tinged with lavender through turquoise and *clair-de-lune*. They so closely resemble Ju, however, that the Ch'ien-lung inscription on a bowl of this ware in the Percival David Foundation describes the piece as 'Chün'. Their fundamental difference lies in the decorative splashes of purple or strawberry pink which are found embellishing, so dramatically, many of the finest Chün specimens, of which there is unluckily no precisely dated example.

We are fortunate, however, in being able to refer to a well-documented piece that is as close to an authenticated example as it is possible to imagine. For this important discovery, we are indebted to the People's Republic of China for the extensive archaeological excavations they have carried out during the past few years. The object in question was unearthed in 1970 at Huhehot, Inner Mongolia, and is normally housed at the Inner Mongolia Autonomous Region Museum. It was displayed, with other treasures excavated in China from 1950 to 1975, at an exhibition in Tokyo in January 1978. According to the official translation from the Catalogue it is an 'Incense burner with lavender blue glaze. Height 42.7 cm. This incense burner was originally kept inside a large jar; a total of six pieces including Chün ware and a large jar of Lung-ch'üan ware were unearthed at the same time. Out of those only this Chün ware incense burner had an inscription, at the front, of fifteen characters: Szu-yu, the nine [ninth] month, the fifteenth, Sung the younger himself made it. Sixty cyclical year corresponds to 1309, Yüan Dynasty.

'This incense burner with a precise date would enable us to establish the standard of chronological form and our studies. The make of this incense burner is exquisitely beautiful and it is a large format. The method of putting on the glaze is called flowing glaze. The glaze is poured from above the object intentionally. When baked the shade of colour of the glaze is not even, making it very characteristic. This is a rare work of art among Chün ware.'

The aesthetic emperors of the Northern Sung Dynasty had devoted themselves to a study of artistic and intellectual pastimes. The Academy of Painting provided the impetus for artists working in a conventional style, whereas those unhampered by court convention drew their inspiration from nature, thereby establishing the tradition of the landscape scene. Into this atmosphere the Imperial court brought an appreciation of the potter's art, and being thus inspired the craftsmen developed glazes and shapes of unbelievable perfection. They concentrated on colour rather than ornament, except for the moulded or incised designs which further enhanced the subtle monochromatic effect. This devotion to artistic pastimes was encouraged by the ministers at court who concerned themselves with the running of government and ignored until too late the impending advance of the Mongols. In 1127 the Mongols invaded Sung territory and forced those citizens that eluded capture to flee across the Yangtze to Hangchou. Here began the Southern Sung Dynasty with Kao-tsung as first emperor, ably assisted by an entourage of courtiers familiar with the past cultural brilliance of their predecessors in the north, who readily immersed themselves again in a similar atmosphere.

A first consideration was naturally given to the setting up of potteries to supply the palace with its customary 'official' ware. For this purpose two kilns were established; one at the Hsiu-nei-ssŭ in the 'Back Park' of the palace grounds which abutted on to the north side of the Phoenix Hill, the other at the Chiao-t'an (Suburban Altar), at both of which every type of northern *kuan* ware was imitated. It was at the former that the general works manager and supervising director of the Imperial ceramic factory tried to keep alive the traditions of the old capital by continuing to call his ware *kuan yao* (official ware). He was Shao Ch'êng-chang, a statesman of the former K'ai-fêng regime, distinguished for his loyalty and uprightness, who had accompanied the Imperial entourage south across the Yangtze. Although there is no precisely dated example, a vase of monumental bronze form in the Foundation is not without interest, for in the Ch'ien-lung inscription on the base the ware is described as 'Hsiu-nei-ssŭ kuan'. The superb quality of the piece was certainly appreciated, for the text goes on to say that if in ancient days this Imperial vessel had been found in unauthorized hands, its possessor would surely have had to pay with his very life!

On the subject of *kuan* ware the *Ko Ku Yao Lun* has this to say: 'Kuan Ware. This was made on the orders of the Palace Works Department (*Hsiu-nei Ssŭ* of Sung). Its paste is fine and unctuous, and its colour *ch'ing* with a pinkish hue. Some pieces are darker than others. It has "crab's claw" markings, dark-brown mouth-rims *(tzŭ-k'ou)* and iron [-coloured] feet *(t'ieh-tsu)*. Those with good colour are similar to Ju ware. Pieces made from black clay are called black-bodied pieces *(wu-ni yao)*. Faked pieces were all produced at Lung-ch'üan, and have no crackle.'

The second area of manufacture was at the Chiao-t'an kiln situated near the Altar of Heaven and Earth—the so-called Suburban Altar—at the foot of the Black Tortoise Hill. The products of both factories were made from a dark body clay; and only the relative distinction of shape and lustrous glaze quality segregates those of the 'Back Park' into a class apart.

With demand exceeding supply, the celadons of Lung-ch'üan in Ch'u-chou Prefecture, some 200 miles to the south of Hangchou, and a centre noted for its potteries since the beginning of the Sung Dynasty, now really came into their own, for the court at Hangchou found itself cut off from the Honan centres of ceramic manufacture, and naturally turned to the nearby kilns of Chekiang. Some of these were thereafter imperially patronized—and no doubt subsidized—so that as a result it is not surprising to find the Lung-ch'üan wares of the Southern Sung Dynasty far superior in quality of material and in craftsmanship to those of an earlier epoch.

The *Ko Ku Yao Lun* has this to say on the subject: 'Lung-ch'üan Ware. Ancient *ch'ing* pieces [of Lung-ch'üan] have a fine and thin paste. Those with blue-green *(ts'ui ch'ing)* colour are valuable, while those which have a pastel *ch'ing* colour are less so. There is one kind of basin with a pair of fish at the bottom and bronze rings handles near the rim, those which are very thick are rather cheap in price.

[A] 'Ancient Lung-ch'üan ware comes from the present day Lung-ch'üan-hsien in Ch'u-chou-fu in Chekiang. Nowadays it is called *Ch'u* ware or *Ch'ing* ware.'

In order to continue our chronological sequence of precisely dated pieces, it is necessary to leave the south for a while and consider a somewhat different group of Chinese wares, generally classified as 'northern celadon', but whose origin may well have been the Tung-ch'ing of later Chinese texts. These seem to imply that this was a class of ware (northern) so seldom seen in southern China in the fourteenth century that it was unfamiliar to most contemporary writers, although the *Ko Ku Yao Lun* makes these comments on the subject: 'Tung Ware. The colour of this type [of ware] is light *ch'ing* with fine crackle. This ware also has a dark brown rim and iron-coloured foot. But compared with Kuan ware, it lacks its pinkish hue as well as the fineness and unctuousness of its paste. It is far inferior to Kuan ware. Tung pieces are also hard to come by nowadays.'

Collating the information that has been published, I think a reasonable explanation is that Tung ware was originally made in certain private factories during the tenth, eleventh and twelfth centuries and that the term Tung-ch'ing refers to the eastern capital K'ai-fêng and the name, Tung-ching, by which it was known in the Later Liang Dynasty (907–22). Being green in colour it was later mistakenly referred to as 'eastern green' (tung-ch'ing). By the time the court had been forced to flee from K'ai-fêng, Tung ware had developed into what we now call 'northern celadon', which might also be extended to include green Chün, certainly a less consistent group, although this is not surprising when the conditions of its manufacture are realistically considered. It was again the product of a private factory which could only have been in restricted circulation in north China at the end of the Northern Sung Dynasty. The true identity of these wares might easily have been forgotten and become confused during the two and a half centuries that elapsed before a reference to any of them appears in the *Ko Ku Yao Lun*. It is certainly so in the case of Tung ware, as is proved by the variant readings of the term Tung-ch'ing that are to be found in various relevant texts. Tung might never have emerged from its obscurity, but for the fragments—and of green Chün as well—picked up at the old kiln sites at Ch'ên-liu, Honan, and in the vicinity of Ju-chou.

The confusion probably gathered momentum when the kilns, which had originally produced simple undecorated wares of the early Chün and Ju types, started making decorated pieces. Their main attraction is the deeply carved and skilfully incised ornament which emerges from the rich olive-green celadon glaze covering the stoneware body. The motifs are numerous: phoenix among flowers, boys carrying flowers, fish and ducks amidst waves, treated separately or as part of a general design.

The kiln site for a group of these decorative wares has now been definitely located at Huang-pao Chen in T'ung-ch'uan Hsien, Shensi Province. They are referred to as *Yao yao* in Chinese texts, because T'ung-ch'uan Hsien, as it was known in the Sung Dynasty, belonged administratively to Yao Chou at the time. An interesting piece which might well be a later specimen of such a ware, for it is precisely dated to the fourteenth century, is the jar in Plate 7.

This incense burner is of particular significance for it appears to be a contemporary version of the *tobi seiji* or spotted celadon of Chekiang. Perhaps, as in the case of the so-called 'northern' celadon, this, too, derived from a southern prototype. Apart from this innovation, the decorative scrolling foliage well illustrates the type of ware that was continuing to be made in the north, now under Mongol occupation but until 1127 part of the Northern Sung Empire. In the south, too, traditions were continuing to be perpetuated, especially around the district of Lung-ch'üan. While the region itself is quite small, it has given its name to a type of ceramic ware which was made over a relatively large area, extending from Yang-chiang of Kuangtung Province in the south to Shou-chou of Anhwei Province in the north. In any event, manufacture of this celebrated ware must have been very extensive, because its areas of dispersal were widespread, covering the trade routes of Central Asia, Persia and India, the Eastern Archipelago, the sea ports of the Persian Gulf, and the east coast of Africa. In mediaeval times, Lung-ch'üan ware was believed to have magical powers, and was highly valued, a poison-detecting quality making it much sought after. In Japan, celadon ware attracted even greater renown from the *Kinuta,* or mallet-shaped vase, which was one of the treasures of the great fifteenth-century shogun, Ashikaga Yoshimasa.

Most of these pieces, however, were of the durable heavy-bodied type, as can be

7. **1303** INCENSE JAR of olive-green celadon, standing on three cloud-scroll feet. It is decorated with chrysanthemums in applied relief ornamented with spots of golden brown glaze. This also covers part of the base and is the medium used for the inscription which reads: 'Made in the seventh year [1303] of the Ta-tê period.' Ta-tê (1297–1307) is the third reign-period of the Yüan Dynasty. Diameter 15 in (38.1 cm) *Museum of Fine Arts, Boston*

seen in the Topkapu Serai in Istanbul, and are one of the principal keys to our understanding of Yüan celadons (see pages 38 and 39). Another particularly significant development of the period is the decorative relief design in unglazed biscuit, burnt in the firing to a reddish brown colour. From a Sung point of view such an intrusion into the pure, jade-like surface of the Lung-ch'üan glaze would have been unthinkable. But with the innovation of blue and white porcelain, the colourful enamelling of Tz'u-chou ware, and the newly developed technique of carved red lacquer, how could celadon have retained its popularity without conforming to this bolder conception of decoration.

Although less dramatic in impact, the emphasis in design was not primarily on unglazed biscuit but much more on carved or applied relief decoration. The following precisely dated example of this technique supplies the key to an unequivocal Yüan dating for a large group of allied Chekiang material, for the inscription is as categorical and circumstantial in its terms as it is unquestionable in its authenticity.

Liu-hua Hill is above the village of Liu-t'ien where the Cheng brothers had their pottery. Chien-ch'üan is the old name for Lung-ch'üan, and Kua-ts'ang for Ch'u-chou Fu. This vase is most celebrated because it has become the yardstick for dating the same class of ware in the Topkapu Serai in Istanbul, and in Teheran, China, Japan and the West, the certain documentation provided by the inscription enabling us to classify a great number of pieces of comparable quality but unmarked.

It is in fact just this category of ware of which Marco Polo (see page 62) speaks when he describes the products of the town of Tingui, as he calls Lung-ch'üan: 'And again I tell you, that the most beautiful vessels and plates of porcelain, large and small, that one could describe, are made in great quantity in a city called Tingui; none are more beautiful that can be found in any other city. And on all sides they are much valued for none of them are made in another place, but in this city and from thence they are carried to many places throughout the world. And there is plenty there, a great sale, so great that for one Venetian groat you would actually have three

8. **1327** TEMPLE VASE (see Plate 9 opposite): the inscription appearing around the lip.

9. **1327** TEMPLE VASE, noble in stature, beaker-shaped with baluster body and tall neck with flaring mouth. Grey stoneware body with rich sea-green glaze of olive tone. Decorated on the body with a peony scroll in boldly sculptured applied relief above a carved petal band; on the neck are similar reliefs between channelled rings. Round the lip is an underglaze inscription reading: 'Chang Chih-ch'eng, of the hamlet (*she*) of Wan-an by the Liu-hua Hill at Chien-ch'üan in Kua-t'sang, a humble believer in the Three Precious Ones (i.e. Buddhism), has baked a pair of large flower-vases to be placed for evermore before the Buddha in the Great Hall of the Chüeh-lin Yuan (temple), with the prayer that the blessing of peace, happiness and prosperity may attend his family. Carefully written on a lucky day in the second month of the fourth year [1327] of the T'ai-ting period.' Height 28 in (71.1 cm) *Percival David Foundation*

bowls, so beautiful that one would not know how to devise them better. And these bowls are made in this way, of this kind of earth, that those of the city gather as from a mine, and make great mounds of it and leave them thus in the wind, in the rain, and in the sun, for thirty or forty years they do not move the mounds. And in this space of time the said earth, being so worked up that the bowls made of it have the colour of azure, and they are very shiny and very beautiful beyond measure. And you must know that when a man gathers it, it is for his sons and grandsons. And it is clear that owing to the long time it must be quiet for its working up, he does not hope to gain profit from it, or to put it into use, but the son who will survive him, or his grandson, will reap the fruit of it.' One cannot vouch for the correctness of this last statement. The Chinese, it is well known, were jealous of, and were resourceful for centuries in guarding, the secret of the manufacture of their porcelain. It seems reasonable therefore that in order to discourage further investigation by foreigners like Marco Polo, his Chinese informants told him that the ingredients for such manufacture could only be found in this small town of Tingui, and that generations of time were needed for their maturing.

The capital of the Mongol Yüan Dynasty (1260–1368) was Khanbalig—city of the Khan—and Marco Polo's Cambaluc. It was Kubilai, the fifth Great Khan and the first of them to rule China, who moved the capital from Karakoram to Yen-ching (near Peking), the Chin Dynasty (1115–1234) capital. In 1267, Kubilai built Khanbalig (Peking) to the north-east of Yen-ching. A hundred and one years later came the expulsion of the Mongols and the beginning of the Ming Dynasty (1368–1644). The founder was Chu Yüan-chang, a Buddhist monk of humble origin but with more than ordinary perspicacity, who assumed the throne in 1368 with the reign-title Hung-wu. His armies had captured Nanking in 1356, and in the year of his accession they had driven the Mongols out of Peking, although not out of China proper until 1371. Quite logically, the centre of his strength, Nanking, now became the capital, surrounded as it was by wealth and population (see also page 113).

There are but few inscribed pieces of Hung-wu's reign, and the only precisely dated celadon is an octagonal ink-palette. This is decorated with the eight trigrams, a motive illustrative of the superstition prevalent in the south of China in those confusing and disturbed days when the native Chinese were striving furiously to win back the country from the occupying Mongols.

The writing of the inscription from left to right is contrary to Chinese style, but in accordance with that of Mongol script. It was in 1269—more than a century earlier—that Pagspa, the Mongolian script, had been introduced by Kubilai Khan. What is particularly significant about this writing accessory is the fact that it was made four years after the Mongols had finally been subdued and the greater part of the country won back by the Chinese, and yet writing from left to right was still the custom in certain remote areas. Pagspa died an early death, however, and after the

10. **1372** Octagonal INK-PALETTE of greyish stoneware with a pea-green glaze. On the top is a disc of unglazed biscuit surrounded by a runnel; on the sides are eight sunk panels with the *pa kua* in low relief. The base is glazed and in its centre is a sunk medallion incised with an inscription reading: 'Fifth year [1372] of the Hung-wu period', in two columns reading from left to right. Diameter 5.4 in (13.6 cm) *Percival David Foundation*

11. **1385** ROCK SHRINE of greyish stoneware covered with a pea-green glaze. A seated Taoist priest in contemplative posture occupies the main compartment which is enclosed by an architrave decorated with cloud and fungus scrolls in high relief. Below the priest two attendants kneel in deferential posture and flank a *chi-lin* reclining on a fungus scroll. On the base is an inscription reading: 'Made in the fourth month of the eighteenth year [1385] of Hung-wu.' Height 40.5 in (102.9 cm) *Edward Chow, Geneva*

accession of Hung-wu in 1368 we see and hear little of it, until a modified form of the script was introduced by the Manchus.

In 1398 Hung-wu died and was succeeded by a grandson who ruled as Chien-wên until 1402. The reign-title of this regime is unknown, to the best of my knowledge, on any reliably authenticated ceramic wares.

Chien-wên's uncle, the Prince of Yen, and fourth son of Hung-wu, resented his accession to the throne and revolted. Civil war ensued, bringing with it countless loss of life and untold devastation. After Chien-wên's brief reign of four years, the Prince of Yen was victorious and in 1403 proclaimed himself emperor with the title of Yung-lo; his occupancy of the throne for twenty-two years brought glory to Chinese annals. He was a Buddhist, like his father, and a man of vision with so deep a concern for the future of his country and so strong a belief in her past greatness that he ordered scholars to compile the opinions of Sung philosophers and to extract the best from her earlier literature. A project of even greater magnitude was the publication of an encyclopaedia in some twenty-two thousand sections that was completed in the first decade of the fifteenth century.

In 1405, two years after the succession of Yung-lo, the eunuch, Admiral Cheng Ho, assembled a fleet of some sixty-three junks at Soochou, from where he set sail for the southern kingdoms. In the course of the next quarter of a century, a total of seven similar expeditions put to sea, during which visits were paid to Java, Sumatra, Ceylon, India, and Arabia.

Yung-lo porcelain is of the finest quality but is rarely marked, and it is again the celadon kilns that supply the only precisely dated object so far recorded.

The eldest son of Yung-lo succeeded his father in 1425, with the reign-title of Hung-hsi. He died in the year of his accession and was in turn succeeded by his eldest son, who adopted the reign-title of Hsüan-tê. This emperor distinguished himself as a statesman and a scholar, and was the guiding spirit behind the Imperial factory at Ching-tê-chên, where during his reign were made many of the most outstanding porcelains of the Ming Dynasty (see also page 114). Other kilns, even without so distinguished a patron, continued to operate successfully throughout the country, from which the following piece from the Ch'u-chou area of Chekiang is a significant example (Plate 13).

After the death of Hsüan-tê in 1435 there was a ceramic twilight of thirty years during which the emperor's eldest son reigned under the respective titles of Chêng-t'ung (1436–49) and T'ien-shun (1457–64) (see also page 88), the intervening gap (1450–7) being filled by his younger brother with the reign-title of Ching-t'ai. The troubled and eventful years of these three decades proved significant in the intellectual growth of the country, especially for the effect they had on the arts and crafts, literature and drama, and the habits and customs of the Chinese people. The mark of Ching-t'ai appears quite frequently on cloisonné but is extremely rare on porcelain. Most of the Imperial factories had closed, and so it was again a time when

12. **1406** ROCK SHRINE with grey-green glaze, divided into three horizontal compartments by cloud scrolls. In the lowest is the God of the North with attendants and guardians. In the middle are the 'Three Holy Ones', Confucius, Buddha and Laotze. In the top is a figure of an Arhat riding on a *chi-lin*. At the back of the lowest section is a relief design of a four-clawed dragon, above which is an inscription reading: 'Made on a lucky day in the fourth year [1406] of the Yung-lo Period.' Height 19.5 in (49.5 cm) *British Museum*

13. **1432** VASE with ovoid body and tall slender neck with flaring mouth. Incised ornament of lotus scrolls above a petal border, and below plantain leaves. The inscription on the neck reads: 'Made on a lucky day in the seventh month of the seventh year [1432] of the Hsüan-tê period for use in the Palace of the T'ien-shih (Taoist Pope).' Height 17.3 in (44 cm) *Percival David Foundation*

private kilns flourished, especially those in Chekiang, of which the following precisely dated piece is yet another product from Ch'u-chou. The floral scroll of a previous era survives, though in a somewhat modified form, while a significant feature is the base which has a curious countersunk disc in the centre, a construction form seldom employed except in pieces of celadon ware of more or less contemporary date.

14. **1454** VASE with slender ovoid body and tall neck with flaring mouth; pea-green glaze. Incised ornament of two bands of lotus scroll separated by a raised ridge; below, petal pattern and a raised ring. On the neck stiff plantain leaves and an inscribed panel reading: 'In the fifth year [1454] of the Ching-t'ai period the believer Yang Tsung-hsin of the hamlet of Chen-an Fu Li (Happy Village) respectfully offers this [vase] to the local Buddhist Temple to be placed before the Buddha, with the prayer that he may have peace and live long.' Height 26.8 in (68 cm) *Percival David Foundation*

In 1457 Ching-t'ai's elder brother returned from captivity, as we have seen, and by a *coup d'état* was restored to the throne. He died in 1465 and was succeeded by his eldest son, aged seventeen, who ruled under the reign-title of Ch'êng-hua for twenty-three years (see page 115). There do not seem to be any precisely dated celadons from this reign, nor dated pieces of the enamelled porcelain from Ching-tê-chên for which it is justly celebrated. In 1488 he was succeeded by his son, who adopted the reign-title of Hung-chih. Like so many of the Ming emperors he ascended the throne as a young man: in this case he was but eighteen years old. Fortunately for our study of precisely dated celadons, this reign supplies two interesting examples, both of which give the name of the maker, Yang Chang-yin.

15. **1492** TABLE-SCREEN with bluish-green glaze, rectangular upright in form with incurved corners and applied ornament. On the front appears a *chi-lin* in a landscape with the sun and clouds in the background. On the back is an inscription reading: 'Made by Yang Chang-yin in the middle of the spring of the fifth year [1492] of the Hung-chih period.' Height 6.3 in (16 cm) *Percival David Foundation*

16. **1492** TABLE-SCREEN with bluish-green glaze, rectangular upright in form with incurved corners and applied ornament. On the front appears a standing official in court attire. On the back is an inscription reading: 'Made by Yang Chang-yin in the middle of the spring of the fifth year [1492] of the Hung-chih period.' Height 6.9 in (17.5 cm) *Percival David Foundation*

The eldest son of Hung-chih succeeded to the throne on the death of his father in 1506 with the reign-title of Chêng-tê (see also pages 90 and 119). He continued to take the same interest in a revival of the Southern Sung traditions of painting and the applied arts that his predecessors had done for more than a century. The effect of this on the celadon industry is readily apparent, for the majority of shapes follow the bronze forms which became popular after Kao-tsung began his reign at Hangchou in 1127, and of which the following are handsome examples.

17. **1506** INCENSE BURNER on three feet; greyish-white ware with thick grey-green glaze. Decorated with rosettes and flower scrolls in relief, and with an inscription reading: 'Made by Ta Fa on a lucky day in the first year [1506] of the Chêng-tê period.' Height 11.2 in (28.7 cm) *Percival David Foundation*

18. **1517** FLOWER POT, tub-shaped, resting on three short cabriole legs. Greyish-white ware with celadon glaze which has split into crackle on the lower part. Inside is a drainage hole, and on the side is an inscription in nine columns reading: 'The believer Ch'en O of the eastern suburb of Li-shin Hsien in the prefecture of Ch'u-chên has resolved to offer joyfully ten pieces (of pottery) to the Liu Ho Ssu (Buddhist Temple), that they may be placed before the Kuan-yin with the prayer that his mother may live a very long life, that he and his wife may grow old together, that every member of his family may be lucky, that he may have many prosperous sons and grandsons, that he may be able to perform meritorious deeds (in the service of Buddha) and that they may all enjoy happiness. Made in the middle ten days of the eighth month of the twelfth year [1517] of the Chêng-tê period.' Diameter 8.8 in (22.4 cm) *Percival David Foundation*

In 1522 Chêng-tê was succeeded by his cousin, who took the reign-title Chia-ching and occupied the throne for forty-five years (see page 91). An event of far-reaching significance had occurred in the year 1517 of his predecessor's regime with the first landing of the Portuguese in Canton. Although they were not granted full concession rights until thirty years later, the date is important for it heralds the beginning of direct commercial contact with Europe, whereby European countries received straight from China the pottery and porcelain they had only been able to acquire with difficulty from the Near East. Their method of payment was not in material exported from Europe but in the produce which came from their colonies in Asia, principally food and spices. A few years earlier the Spaniards, having tried in vain to secure a foothold on the Chinese mainland, had turned their attention instead to the Philippines, where in 1565 they began an occupation of more than three centuries.

The celadon industry of Lung-ch'üan continued to maintain its considerable output. This was achieved by the addition of eight kiln sites over and above the Sung figure of twelve, making a total of twenty in active operation from the beginning of the Yüan Dynasty. It was at this time, too, that an increase in the size and thickness of all vessels was being introduced. An example of this change is the following piece of stout construction.

19. **1547** VASE, one of a pair, with pale grey-green glaze; the neck ornamented with two 's'-shaped handles and the body decorated with an incised peony scroll. Surrounding the shoulders of the vase is an inscription reading: 'At Wan-shou village, in the lower Hsiao quarters, the lady believer K'ang I-chieh, in the first moon of the twenty-sixth year [1547] of Chia-ching, having asked for and obtained a son, joyfully sets a pair of flower vases in front of the incense burner for the revered ancestors in the Hou-feng Hall, to return thanks and to pray for protection for her son, that he may grow big and become a man.' Height 12 in (30.5 cm) *Victoria and Albert Museum*

It is perhaps strange that the reign-title of Wan-li (1573–1619) (see page 97) which is so frequently found on the blue and white porcelain from Ching-tê-chên, should appear on so few pieces emanating from the celadon kilns of Chekiang, and not at all on any precisely dated objects. We have to bypass, too, the reign of his eldest son, T'ai-ch'ang, and accept for our next piece a vase made during the reign of Wan-li's grandson, T'ien-ch'i, who came to the throne in 1621 (see page 105).

20. **1626** VASE with ovoid body tapering to a broad shallow foot-rim, freely carved with flower sprays alternating with entwined leafy stems, the leaves and petals with combed details between a band of vertical flutes around the base and pendent over-lapping petals on the domed shoulders. The tall flared neck with upright stiff leaves, combed with veining, rises from a band of incised petal motifs and is divided on one side by a panel enclosing a long dated inscription reading: 'The believer Chou Kuei of Fêng-tang has carried out his wish to offer joyfully a pair of precious vases to [the temple] Ch'ing Fêng An with the prayer that his eyes be cleared and brightened and that the whole families of his two sons Chou Ch'êng-chiao and Chou Ch'êng-tê may have peace. Tenth month of the fifth year [1626] of T'ien-ch'i.' Height 20 in (50.8 cm) *Private Collector*

2

TZ'U-CHOU WARES

Tz'u-chou, in the southern corner of chihli and near the border of Northern Honan, has become the accepted description for a large group of highly decorative wares. The name is derived, according to Chinese authorities, from the *tz'u* (stone) of which the ware is made, and one can safely deduce that this gained importance some time in the Sui Dynasty (589–617), since which era the district acquired the name and its products have been discovered in so many far-off places. Fragments decorated with brown spots have been found at Samarra, and a finely painted fragment of a vase, discovered on a tenth-century site in Turfan, is reported to be in the Anthropological Museum in Leningrad. The whole district of Tz'u-chou, and indeed considerable areas around it, are prolific in ceramic production, and a number of kilns must have been in operation prior to the T'ang Dynasty for many complete pieces have been found in tombs of this period. At any rate, one can say with certainty that from the early part of the ninth century these highly decorative wares found a place in the repertoire of many kilns in north China, notably those at Chiao-tso in Northern Honan and Tzu-hsien in Chihli Province. The vessels are of stoneware, rather heavily potted, and take the form of vases, wine jars, brush holders and pillows. Although not highly esteemed by the literati, the ware plays a significant role in the history of Chinese ceramics as the earliest type to be painted in colour under the glaze. At first the palette was confined to black or dark brown on a white or cream ground, but later the practice developed of enamelling the wares in red, green and burnt ochre. A piece with a precise date on an example of the earlier palette is the following jar in the Percival David Foundation.

This jar is an excellent example of the spirited drawing we have come to expect from such pieces. The tiger is the Chinese 'King of Beasts' and is here portrayed with ferocious mien as if to strike terror into the hearts of all who disobeyed. The beast is so called because the character for king *(wang)* is written by three parallel horizontal lines joined down the middle by a vertical stroke and resembles very closely the markings on the animal's forehead.

49

21. **823** JAR of buff stoneware, ornamented in dark brown on its drab-coloured glaze with a fire-breathing tiger under a tree on one side, and on the other with a long dedicatory inscription recording an event which occurred only a few years before the official repression of Buddhism. The inscription reads: 'In the third year [823] of the Ch'ang-ch'ing period, the disciple Ssu-tu Po respectfully made this vessel as an offering to be placed before the Great Buddha.' Height 9.2 in (23.5 cm) *Percival David Foundation*

Unlike its contemporaries, Tz'u-chou has never claimed the refinement of Ting as one of its characteristics, nor has it aspired to emulate either the subtlety of celadon or the variety of Chün. Tz'u-chou is a ware of the people, a simple ware made for practical everyday use, and yet frequently decorated with the same skilful brush strokes that would be applied by the well-trained hand to the finest silk or paper. The interpretation of the design on the finished project differs in almost every example for they are a variegated group with little in common except the basic ingredients. There were naturally those who spurned the conventional method of painting in black or brown on a creamy surface and introduced original effects, such as employing 'slips' in contrasting colours in which the designs would be revealed either by incising or carving away the ground before the final glaze was applied.

Several examples of Tz'u-chou ware have been found in Korean tombs of the Koryo period, and in the Liao country, including a tomb in Manchuria which contained a sarcophagus with the date of 1018, the second year of T'ien-hsi (1017–21). This is one of the reign-titles of the Emperor Jên-tsung (1010–63), who ascended the throne at the age of thirteen and who later distinguished himself as a painter and as a patron of the arts. The vase illustrated here supports the evidence of the tomb and is the second claimant to a precise early dating for these wares.

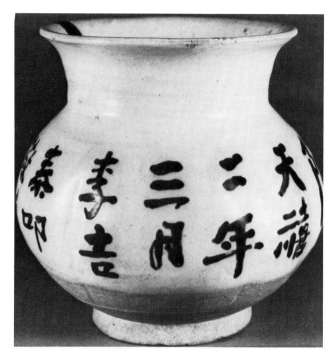

22. **1018** VASE with short neck, everted lip and gently curving body. Grey stoneware covered with a creamy-white glaze. Decorated with two inscriptions in brownish-black round the middle of the vase. On one side are four characters reading: 'Amitabha Buddha', and on the other are twelve characters reading: 'Respectfully made by Li Chi Tai in the third month, second year [1018] of T'ien-hsi.' Height 13.5 in (34.3 cm) *S. Lee, Tokyo*

A vase with an identical date was found at Chü-lu Hsien, a market-place inundated by a flood in 1108. To fully appreciate the significant part played by this sub-prefecture in the study of Chinese ceramics, it is helpful to know something of the turbulent history of the Yellow River. This rises in the Kokonor region of Sinkiang, runs a tortuous course through the Kun-lun mountains, and divides the provinces of Shensi and Shansi before it reaches the great plain. Here it receives its largest tributary, the Wei, and then flows east along the northern parts of Honan and Shantung, until it finally reaches the Gulf of Chihli. Although most unsuitable for navigation, it is in the Yellow River basin that Chinese history and civilization begin, and it was for long the political and economic centre of the nation. But throughout its career the river has been notorious for the havoc it has caused. Records going back some three thousand years describe breaches and inundations on more than fifteen hundred occasions, and no less than twenty-six important changes of course, the penultimate being in 1108 when it flowed south into the Huai River and thence into the Yellow Sea. It retained this course until 1855 when, weakened by inadequate dyking, it returned to its old Ta-ch'ing course, which in the third century of our era was the only sea outlet of the Yellow River.

In 1920 it came to the notice of the Tientsin Museum officials that a number of Sung Dynasty wares had been found in the district around Chü-lu Hsien and that because of the persistent drought which prevented the normal work of tillage, the farmers had turned to amateur archaeology. Fortunately for posterity, their digging was only superficial so that when the Museum authorities arrived they were able to excavate on a scientific basis. Many inscribed pieces were found, some giving the names of their ancient owners as well as their dates. A jar in the Percival David Foundation inscribed with the date of 1107 came from this site when under official supervision, and will be described later in chronological sequence (see page 55). Chü-lu provides us with no clue as to the provenance of its relics, only to their date which must be earlier than the autumn of 1108.

We have digressed for a moment from our chronological sequence, so we will return to the middle years of the eleventh century for our next precisely dated piece. This brings us to the period of the Northern Sung Dynasty which is most intellectually stimulating, for the level of education, under whatever auspices, was higher than ever before. Certainly the system of competitive examinations for the official classes had begun in the T'ang Dynasty, but under the direction of that illustrious prime minister Wang An-chih (1021–86), the curriculum was modified. Now the emphasis was on the fundamental principles of philosophy and government rather than on the composition of poetry and rhyming couplets, as it had been in the past. Private education flourished, too, and centres of learning were established in the quiet of the countryside where research and philosophic deliberations could continue without government interference. The foremost poet of the century was Su Shih (1037–1101), whose accomplishments included art criticism, authorship of the essay on the Red Cliff, and the building of a causeway at the West Lake, Hangchou. The outstanding essayist was Ou-yang Hsiu (1007–72), while the role of historian was admirably filled by Ssu-ma Kuang (1019–88), whose great work was the history of China from 403 B.C. to A.D. 959.

There are many pieces of Tz'u-chou that can be attributed to the eleventh century, when Sung culture flowered thus and attained such brilliant heights. They display a variety of shapes and techniques, and the individuality of the potter is clearly discernible. Pillows are amongst the most numerous shapes and employ several techniques to achieve the variety of decorative motifs so characteristic of the ware. One such method is used to embellish the following example (Plate 23), the first of three precisely dated pillows from this period of the Sung Dynasty.

A third pillow attributable to the same family of potters is in the British Museum. Decorated in black on a cream ground, it has a stamped mark reading: 'Made by the Chang Family at Old Hsiang.' It thus connects the Chang *fabrique* with Tz'u-chou, since Hsiang is the old name for Chang-te Fu, the prefecture in which Tz'u-chou was formerly situated.

Yet another pillow attributable to this family is in the Art Institute, Chicago (Russell Tyson Collection). It is cloud-shaped and decorated with a swimming carp amidst water-plants. On the base is a stamped mark reading: 'Made in the inner precincts of the Chang Family.' Width 15.25 in (38.7 cm).

23. **1056** PILLOW of rectangular section, its concave sides being ornamented with chrysanthemum scrolls moulded in low relief. At each end is an oblong cartouche inscribed respectively: 'Third year [1056] of Chih-ho', and 'Made by the Chang Family'. The pillow is of buff stoneware and is covered by a dull black glaze mottled with reddish-brown spots. Length 7.5 in (18.7 cm) *Percival David Foundation*

24. **1056** Another PILLOW decorated with the same cartouche is this example of shovel shape on a pentagonal base. It is of marbled stoneware with a coating of slip over a neutral glaze, and is decorated with a bird and flowers carved in white on an olive ground on its concave top. On two of the four sides appear stamped marks reading: 'Third year [1056] of Chih-ho' and 'Made by the Chang Family'. This pillow was also found at Chü-lu Hsien, inundated in 1108. Width 12 in (30.5 cm) *Percival David Foundation*

A popular style of decoration, and certainly the most picturesque, was the use of a simple motif—groups of foliage, bamboo and orchid, lotus and chrysanthemum—applied with brushed calligraphic strokes in brownish-black slip. Sometimes the surrounding area is carved away to leave the design in relief. In both cases the surface is finally covered with a colourless or coloured glaze. The latter technique appears to advantage on the following example.

25. **1071** PILLOW, rectangular in shape and decorated with formal lotus panels on the sides. Three inscriptions appear on the upper surface, one giving the date of the 'Fourth year [1071] of Hsi-ning'. Length 8.5 in (21.6 cm) *British Museum*

Since we can establish a *terminus ante quem* for the objects found at Chü-lu Hsien, which was inundated in 1108 as we have seen, those with inscriptions from this market-place have a double claim to authenticity. The following jar is interesting because it is dated to 1107, the year before the inundation, since it is recorded that in the eight month of 1108, the Yellow River having overflowed its banks, a special tax was levied for the assistance of the neighbouring families, and an Imperial edict ordered the removal of the location to a site higher up the river. Prior to the inundation, ceramic wares from all parts of the country were brought to Chü-lu

Hsien for sale. These included Tz'u-chou and Ting-chou, Lung-ch'üan and Yüeh, Chien, and the bluish-greenish-white translucent porcelain from Ching-tê-chên.

26. **1107** JAR of grey stoneware with buff coloured glaze, decorated in dark brown with floral medallions between ring borders. Round the shoulders is an inscription reading: 'Made in the first year [1107] of Ta-kuan.' Height 7 in (18.3 cm) *Percival David Foundation*

27. **1112** This DISH is an early example of a dated piece employing the advanced technique of enamelling in colour, in addition to black, over the glaze. It is decorated with a design of ducks and lotus incised through a white slip and filled in with green and yellow enamels. An ink inscription on the back reads: 'Made by Ch'en in the second year [1112] of the Chêng-ho period.' Diameter 8 in (20.3 cm) *M. Calmann, Paris*

Although a shadow of doubt has been cast on some of the inscriptions applied in this way, there are many, I think, that are acceptable as being contemporary with the object they adorn. There is even a scarcity of pieces dated in this rather unusual manner, which may be accounted for by the frequent change of reign-period in the latter days of the Northern Sung regime. These were of such short duration that the last ten emperors averaged between them but four years on the throne. This supports the authenticity of the ink inscription, for the calligraphic minded Chinese, anxious to record accurately the quickly changing face of history, delayed inscribing his vessel until the pertinent facts were available. If he made his inscription when the piece was originally fired, it would have been too late to alter the text, had any of the facts become incorrect.

A variety of stoneware with black and brown glazes was made in both north and south China under the Sung Dynasty. Many of those from the north were produced at kiln centres of 'Tz'u-chou' type, which often made white wares as well, in addition to the several kinds of decorated ware for which they were best known. The brown-black glazes are due to oxidized iron, and through improvement in techniques a number of new and attractive styles were developed. By variations in both glaze content and kiln conditions many different decorative patterns emerged, such as 'hare's-fur' streaks of rusty brown or 'oil-spots' of metallic silver. According to tradition, these were a speciality of kilns in the region of Yu-hsien. A further range of such wares were also made in the south of China, and of these the most celebrated are the Chien wares made in the province of Fukien, first at Chien-an, then at Chien-yang, both in the northern prefecture of Chien-ning. The glaze is seldom totally black, more generally a very dark brown or a purple streaked with a deep lustrous silvery blue. Sometimes it is flecked with a warm tawny brown which shades at the mouth-rim to a rich gold. The potter's use of this type of ware was limited almost entirely to the tea bowls which had already in the tenth century come into favour in Chinese literary circles for their tea-tasting parties. This was an interlude in history when scholars turned to the philosophic pleasures of conversation and tea-drinking as a refuge from the many trials and tribulations caused by misrule under the Five Dynasties sovereigns. The date of the beginning of the manufacture of Chien ware is not exactly known, but from the fact that it is mentioned in laudatory terms in contemporary literature it seems reasonable to suppose that its origin might be datable to the last years of the T'ang Dynasty.

It is said there that the bowls of Min, the old inhabitants of Fukien, with the mottlings and speckles of a partridge were greatly prized for tea-tasting parties. The prevailing dark colour of the Chien glazes made them especially suitable for tea-tasting competitions, then popular amongst the scholar-class and particularly so in Fukien which had always been celebrated for its tea. The object of the contest was to see whose tea would stand the largest number of waterings, and it was found that the least trace of tea was visible against the dark glaze of the Chien bowls, thus making them eminently suitable. These ceremonies were later adopted by the Japanese who elaborated them into a curious ritualistic affair which subsequently assumed certain political overtones.

Fukien Chien was soon imitated in other provinces, especially in Honan and

Chihli, and to some extent in Kiangsi. In the north, one of these factories is said to have been at Shen-hou Shan, a site in the neighbourhood of many of the Chün factories, where there was produced a ware with a white body and a sleek black glaze. The Honan glazes were capable of even greater varieties of colour modification than the Fukien Chien, and the northern potter learned to control their markings with skill, such as his southern colleagues could not achieve. The silvery crystals were brought together to form a regular and most attractive pattern of dots or 'oil-spots' as they have been appropriately called, which were especially admired by the Japanese tea-master. The last of the three varieties of Chien is the Kiangsi imitation. The kilns are situated at Yung-ho, near Chi-chou (formerly Chi-an), and during the Sung period produced several kinds of pottery, but they are best known for their brownish black glazed wares. The majority of pieces were tea bowls, and the most popular types were those with this dark glaze variegated with 'tortoiseshell' splashes, and a hare's fur glaze ranging from this basic colour to a golden yellow. Other attractive types are those in which the decoration is reserved in white on a golden brown ground, or in which the veined imprint of a leaf appears in light golden yellow on a brownish black ground.

Chien ware is seldom inscribed, although in some cases it seems that the artist may have attempted to form a character when he applied the necessary ingredients for what eventuated as a splash. Fortunately, one precisely dated piece has appeared.

28. **1119** JAR with wide flat mouth and short neck above a rounded body. It is covered with a deep bluish-black glaze and is splashed with hare's fur markings in silvery brown. On the base is an ink inscription reading: 'Made in the fifth month of the first year [20 May 1119] of the Hsüan-ho period.' Height 10 in (25.4 cm) *Idemitsu Museum, Tokyo*

At one time it was thought that Tz'u-chou ware was exclusively a northern product. Post-war excavations and precisely dated material have proved the contrary, since the southern kilns reveal the existence of a comparable output of this basic, unsophisticated ware of the people. It is often gaily decorated, it displays originality in shape and design, and it is unhampered by the demanding requirements of the refined classic wares made for the nobility, the Ju, the Kuan, the Ko, and the Ting. Tz'u-chou was thus already in production when the Sungs fled from the north in 1127 and established their capital in Hangchou, as we have seen, although it is not until six years after this event that a precisely dated piece has so far been recorded.

29. **1133** PILLOW of Tz'u-chou type of oblong rectangular form covered with a brilliant green glaze. The long inscription on the upper surface describes the conflict raging between the Sungs and the Mongols, and includes the information that it was 'Made on the day before the Ching Ho Festival in the third year [1133] of the Shao-hsing period.' On the base is an oblong seal reading: 'Made by Chu Chia.' Length 12 in (30.5 cm) *Mr Umezawa, Tokyo*

Another object of Tz'u-chou type, although not precisely dated, is worthy of mention in establishing a southern provenance for these wares. It is a bust of Chao Tun, the third Southern Sung emperor who reigned from 1190 to 1195 and died in 1200. It portrays the head and shoulders of a bearded man with elaborate head-dress, in hard red ware with a wash of white slip and details of eyes, eyebrows, beard and hair painted in brown slip under a creamy-white glaze. Across the back in brown is an inscription reading: 'The Emperor Kuang Tsung of the Great Sung Dynasty.'

(Height 8.4 in (21.2 cm) Percival David Foundation.) The title Kuang Tsung is his canonized name and would not be used until after his death. Probably this is one of a series of 'portraits' of Sung emperors.

The disruption caused by the hasty retreat south of the Sung regime seems to have had little effect on the population who remained behind, for life continued much as before. This was certainly true of the ceramic world, for under Mongol domination the northern Tz'u-chou wares continued to be both restrained and imaginative in their decorative designs—as they had been under the former regime—of which these two pillows are worthy representations.

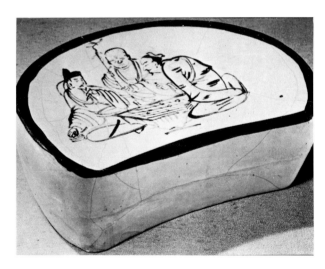

30. **1156** PILLOW of oval shape with a design of flowering peony and leaves within a quatrefoil border in yellow and white on a green ground. On the base is an inscription reading: 'Made in the first year [1156] of the Chêng-lung period.' Length 8.3 in (21 cm) *National Museum, Tokyo*

31. **1179** PILLOW of oval flattened form embellished with the decorative theme of the 'Three Holy Ones' engaged in the secular pastime of chess. They are represented by a Confucian scholar, on the left; a Taoist sage, on the right; and, in the centre, a Buddhist priest who plays the interested spectator. The pillow is decorated in brown on a white slip body and bears an inscription on the base which includes the date 'Eighteenth year [1179] of Ta-ting'; the sixth, seventh, and eighth characters cannot be read. Length 19.8 in (50.3 cm) *Philadelphia Museum of Art, Mrs Carroll S. Tyson Collection*

The output of these northern kilns at this time was tremendous, especially during the reign of Chih-tsung (1161–90), the fifth emperor of the Chin Dynasty, who took the reign-title of Ta-ting. The foregoing is such a piece which is said to have come from T'ang Yang-hu on the Honan border.

The popularity of Tz'u-chou wares continued well into the thirteenth century, but with the advent of Mongol taste for a more colourful palette the somewhat showy combination of red, green, and yellow was introduced to augment the restrained use of black and white which appealed to the aesthetic Sungs. This innovation also reflected a revival of the traditional T'ang 'three colour' glazed earthenware, later imitated with such individuality by the Liao potters. Three of the following five pieces are decorated in this colourful Chin Dynasty style. The earliest, a pillow, confines itself to yellow and green in addition to the customary black, while the penultimate, a jar of monumental form, harkens back to the days of the Sung regime and the celadon type glaze which they so admired.

32. **1200** PILLOW of Tz'u-chou type decorated on the upper surface with the figure of Shou Lao delineated in black under a green glaze. An inscription on the base reads: 'Made in the fifth year [30 May 1200] of the Ch'êng-an period.' Width 11.8 in (30 cm) *National Museum, Tokyo*

33. **1201** SAUCER of Tz'u-chou type decorated in red, bluish-green, and black with a floral medallion surrounded by interlacing black lines, the interior giving the impression of a flowering chrysanthemum. On the back is an ink inscription reading: 'Made in the first year [28 February 1201] of the T'ai-ho period.' Diameter 6 in (15.3 cm) *National Museum, Tokyo*

34. **1230** SAUCER DISH decorated with a conventional design of a single peony surrounded by black lines. On the base is an ink inscription reading: 'Made in the seventh year [28 December 1230] of the Chêng-ta period.' Diameter 6 in (15.3 cm) *National Museum, Tokyo*

35. **1256** JAR of monumental form covered with a greyish-green glaze, and decorated with bands of ornamental rope design. Between the bands is an inscription of twenty-six characters and which includes the date of the 'Fourth year [1256] of the Pao-yu period.' Height 32 in (81.3 cm) *National Museum, Tokyo*

36. **1269** DISH decorated in green, white, yellow, and black with a freely drawn hare among

foliage, surrounded by black lines and a deep green border. On the back is an ink inscription reading: 'Made in the sixth year [1269] of the Chin-yüan period.' Diameter 12 in (30.5 cm) *National Museum, Tokyo*

In 1260, Kubilai, grandson of Genghis Khan, was proclaimed emperor in K'ai-fêng, Coleridge's Xanadu. This 'Lord of Lords', this 'intrepid warrior' was a wise and benign administrator, although less successful as a conqueror, for a great part of the vast territory of China still remained unsubdued. The Yangtze was not crossed until 1273, Hangchou did not open its gates to him until 1276, nor was it until 1279 that consolidation of Mongol suzerainty came to full fruition, the last scion of the reigning Sung family having perished. It was only then, when Kubilai became the first emperor of the Yüan Dynasty, that he regarded himself master of all China.

Four years prior to this momentous happening a party of Italians arrived in K'ai-fêng, having left their native homeland in 1271. Thas was the second expedition for the two senior participants, who came as the emissaries of Pope Gregory X. They were accompanied by a young man—Marco Polo—son of one and nephew of the other. It was his unusual intellectual resources and remarkable linguistic ability that had enabled him to transcribe the oral traditions and written records of the diverse cultures he had encountered. These attributes soon caught the attention of the khan and he was at once given service in the administration. He rose swiftly in the emperor's favour, delighting him with his ready wit and quick repartee. In one capacity or another he served Kubilai continuously for sixteen years, and became in a sense his eyes and ears, especially on expeditions to south-east Asia, to Burma, and to Tibet, which preoccupied the Mongols during the course of Polo's visit.

It was during this period, too, that the great Tibetan reformer Pagspa promulgated the short-lived script which was named after him and which is used to inscribe a piece in the British Museum. This is a tall jar with a short neck and four loop handles, the lower half of the body black, the upper white and inscribed in black with the characters for 'good wine'. Another piece of similar shape, although fully covered with a creamy white glaze is inscribed round the neck with four characters reading: 'Enough to spare year after year.'

The decorative technique of Yüan Tz'u-chou brush drawing may have influenced some of the designs on contemporary blue and white, and the same observation might equally well apply to the wide-mouthed jars. The Tz'u-chou examples of this shape were a successful innovation, in particular perhaps when a turquoise blue glaze was applied over a slip-painted decoration. This embellishment would have pleased Mongol taste much more than the following piece which displays some delightful brush work but has the simple aesthetic appeal of black on white (Plate 37).

Another technical achievement of Yüan Tz'u-chou pieces is the employment of a dark slip-carved decoration applied directly to the stoneware body. This then appears as a matt background against which the lustrous black glaze stands out in striking contrast. The second piece gives positive evidence for this new technique (Plate 38).

37. **1303** JAR of ovoid shape with short neck, on either side of which are two loop handles. Buff stoneware decorated in brown slip on top of a creamy-white glaze with orchids and leaves. On the base is an inscription reading: 'Tenth day, first week, third moon, seventh year [1303] of the Ta-tê period [?] made this glaze jar and record.' Height 6.3 in (16 cm) *British Museum*

38. **1304** JAR covered with a brown glaze which is cut away to reveal a powerfully carved decoration of boys among floral scrolls in a background of creamy-white ware; a vigorous sloping meander on the small neck around which runs a raised ring. The inscription on the base reads: 'Made in the seventh month of the eighth year [1304] of the Ta-tê period.' Height 10 in (25.4 cm) *British Museum, Eumorfopoulos Collection*

A dated example of the fourteenth century, one of the fifteenth, and another of the sixteenth century, all employing the simple technique of decorating the surface in brown or black slip, are again significant in allowing us to place less well authenticated pieces.

39. **1336** PILLOW in the shape of a bottle, of oval flattened form with high shoulders. The stoneware body is painted in brown with a decorative design of chrysanthemums with intertwining leaves separated by sketchy scrolls. The inscription in brown on the neck gives the date of the 'Twenty-fourth day, fourth month, second year [1336] of Chih-yüan' and says that it is the 'Jar pillow of Li Ming-chi'. Length 11.5 in (29.2 cm) *Museum of Fine Arts, Boston*

40. **1446** WINE JAR painted in dark brown on a white slip with a design of scrolling peonies round the body; and with an inscription round the shoulders reading: 'Made on the first day, fifth month, eleventh year [1446] of the Chêng-t'ung period.' Height 9.6 in (24.4 cm) *British Museum*

41. **1571** WINE JAR of buff stoneware with decoration in brown slip on top of a white glaze. Truncated ovoid form. Broad band of stylized flowers surrounded by two bands of characters in reserves. The upper band reads: 'An auspicious day, twelfth month, fifth year [1571] of Lung-ch'ing, the jar is one of our own manufacture.' The lower band reads: 'During the season of the vernal equinox, from beautiful rice, fragrant sweet fine wine, one jar, Tz'u-chou.' Height 23.5 in (59.7 cm) *Royal Ontario Museum of Archaeology, Toronto*

3

WHITE WARES

THE IDENTIFICATION OF TING WARE has now been firmly established. It was
really only a question of locating the kiln site, for its description in Chinese texts was,
for once, unanimous and quite explicit on the colour and nature of the ware. It was
white and it was porcelain. As a result it was easy to recognize, and it was generally
agreed that most of the finer Ting pieces had a more or less translucent white body,
that their colourless glaze was apt to collect in gummy drops or 'tear stains', and that
the vessels had been fired in an inverted position. This exposed an unglazed mouth-
rim, which was in turn generally concealed by a thin metal collar. Early attempts to
locate the kiln-site failed because of the misleading tradition that Ting ware was
made at Ting-chou, whereas the actual site was located at Chien-tz'ǔ Ts'un in the
Ch'ü-yang Hsien region of Hopei (Chihli), a hundred and thirty-three miles south-
west of Peking. This came about because in the Northern Sung period, Ch'ü-yang
was one of the eight counties comprising the prefecture of Ting-chou, which then
naturally became identified as the source of the white porcelain, even though the
kilns were actually located in the Ch'ü-yang area. In addition to the discovery of the
main kiln-site at Chien-tz'ǔ Ts'un, which lay a mile to the west of Lung-ch'üan
Chên—a prosperous market town and seat of local government—a secondary site
was discovered at Yen-shan Ts'un, some nine miles further west.

Among the many questions concerning Ting ware which remain to be settled is
the problem of dating these kilns. The shards from Chien-tz'ǔ Ts'un suggest a period
of manufacture prior to the tenth century, for already at this time there is the record
of a stele in the precincts of the Fa-hsing Monastery bearing an inscription dating it
to the 'Fourth year [957] of Hsien-tê'. This is said to have been located about three-
quarters of a mile west of Lung-ch'üan Chên. Among the donors who set up the
stele was Feng Ao, the officer in charge of the Ceramic Taxation at Lung-ch'üan
Chên. This is indeed evidence that by the tenth century the output of the kilns
around Lung-ch'üan Chên was sufficiently large to justify the presence of such an
official.

66

42. **977** A precisely dated Ting ware piece of the tenth century was excavated in 1969 by the Institute of Archaeology in the People's Republic of China. It is a white-glazed porcelain SAUCER with lobed lip and marked *kuan* (official). On the back of the saucer is written in ink: 'Second year of the period T'ai-p'ing hsing-kuo [977] fifth month twenty-second day; dedicated by the male believer Wu Ch'eng-hsun, who also dedicated in money thirty *wen* sufficient for prayer to comfort the soul of his father.' Diameter 4.7 in (12 cm) *People's Republic of China*

It is of interest, I think, to mention in relation to the above, a five-lobed saucer of Ting ware in the Foundation which is marked *hsin kuan* (new official) (Diameter 5.1 in (13 cm)).

While on the subject of Ting-chou generally I must mention an interesting item in the Foundation: although it is not precisely dated, it is a piece of some consequence. It is a small circular dish marked 'Ting-chou kung-yung', which can be translated 'Ting-chou for general use' or 'Ting-chou ordinary quality'. In either case, the mark connects the piece irrevocably with Ting-chou, or Ting-chou Shu-wu Chun as it was called in the Five Dynasties period (907–60). The mark suggests that being a vessel made for common use, it is rather inferior in quality, the glaze having the clinical whiteness typical of most T'ang pieces. These characteristics are amplified by a small constructional particularity of the dish, which unlike so many other Ting pieces, has a glazed mouth-rim and is furthermore strengthened with a band of clay on the exterior, a feature appearing on some fragments excavated at Samarra on the River Tigris, the capital of the 'Abbasid caliphs from 836–83. The Foundation dish was found at Chü-lu Hsien, the marketing centre inundated by flood in 1108.

So already in the tenth century there is evidence that the potters of Ting-chou were well advanced in ceramic technique, a fact made known throughout much of the world by the ever-increasing export trade. Among their accomplishments was the ability to make a translucent white porcelain, although this achievement did not apparently lead to full-scale production until the latter part of the Northern Sung Dynasty. This translucency brought about a change in the texture and colour of the glaze, altering the former to a subtle smoothness and the latter to a warm ivory-white. The visual eye-appeal of this very lovely porcelain could be threefold. Sometimes the attraction was mainly in its form, while its delicately incised designs were an additional pleasure, and the most discerning connoisseur would have admired its boldly carved or moulded decoration. The artists were indeed great craftsmen and developed from their repertoire of motifs a variety of subjects: a phoenix among flowers, ducks among reeds or in a lotus pond, fish among waves, or a dragon battling his way against a stormy sea. Our second precisely dated piece from Ting-chou, although undecorated, is a fine example of this attractive ware.

43. **1089** BOX, with four-lobed cover, circular with straight sides and flat base, on which there is an inscription reading: 'Fourth year [1089] of Yüan-yu'. Diameter 4.5 in (11.4 cm) *Carl Kempe Collection, Stockholm*

There is no doubt that Ting ware reflected the mood of contemporary Chinese painting, which as a fine art now came to be officially recognized and, under Imperial patronage, flourished along with all branches of the arts and literature. This was particularly true in the reign of Hui-tsung (1101–25), a painter in his own right, as I have mentioned (page 30), whose favourite subject was the idyllic genre known as 'birds and flowers'; a genre which became so popular with Ting ware decorators, and of which many examples must have graced the emperor's dining table. That they did so is supported by the painting in the Palace Museum, Taiwan, attributed to Hui-tsung, although generally believed to be the work of one of the court artists. It is entitled *A Literary Gathering* and depicts a garden scene in which twelve men of letters and their attendants are grouped around a dining table suitably prepared with ceramic and lacquer vessels in T'ang and Sung shapes. Amongst the porcelain are examples of Ting ware and, judging by the delicate shapes of the bowls and cup-stands, the pieces represent Ting ware at its most Imperial best.

This painting thus places some specimens of Ting ware in the same category as Ju and the earlier *pi sê* variety of Yüeh, although if one takes into account the number of complete pieces that exist and the vast quantity of fragments that have been seen, it was without doubt primarily a utilitarian ware. The great majority of shapes were practical: bowls, dishes and basins. The vase, that elegant holder of a single perfect flower, is found in almost negligible quantities. Vessels in bronze form are virtually non-existent, too, as in the case of Ju ware. But that is only to be expected for it was not until the establishment of the Sung court at Hangchou, following its flight from the north in 1127, that vessels in bronze form became an accepted ceramic shape. This was the traditional approach of the antiquarian scholar, who wanted to recapture the glorious past by creating in ceramic form the bronze vessels that had been melted down or had been left behind.

A contemporary mention of Ting ware is to be found in the written report of Hsu Ching who visited Korea in 1123 with a Chinese mission. Hsu spent a month in Korea, and in his Memorial presented to the throne in 1124, he describes the ceramic industry, saying: 'In recent years they have been making good pottery with fine glazes; their bowls, dishes, wine-cups, tea-cups, flower vases and soup bowls are generally copied from Ting ware forms.'

Ting ware is the subject of these interesting comments in the *Ko Ku Yao Lun*: 'Ancient Ting Ware. Of ancient Ting ware, specimens with a fine (and unctuous) paste and white and lustrous glaze are valuable; while those which are coarse and yellow in colour are less so. Genuine pieces have 'tear drops' on the outside. The best have incised designs; the second best are plain; and of third quality are those with very elaborate patterns. The best Ting wares were produced in the Hsüan-ho and Chêng-ho reign-periods [1119–25 and 1111–17 respectively], but it is very difficult to procure them in sets.

'There are also purple Ting and ink Ting wares, the latter as black as lacquer.

Their paste, however, is white. Like white Ting pieces, they were also produced at Ting-chou, but are more expensive. Su Tung-po's line records: "The adorned porcelain of Ting-chou is incised like jade."

'White Ting pieces, if they are damaged, cracked, or lack unctuousness, are inexpensive.'

Until 1933, it had been generally agreed that the ivory-white porcelain from Ting-chou could definitely be associated with the kilns in that prefecture, and that some sort of finality in this connection had been reached. Our complacency was, however, disturbed at this time by the appearance of some labels in the Palace Museum, Peking, which suddenly adopted the description 'Chi-chou' ware for what had been previously called 'Ting-chou'. No reasoned explanation was given, and how were we in the West, nine centuries removed, going to distinguish between northern and southern Ting when it was said by the Chinese in the seventeenth century that 'lovers of ancient art work who can distinguish them and are not deceived by later imitations, have no reason for shame and may well be reckoned connoisseurs.' It was not until certain marked pieces came to light that the opinion was substantiated. A dish in the Foundation was the first in the West to establish beyond doubt that a ware indistinguishable from that of Ting-chou was made in the southern province of Kiangsi at Chi-chou. This was further substantiated by large mounds of kiln waste from both kilns being compared and found to be exactly similar in every particular. The Foundation dish, which is fired on the mouth-rim, has a metal collar and is decorated with incised lotus in the interior. On the base under the glaze is an inscription reading: 'Made by the Shu Family at Yung-ho in the Shao-hsing period' (1131–63). Not a precise date, indeed, but material evidence in support of the change in attribution. An even more important piece, though, was found in the Palace Museum, Peking, formerly the Kuo Pao-ch'ang Collection. The inscription on this second dish—which is undecorated—states that it was, like the one in the Foundation, made by the Shu Family and at Yung-ho, but actually gives the precise year of its manufacture—1145—the fifteenth year of the Shao-hsing period.

The Shu Family are referred to thus in the *Ko Ku Yao Lun*: 'Chi-chou Ware. The colour of this ware is similar to that of Brown Ting. The body is thick and the substance is coarse paste. The ware was produced at Chi-chou and its price is low.

[A] 'Chi-chou ware came from what is now Yung-ho in Lu-ling hsien, Chi-an-fu.

'In the Sung Dynasty, there were [here] five kilns, among which Shu Kung produced the most commendable pieces in white and brown. The big vases are worth several taels of silver; the smaller were decorated with delightful designs. It also produced very good crackled wares.

'It is said that when Chief Minister Wên passed by the kilns, the wares in them turned to jade. Later, the kilns ceased to operate. The site of the kilns is still to be seen although dwelling houses have been built on it. It is also said that jade cups and bowls were discovered there during the Yung-lo reign-period [1401–26]. This might be true . . . [characters illegible]. It has been so from the Yüan Dynasty to the present day.' Another Chinese authority says that Shu Kung's daughter, Shu Chiao (beautiful Shu), was still more clever, and the feminine character of the script suggests that this was her work.

The dating of these two pieces is substantiated by the tradition that some of the Ting potters fled south to Chi-chou in 1127 when the Tartars swept down from the north. Although there is no reliable native authority for the rumour that these potters accompanied the court to Hangchou, it is probable that Shao Ch'êng-chang, director of works in the Imperial household, and a few chiefs of the various departments under his control left with him. There would certainly have been no general exodus of the potters with the confused mass of court followers in their hurried and frequently interrupted flight south, and the fame of the ware of Ting-chou undoubtedly did not come to an end with the fall of the Northern Sung Dynasty. We have material evidence of the continuation of its production in the following six precisely dated pieces, which have the reign marks of the Chin Dynasty (1115–1234), and a single example from the Yüan Dynasty (1260–1368).

44. **1162** COVERED BOWL decorated with a moulded petal design on the sides; the lid with everted lip has incised lines radiating from a looped knob which serves as a handle. On the base is an ink inscription reading: 'Shih Liang-mu (née Ch'en), recorded as a memorial for her on the fourteenth day, second moon, second year [1162] of the Ta-ting period.' Height 5 in (12.7 cm) *British Museum*

45. **1184** MOULD for impressing decoration on the interior of bowls. It is of hard stoneware and unglazed. The centre of the convex side is decorated with an elegant floral scroll with small star-like five-petalled flowers and a melon vine with two fruits, surrounded by a border of phoenixes and chrysanthemums; a narrow scroll band near the lip. On the concave side is incised an inscription reading: 'Made by Wang Shen-chi on the twenty-sixth day of the fourth moon of the twenty-fourth year [1184] of the Ta-ting period.' Diameter 8.6 in (21.9 cm) *Percival David Foundation*

46. **1185** PILLOW of oval flattened form with a carved design of waves on the upper surface under a creamy-white glaze. On the base is an inscription in black ink reading: 'National Mourning on the eighteenth day of the previous fifth moon of the twenty-fifth year [1185] of Ta-ting.' Signed, 'Shu Ching at Ho P'ing Hsien.' This was a leap year in which there were two months of May (fifth month) and the second of May was an intercalary moon or month. Length 13.8 in (35.1 cm) *S. Lee, Tokyo*

47. **1189** MOULD for impressing decoration on the interior of bowls. It is of hard stoneware and unglazed. The convex side has in the centre a round panel decorated with two peony sprays, which is surrounded on the sides by scrolling peonies of similar design. On the concave side is an inscription reading: 'Twenty-ninth year [1189] of Ta-ting.' Diameter 8.2 in (20.8 cm) *British Museum*

48. **1203** MOULD for impressing decoration on the interior of bowls. It is of hard stoneware and unglazed. The convex side has in the centre a round panel decorated with a realistic peony with leaves, surrounded on the sides with a scroll of palmette-like leaves. Below the rim is a classic scroll border. On the concave side is an inscription reading: 'Third year [1203] of T'ai-ho.' Diameter 7.8 in (19.8 cm) *British Museum*

49. **1210** SAUCER with foliated rim which continues the traditional form introduced in the

Sung Dynasty. The sides are divided into five lobes by low ridges on the interior. In the centre is a lightly moulded flower design, barely visible. The inscription on the base, incised before firing, reads: 'Third piece in the third year [1210] of Chia-ting.' The characters 'Ever Precious' appear after the date and perhaps express the potter's wish that the piece be treasured. Diameter 5.25 in (13.3 cm) *Percival David Foundation*

50. **1271** DISH of white porcellaneous stoneware with a flat horizontal rim, slightly thickened at the edge, covered with a creamy-white glaze and decorated inside with a large fish and a floral spray of mallow-like flowers in a circular medallion. On the base is an inscription reading: 'Made in the eighth year [1271] of Chih-yüan.' There is also a horizontal mark reading: 'Kung yung', which has been interpreted as 'general use' or 'ordinary quality'. This phrase also forms part of the inscription reading: 'Ting-chou kung-yung' which appears on a dish in the Foundation described previously (page 67). Whatever its precise meaning, this dish furnishes a link with the earlier piece and indicates a common provenance. Diameter 7.75 in (19.7 cm) *British Museum*

The second main group of Sung porcelain is the so-called *ch'ing pai*. It is unquestionably among the finest porcelain ever produced, its most evident characteristic being its glaze which varies from a bluish-green through a pale blue to an almost blue-white tone. It is generally more thinly potted than the wares of Chien-tz'ŭ Ts'un or Chi-chou that we have been discussing, for the translucency of body and high glaze results in an effect of far greater brilliance than is achieved by either of the foregoing. *Ch'ing pai* has in common with them, however, the essential elements of decoration, for all were frequently embellished with similar interpretations of the same motif, be it a bird, animal, or floral design.

The kilns of *ch'ing pai* were situated chiefly in the neighbourhood of Ching-tê-chên, Kiangsi, where the vast ceramic industry of later times was to be concentrated. It is recorded that in the Ching-tê period (1004–7) the Emperor Ch'ên Tsung appointed an official to oversee the affairs of Ch'ang-nan Ch'ên, which thereafter came to be known as Ching-tê-chên. Imperial factories, called *kuan yao*—official kilns—were established there and supplied the needs of the palace. It was further ordered that the reign mark of Ching-tê be inscribed on the base of a vessel. Although there are no dated pieces of this period, by the middle of the eleventh century all forms of distinctive tableware appeared in considerable quantities, much of it ornamented in the customary Sung style; the designs being incised, carved, or moulded. Other centres of production are all in the south—for it was never a northern ware—and kiln sites have been located in Fukien, Chekiang, Anhwei and even Yunnan. Complete specimens of the ware have been excavated from a number of Sung tombs, especially around the neighbourhood of Cheng-tê-chên in Kiangsi. In the Yüan Dynasty the kilns of this area experienced what was to be a turning-point in Chinese porcelain, for what had been a rather fragile ware for general use became a strong, durable porcelain suitable for the nobility. While no marked pieces of Imperial quality are known, it is stated in Chiang Ch'i's *Abstract of Ceramic Records*

74

that a Mongol commissioner was in charge of the Ching-tê-chên kilns, and that this porcelain was in demand throughout most of southern China. Undoubtedly taste was moving away from the well-established wares of the Sung Dynasty with their glazes of warm-white, blue, and jade-like green, with the realization of the need for a cool white ware of greater substance. Such a choice, both of colour and fabric, would lend itself to the heavier type of decoration which ornamented the large celadon bowls and dishes, and thus provide an alternative, though equally appropriate ware, for the Mongol dining tables with their similarly constructed vessels of glittering gold and silver. The change was gradual, for delicately incised designs and lightly moulded or carved decoration continued to decorate pieces of finer quality porcelain, while others used a simple formula of recurring motifs, not unlike the *'guri'* lacquers of contemporary date. But soon the majority of pieces were made of more substantial fabric, which dictated a less delicate type of incising and demanded instead a bolder approach to the design in order to fill out the massive shapes coming into vogue. It is this group with which we are directly concerned because it numbers among its many adherents a precisely dated example. The pieces in question are so heavily constructed that it might be more accurate to designate them as sculptural forms, the revival in fact of a T'ang original as interpreted through intervening dynastic tradition.

The prime specimen of the group is the well-known 'Fonthill Vase', now in the National Museum of Ireland. This vase, besides the value it derives from the historical circumstances connected with it, is further curious in being the earliest known specimen of porcelain imported from China into Europe. It comes from a period prior to the circumnavigation of the Cape of Good Hope by the Portuguese. Its first Western owner was Louis of Hungary, who died in 1382. The subsequent vicissitudes of the vase have not been fully traced, and so we shall bring it forward to the eighteenth century when it is known to have belonged to the Grand Dauphin, son of Louis XIV, who died in 1711. It then passed into the collection of Monsieur Louis de Caumartin, Counsellor of State to Louis XIV and Louis XV. In the confusion of the French Revolution, the vase found its way to England and into the collection of that well-known eccentric, William Beckford of Fonthill Abbey. It was sold at auction in 1823, since when it vanished until discovered by the late Arthur Lane in the National Museum of Ireland. The documentation provided by the now-lost silver-gilt mounts and handle is quite precise. These are encrusted with figures in relief in compartments, in Gothic taste and further embellished with paintings in enamels in colours, with the arms of Joan of Aragon, Queen of Naples, the friend of Petrarch. The handle, rim, and foot bear the legend of the House of Anjou in Gothic characters upon blue enamel. In addition, supporting evidence for the dating of this *ch'ing pai* vase comes from its beaded, moulded and *ajouré* decoration. It can be further pinpointed since this decoration is comparable with that of some of the *ch'ing pai* sculptures, and with the following example in particular.

51. **1298** WATER-MOON KUAN-YIN, seated and garbed in flowing drapery, adorned with jewellery; the lower robe in unglazed biscuit. On the unglazed base is an inscription written in ink which reads, except for the characters which are illegible: 'Eighth month, second (or third) year [1298 or 1299] of Ta-tê.' Height 20.25 in (51.4 cm) *William Rockhill Nelson Gallery of Art, Atkins Museum of Fine Arts, Kansas City*

Sculpture in porcelain, especially a group of Buddhist images similar to the foregoing, can now be securely localized in Kiangsi Province, the centre for Yüan and later white porcelain development. The characteristic milky greenish-white glaze of these figures, combined with their white body flecked with iron impurities, mark them as products of the same southern kilns, which produced the *ch'ing pai* and *shu-fu* utensils.

Sculpturally, their Liao-Chin heritage, and the 'beaded' decor in the jewellery and ornament, support the evidence already affirmed for their Yüan dating. The supple, plastic grace of most of these porcelain sculptures marks the first substantial sculptural achievement by the Chinese in the porcelain medium, and provides the ancestry for the more numerous products of the later *blanc-de-chine* of Tê-hua and related kilns in Fukien.

The fourteenth century brought about a notable change in the fabric of all but the purely traditional *ch'ing pai* porcelain. In place of the flimsy body of the Sung wares, a more homogeneous paste was introduced, thereby creating a substantially harder product. Although the differences are readily apparent, both types continued to employ the somewhat glassy, very translucent greenish-blue glaze. About the middle of the fourteenth century, this *ch'ing pai* porcelain inspired the introduction of an important new type, the so-called *shu-fu* ware. This phrase has been rendered as 'Imperial palace', 'central palace', and even 'privy council', but no satisfactory conclusion has yet been reached as to the correct interpretation. '*Shu-fu*' appears under the heading 'Ancient Jao-chou Ware' in the *Ko Ku Yao Lun* and is referred to thus: 'Wares made of imperial paste have a fine, unctuous body. These are the best. Also fine are the plain pieces with an inturned waist and unglazed rim. Although these are thick [in paste], they are in colour both white and mellow. They are not as expensive as Ting ware. Pieces made in the Yüan Dynasty with small feet, impressed patterns, and bearing the mark, *Shu Fu*, are of a very high order. New pieces, however, have large feet. Among them the plain pieces lack unctuousness and the blue-and-white *(ch'ing hua)* and the multicoloured *(wu-sě)* specimens are vulgar in taste'. The ware is also known as *shu-fu* because these characters are frequently found as part of the decorative scheme, in raised slip under the characteristically milky, semi-opaque glaze which covers a fine and firmly homogeneous porcelain body with iron impurities.

The *Ko Ku Yao Lun* [A] in its reference to 'Ancient Jao-chou Ware' describes it as coming 'from present day Fou-liang-hsien in Jao-chou, Chiangsi. The present day products in white and lustrous ware are the best. There are also (dark blue as well as black) wares with gold decoration. These are mostly wine-cups, and are delightful objects.' A few pieces exist of the somewhat heavy-bodied Yüan type of ware on which traces of a former gilt decoration are still discernible.

The following precisely dated example is of a mould which embodies the characteristics of these rather substantial pieces.

52. **1301** MOULD for impressing decoration on the interior of bowls; of light brown pottery. The convex side is decorated with a flowering lotus and leaves skilfully contained within a circular medallion. On the concave side is incised an inscription reading: 'On the fifteenth day of the fifth month of the fifth year [1301] of the Ta-tê period, the Chiu Tien Wan Man Wang Sze bought and respectfully presented to a superior, the Fan Bowl. Moreover (if it is borrowed) it is non-returnable.' Diameter 7.7 in (19.6 cm) *Asian Art Museum of San Francisco, Avery Brundage Collection*

An interesting piece in the Foundation which seems to bridge the gap between *ch'ing pai* and *shu-fu* is a dish having neither the glossy brilliance of the former nor the dull opaque quality of the latter.

53. **1328** DISH covered with a bluish-green glaze and decorated in low relief with phoenix among clouds, two in the centre and two round the sides. The mark which is written in extremely fine slip on the body before glazing reads: 'Made in the T'ien-shun period [1328].' It has an unglazed base and foot-rim which have burnt reddish brown. Diameter 8.2 in (20.8 cm) *Percival David Foundation*

In 1328 the Emperor T'ai-ting moved to Shang-tu, the northern capital, where he died in August of the same year. He was succeeded by his nine-year-old son who reigned as T'ien-shun for ninety days.

Alongside the production of these typically fourteenth-century wares, the kilns at Chi-chou continued to make representative facsimiles of the celebrated Ting-chou porcelain. This practice was maintained until well into the Ming Dynasty as the following reference shows.

54. **1343** Another interesting piece of the fourteenth century, which is so rare in marked specimens, is this JAR AND COVER with pointed knop. Creamy-white porcelain with close crackle, stained brown in places, and decorated with incised floral scrolls. Incised under the glaze round the neck is an inscription reading: 'Made in the third year [1343] of the Chih-chêng period.' It has been described as Tung-ch'i ware. Height 12 in (30.5 cm) *Museum of Fine Arts, Boston*

It is recorded in the history of the Ming Government that the Ch'ü-yang kilns were ordered to make hundreds of wine jars and vases for the Imperial court in the Hsüan-tê period (1426–35). By the end of the sixteenth century, Ting ware of the Sung Dynasty had achieved an exalted reputation, as well as the further compliment of being imitated, one of the greatest copyists being Chou T'an-ch'uan, a native of Wu-men, Kiangsi. The story goes that during the Lung-ch'ing and Wan-li periods (1567–1619), he went to Ching-tê-chên where he made imitations of Sung Ting wares. He came to be recognized as a craftsman of great skill. His copies of Ting vessels (cauldrons) were said to have deceived the most experienced connoisseurs of the time. A cauldron of steatitic ware with a lemon glaze and decorated with *t'ao tieh* masks was lent by the Chinese Government to the International Exhibition of Chinese Art in London in 1935 and described as 'Chou Yao'.

Unfortunately, there are no precisely dated pieces of the Hsüan-tê period, nor of the reign of T'ien-shun (1457–64), although an example of the extremely rare porcelain of the latter exists with the four-character mark of the period. This is a white stem-bowl decorated on the exterior with three flying animals—a horse, an elephant, and a lion—and in the centre of the interior with an inscription reading: 'T'ien-shun nien tsao' under the lustrous creamy-white glaze (Height 4.2 in (10.7 cm)).

The reign of Ch'êng-hua (1465–87) is also lacking in precisely dated material, although a most interesting document of the period exists in the form of a seal of Tê-hua porcelain. A product of the province of Fukien, it was actually made for the director of the Imperial porcelain manufactory at Ching-tê-chên in the adjacent

province of Kiangsi. It is a finely modelled piece of exceptional rarity, and intended
for the exclusive use of this eminent director, Chu Yuan-tso, his name being
engraved on the seal before it was fired.

Fukien Province had been noted for its pottery since Sung times, when it became
famous for Chien ware bowls, the black-glazed products of Chien-an Hsien and
Chien-yang Hsien, both in the prefecture of Chien-ning Fu. In recent years, no
fewer than twenty-two areas have been discovered by excavation to have been
producing pre-Ming wares, in addition to Tê-hua, and many more are known to
have existed, for Fukien abounds in kiln sites, and shards are everywhere, dating
from Sung times almost to the present day.

It is not until the reign of Chêng-tê (1506–21) that we can produce a precisely
dated example of Fukien ware, although probably not from a Tê-hua kiln.
Nevertheless, it is again an object of documentary interest.

55. **1511** BOWL with inturned mouth and rounded sides terminating in a small foot. Round
the shoulders is an inscription in greenish-brown glaze which includes the date of the 'Sixth
year [1511] of Chêng-tê'. Diameter 7 in (17.8 cm) *British Museum*

The reigns of Chia-ching and Lung-ch'ing are not represented by precisely dated
pieces in any of the vast range of white wares, and so we must wait until the Emperor
Wan-li ascends the throne in 1573 before we can continue our story.

56. **1575** BELL, drum-shaped, with pale greyish-white glaze and decorated with a row of bosses on the shoulders and a dragon in high relief on the top. The body is embellished with moulded Buddhist figures on either side of an inscription which reads: 'An-kuo Ssu [Temple for Pacifying the Nation], eighth day, fourth month, third year [1575] of Wan-li.' Height 9.2 in (23.4 cm) *Asian Art Museum of San Francisco, Avery Brundage Collection*

The most famous temple of this name was the old dwelling-place of the T'ang emperor Jui Tsung (710–13) built in the first year of his reign in the eastern part of the Hsien-ning district of Shensi. This is probably not the same temple as the one named in the inscription, however, since An-kuo is a name which was used for many temples.

57. **1593** VASE of baluster form with two elephant-head handles. On the neck and round the body below a flanged rim is a long dedicatory inscription which gives the information that 'One [?] Hui, resident of Ch'ing-t'ai-li, Chia-ch'i fu, offers (to the temple) this handsome pair of flower vases for the protection of his family, to ensure prosperity and good fortune, bumper crops and flourishing herds. Twelfth day, first month, twenty-first year [1593] of Wan-li.' Height 11.7 in (29.7 cm) *Private Collector*

It is perhaps strange that more than three hundred years were to elapse between our dated Kuan-yin of 1298 and the reappearance of sculptural figures as a serious ceramic shape from a particular area. As predicted, these were from the famous kilns of Tê-hua, Ch'uan-chou Prefecture, Fukien Province, some one hundred miles north of Amoy. This district was originally formed in the T'ang Dynasty, when it was known as Tê-chen. In 824 the area was re-named Tê-hua, by which it has been known throughout the intervening centuries. The following are precisely dated pieces of exceptionally fine quality.

58. **1610** FIGURE OF THE GOD OF WEALTH, TSAI-SHÊN, in creamy-white porcelain tinged with green, and with appropriate emblems in relief. Chain-mail armour is to be seen at the knee and below the collar, while almost the entire surface is incised with flower scrolls; appropriate slits appear at ears, nostrils, mouth and chin for the insertion of hair. Incised under the glaze in four vertical columns at the rear of the stand on which the figure is seated

is an inscription reading: 'Made at the *wei* hour of the *jen-yin* day, the sixteenth day of the third month of spring in the thirty-seventh year [1610—between one and three o'clock in the afternoon of the 19 April] of the reign-period of Wan-li.' Height 10.5 in (26.7 cm) *British Museum*

59. **1615** SEATED FIGURE OF KUAN-YIN covered with a creamy-white glaze. On the base is an inscription reading: 'K'ai-yuan Buddhist Monastery, village of Tung-ch'i outside the eastern gate [of the city wall] of Tung-an Hsien, Chang-chou Fu, in the forty-second year [1615] of the Wan-li period of the Great Ming Dynasty. Respectfully offered by Mrs Lin (neé Shih) a lay disciple.' Height 19.25 in (48.9 cm) *Asian Art Museum of San Francisco, Avery Brundage Collection*

60. **1629** FIGURE OF KUAN-YIN, seated on a high rock with one knee upraised; an attendant on either side, forming a characteristic pose of the Goddess of Mercy. Fine white porcelain covered with a cream glaze of greenish tone. The ornament is simple; a few beads in relief form the necklace, the hair depicted by slight incisions. On the base is an inscription reading: 'Peace and pure good luck for a birth at the *ch'ou* hour of the ninth day of the seventh month of the second year [1629—between one and three o'clock of the 6 August] of the Ch'ung-chêng period.' It is thus a thank-offering for the birth of a son, showing Kuan-yin the Maternal to be firmly established quite early in the seventeenth century. Height 9.75 in (24.8 cm) *City Museum and Art Gallery, Hong Kong*

61. **1639** VASE of baluster form with two mask and ring handles. Fine white porcelain with warm white glaze. On the base is an inscription in a single column in greenish brown glaze reading: 'Made in the twelfth month of the twelfth year [1639] of Ch'ung-chêng.' Height 11.9 in (30.2 cm) *Percival David Foundation*

4

BLUE AND WHITE

ONE OF THE MANY UNSOLVED MYSTERIES OF Chinese ceramics is the period when they were first decorated with painting in blue. In the T'ang Dynasty, a method was evolved for the use of a cobalt oxide, applied as a single colour, or in combination with the familiar yellow, green, and white glazes of the period. Sometimes these were employed as part of a splashed technique, but more frequently the colours were applied to enrich the designs of a decorative pattern. Remarkably advanced as this method then appeared to be, it is a long way from the blue and white porcelain concerning us now, for it is not until 1351 that we can produce the precisely dated examples which have made this particular category familiar to all connoisseurs of Chinese ceramics. This present type developed in a way which has little in common with the earlier T'ang methods, where the painting was applied directly to the clay body, and the surface left uncovered. At a later date, the technique varied, whereby a slip or opaque glaze was applied to the body of the vessel before it was decorated; the surface was then covered with a transparent glaze and fired at a high temperature. The potter had by now learnt the importance of felspathic ingredients, and had so mastered the development and control of the blue pigment that he achieved success to a remarkable degree.

Although it is reasonably certain that this method of procedure began in the Sung Dynasty, and many authorities believe that it did, the fact remains that no piece as yet has been linked conclusively to that period. So it is for lack of earlier dated material that we begin our discussion of blue and white porcelain with the Yüan Dynasty (1260–1368), and with a pair of temple vases in the Percival David Foundation. These are still the earliest authenticated specimens of this ware, and as such have formed the standard for the dating of all similar pieces. Amongst the most important of these are the fourteenth-century items included in the gift made by Shah ʿAbbas to the Ardebil Shrine in 1612, since moved to the Archaeological Museum in Teheran, and those of similar date in the large collection accumulated by the Ottoman sultans, and now in the Topkapu Serai, Istanbul. It has, however, been

62. **1351** Pair of TEMPLE VASES, of monumental form, with high hollow foot and elephant handles. The decoration, executed in brilliant blue, is distributed in a series of bands, the main field bearing a vigorous four-clawed dragon pursuing a pearl through clouds, with a wave pattern below. On one vase the mouth of the dragon is closed, on the other it is open. Round the foot is a peony scroll above a band of auspicious symbols. On the shoulder is a floral scroll and the lower part of the neck is decorated with a phoenix among clouds; the upper part with plantain leaves, interrupted on one side to make space for a long inscription

which reads: 'The faithful disciple and member of the Ching-t'ang Society, Chang Wen-chin of Te-hsiao lane in the village of Hsin-chou, is happy to present an altar set of an incense burner and vases as a prayer for the protection of the whole family and for the peace and prosperity of his descendants. Recorded on a lucky day in the fourth month of the eleventh year [1351] of Chih-chen. Dedicated before the Hsing Yuan Altar of the General Hu Ching-i.' Height 25 in (63.5 cm) *Percival David Foundation*

the sophistication of the complex decorative designs on the pair of dated vases in the Percival David Foundation which has prolonged the search for earlier precisely documented material, since these represent the apogee of endeavour and must therefore post-date a less ambitious undertaking. It will be interesting to see whether future excavations by the Chinese produce positive evidence for a date earlier than this.

Apart from the basic importance of the date, the Buddhist context of the offering is not without interest, for the Ching-t'ang Society may have been a religious club attached to the monastery for the promotion of social and economic functions. Such institutions are referred to in manuscripts found at Tun-huang, and give as their objective the financing of activities to promote the Buddhist religion. The complex and varied nature of the numerous decorative motifs is also worthy of detailed study, recalling, as it does, certain elements from earlier techniques of Tz'u-chou and *ch'ing pai*. The banded floral arabesque, the cloud patterns and the waving water-weeds (eel-grass) sprouting like hairs from the dragon's leg joints have a close affinity with Tz'u-chou, while the lotus-petal base and the rising plantain leaves of the neck proclaim a *ch'ing pai* tradition. Even the Southern Sung academic style of painting is represented by the technical refinement of the brush-drawing in the carefully delineated waves and the precisely constructed dragon.

There has been nothing in the way of convincing proof for a positive date earlier than 1351 from recent excavations. Fragments of blue and white, datable from the eleventh to the late fourteenth century, have been found at Kharakhoto, Inner Mongolia; at Aidhab, a port on the African coast of the Red Sea, where trading with the Far East continued until the destruction of the city in 1426; and at Fostât (Old Cairo), a site which has yielded many pieces bearing fifteenth-century reign-marks.

Underglaze blue was also used for a type of porcelain which has been well described as 'white on blue'. Few of these have survived, and none are precisely dated. One of the most splendid examples is a *mei-p'ing* in the Musée Guimet, Paris, decorated in white relief on a blue ground with a typical Yüan dragon.

Still another related porcelain type used underglaze blue as a monochrome, wholly or in part, with both incised and moulded decoration. A bowl, formerly in the author's collection, at present unique, combines a blue exterior with a red interior, and leads us to the most unusual Yüan Dynasty ceramic innovation, white porcelain decorated with underglaze copper red. This technique, whose relationship to the blue and white of contemporary date is readily apparent, was in actual fact far less successful, for the critical firing conditions were not usually solved by the potter, with the result that most examples are either dull red or grey black in colour. There are exceptions, however, which are of a pronounced vermilion tint, although it was not until the early years of the fifteenth century that a really brilliant red was achieved. There are, unluckily, no precisely dated pieces of the Yüan Dynasty.

The Chinese scholar in the fourteenth century carried on the cultural traditions of his past heritage. He was thus endowed with an aesthetic appreciation of refinement in the arts. With such a background he naturally regarded blue and white decorated porcelain as rather vulgar in taste and therefore unsuitable for his environment. But since he represented only a small segment of the population, the richly ornamented pieces of blue and white made in such great quantity at this time were in response to the requirements of the every-growing export trade with the Near East. This elaborate style gradually evolved into the restrained elegance of the fifteenth century, when the kilns at Ching-tê-chên submitted to Imperial patronage and produced some of the finest specimens in China's ceramic history. But such pieces were so dominated by empirical standards as to design, shape and mark that the occasion for a precisely dated specimen would have been almost non-existent. In this way passed the reign of Yung-lo (1403–24), the first of the early fifteenth-century periods which we associate with ceramic perfection, as we have seen. This era was equally famous for its white and copper-red monochromes, which even excelled those of the Hsüan-tê period (1426–35), a reign most celebrated for its blue and white porcelain, and a worthy example of which is represented by our next piece.

63. **1433** Square SEAL surmounted by a half-circular handle decorated with two dragons pursuing a pearl, with appropriate emblems on either side of the surface below. On the sides of the base at each end of the handle appear two inscriptions. The first reads: 'Made in the eighth year [1433] of the Hsüan-tê period', and the second: 'Kindness to all is your duty.' The seal was probably presented to a provincial magistrate. Height 3.5 in (8.9 cm) *Mr F. Gordon Morrill, Boston*

Hsüan-tê, grandson of Yung-lo, was a lover of music, and a patron of the arts who took a keen personal interest in the Imperial factory at Ching-tê-chên, from where this delightful piece very probably emanated. He was succeeded in 1435 by his suppositious nine-year-old son, Chêng-t'ung, as already mentioned, who became the sixth emperor of the Ming Dynasty. Chêng-t'ung was completely dominated by his mother and by the palace eunuchs, who in their effort to gain control divided the court into contending factions. Despite these internal dissensions, the Imperial palaces in Peking were completed and equipped. In 1449 Chêng-t'ung commanded an expeditionary force against the Tartars (Weilate) by whom he was defeated and taken prisoner. In 1450 he was succeeded by his younger brother Ching-t'ai, the year in which Chêng-t'ung was released by Weilate. On his brother's death in 1457 he re-ascended the throne as T'ien-shun. He was, incidentally, the first Ming emperor to forbid the sacrifice of his concubines on his death.

I have explained that inscribed pieces of this thirty year 'ceramic interregnum' are exceptionally rare, for it was a period when political turbulence and civil war alternated with brief interludes of uneasy peace. There were seven reigns, four representing three monarchs and three more of rebel claimants. The political confusion caused by this pursuit of power was reflected in the far-away provinces of Kiangsi, Chekiang, and Fukien, where many of the potter inhabitants were enlisted for military service and so limited was the number of private kilns operating, that the manufacture of ceramics became greatly restricted. No longer could the officials in Peking rely on Ching-tê-chên to replenish their orders after the closure of the Imperial factory. It was again, as throughout history, that the resourceful individual made a virtue of necessity; and the scholar-potter was not found wanting. There is a remarkably interesting group of blue and white pieces—very few marked, and none precisely so—that can be assigned to this period. Naturally, many of them reflect the characteristics of Hsüan-tê and earlier porcelain. Others reveal a spontaneity and freedom of drawing for which their imaginative artists were so ideally suited, and the resulting creations have delighted the most discerning critic.

Ch'êng-hua, eldest son of Chêng-t'ung, ascended to the throne in 1465, the year in which the Imperial factory was re-opened and many of the private potters were induced to return to Ching-tê-chên. From here emerged some of the finest porcelain that ever graced the ancestral temples and the banqueting halls of the nation's capital. The Chinese have expressed the opinion, in their appraisement of Ming wares, that the products of this reign rank second only to those of Hsüan-tê.

After Ch'êng-hua's death in 1487, a new style of decoration on porcelain gradually emerged whereby the boldly imaginative splashes of colour were replaced by a method in which carefully drawn outlines were filled in with a uniform wash. With this came a conformity that resulted in a decline in the execution of the drawing and in the control of the cobalt. The following year Ch'êng-hua was succeeded by his son Hung-chih, as I have already described, whose reign lasted eighteen years and was comparatively peaceful, except for a minor earthquake and for the disastrous occasion in 1489 when the Yellow River broke through its high embankment, only to repeat the calamity four years later (see also page 118). Taoism was out of favour at court, and all relevant literature was ordered to be burnt. This was soon followed by the expulsion of every foreign monk, and the restoration to power of the Confucian officials. Information regarding the reopening of the Imperial factory is not well documented, and it may well be that it remained closed during this reign-period. It is true that the potters at Ching-tê-chên continued to work in the earlier traditions, and made pieces that were thin and resonant, but somehow the magic touch of the artist was lacking. Altogether there are very few marked specimens of this reign and it is a piece of provincial manufacture which supplies our late fifteenth-century precisely dated item. The inscription even includes the name of the potter himself.

64. **1496** TEMPLE VASE of baluster form with two handles springing from animal masks on the neck. The central zone is decorated with formalized lotus scrolls, with rocks, bamboo and clouds below, and with upward pointing leaves above. Under the rolled lip is an inscription reading: 'The faithful disciple Ch'eng Piao, of the Ch'eng Family in the Li-jen village in the Fou-liang district of Jao-chou prefecture in the province of Kiangsi, rejoices to send as an offering to the Kuang-wang Temple in Peking, in the prefecture of Shun-t'ien, this altar set of an incense burner and (two) vases, to remain there as a perpetual prayer for the support and protection of the whole family, that they may have peace and prosperity, and that their business affairs may flourish. Made on a lucky day in the fifth month of the ninth year [20 June 1496] of the Hung-chih period by the disciple Ch'eng Ts'un-erh.' Height 24.5 in (62.2 cm) *Percival David Foundation*

In 1497 the Portuguese navigator, Vasco da Gama, was sent in command of a naval expedition to discover the Cape route to India. On Christmas Day of this same year he touched land on the east coast of Africa which he named Natal. Crossing the Indian Ocean brought him to Calicut in May of the following year. His ship was the first from Portugal to reach India, an exploit which led eventually to a trade route with the Far East, beginning in 1511 with the establishment of a base at Malacca, from which periodic visits were made to Canton, Ch'ang-chou, Ch'uan-chou, and Ningpo.

Chêng-tê, grandson of Ch'êng-hua and eldest son of Hung-chih, succeeded to the throne in 1506 on the death of his father (see Chapter 1 and Chapter 5). He reigned for sixteen years and died at the untimely age of thirty, partly as a result, no doubt, of his misspent youth, for which the palace eunuchs must be held responsible. His interest in foreign affairs seems to have been confined to languages and religions. The Muslim merchant and traveller, Ali Akbar, who visited China in the year of his accession, when the emperor was but fifteen years old, reports that among the palace courtiers were many of his countrymen, and even a number of Muslim ladies in the emperor's harem. The power of Islam was exercised in other directions, too, for some of the best blue and white porcelain made during this reign bear inscriptions in Arabic or, more rarely, Persian. Most of these were designed for the scholar's writing table, and were of good quality, although the majority of other pieces display the declining technique which was to herald the beginning of a new era, and mark the final transition from the fifteenth-century style.

It is not from this category, however, that we can produce our next precisely dated piece, which is an example in purely Chinese taste and displays much of the spirited drawing we associate with the previous century.

65. **1520** ALMS BOWL decorated with winged dragons on the outside; a carp surrounded by waves on the inside. There is an inscription along the outside rim reading: 'Made in the fifteenth year [1520] of the Chêng-tê period of the Great Ming Dynasty to the order of Mr Wu Tzu-yen, a merchant who travelled through the Jao-chou district of Fouliang. He offered the bowl to a temple and prayed for success in business, and well-being and good fortune for his family.' Diameter 7 in (17.8 cm) *City Museum and Art Gallery, Hong Kong*

Chia-ching, another grandson of Ch'êng-hua, and first cousin of Chêng-tê, succeeded to the throne in 1522 and reigned for forty-five years. Unlike some of his predecessors he was strong-willed and, contrary to accepted practice, selected his immediate entourage without first consulting the ever-powerful eunuchs. In 1536 he became attracted to Taoism, and cleared the Forbidden City of all Buddhist images. Fourteen years later he reverted to the cult of Buddhism, although in his declining years he turned back to the lure of Taoist magic, and died, it is said, from taking drugs to achieve the goal of his lifetime—the elixir of immortality.

It was a period of internal disturbances and Tartar incursions around Peking, while the south-east coastline was raided by the Japanese several times between 1555 and 1562. One event of a peaceful nature in the history of foreign relations occurred in 1536 when China allowed the Portuguese to settle in Macau.

The morale of the potters at Ching-tê-chên seems to have reached an all-time low throughout the reign, owing to maladministration on the part of the government officials. Much pilfering took place, especially of the Mohammedan blue, and the controls that were of necessity introduced alienated many of the potters who left to work in private kilns. Nevertheless, great quantities of porcelain of Imperial quality were produced. There was even a determined effort to emulate the early fifteenth-century wares and traditional designs of that time were revived. (See also page 98.) However, they are not convincing copies, and it is rather with an original theme that the artist excels as an individualist. The following pieces indicate the great heights to which the craftsmen of this period could ascend.

66. **1543** JAR with wide mouth, decorated with gentlemen at leisure in a landscape; round the rim is a band of feather decoration. On the base is an inscription reading: 'Made in the twenty-second year [1543] of the Chia-ching period' within a double blue ring. Diameter 5.3 in (13.5 cm) *Percival David Foundation*

67. **1549** WINE JAR decorated with a band of phoenix among lotus on the shoulders and with four winged fish-dragons between clouds and breaking waves on the main zone; a deep band of petal panels above the foot. The dedicatory inscription of one hundred and seventy-five characters is contained within a cartouche and reads: 'At Wu-yun of Chi [i.e. in Chi-an Prefecture, Wu-yun township] in the suburb of Shih-san-tu li; Hu Tsung-yao, Buddhist of strict observance, makes a donation, in prayer for the family succession and for the protection of his life, and with his wife Ch'en Chin-yu, his father I-ch'ao, his mother Lo Hsin-hsiu, his younger brothers, Tsung-wei, Tsung-hsiu and Tsung-hsi, his nephew Hsuan, his younger sisters-in-law Ou-yang, Lai and K'ang, his daughter I-shun and his niece I-tung—being all members the family, sincerely adores the condescending benevolence of the Great Creator. I, Tsung-yao, thankful for existence but concerned at the lack of offspring in this life, hereby devoutly purchase a water-pot [shui-hu] and present it as an offering to the Shrine of Eternal Peace; at the same time I light candles and acknowledge the Almighty praying for the mercy of all-scrutinizing Providence; and I may forthwith be granted wise sons, and that I may fare well in acquiring wealth, that my family goods may be abundant, that all my wishes be fulfilled, that all my prayers be answered. Moreover, my wife and I are ill-fated and have great difficulty in bearing children. Furthermore, my parents are suffering from misfortunes and are distressed as the result of farm taxes. For all these reasons I vowed to donate this water-pot to the Pavilion of the Clear Spring, in token of my sincere sentiments, and at the same time I lay sacrificial fruits before the altar of Universal Mercy, and with the prayer; that my wife be blessed with many sons, that my parents be granted long life and good health, that I may be successful in my plans and in acquiring good renown, that my family may prosper, I purchase one water-pot and present it to the Pavilion of the Clear Spring as an offering for ever. I humbly pray that favourable notice may be taken of this. Inscribed by the Monk Ch'ung-teh, who solicited this donation, on an auspicious day in the first month of the twenty-seventh year [1549] of the Chia-ching reign of the Great Ming Dynasty.' Height 14.5 in (36.8 cm) *Sir John Addis*

Wu-yun township which dates back to the Sung Dynasty is in the district of Wan-an which is within the prefecture of Chi-an and five miles south-south-west of Chi-an in Kiangsi Province. 'Wu-yun of Chi' is an abbreviated but sufficiently clear way of indicating the location. Chi-an is of course familiar as the source of the *temmoku* bowls, but what is more significant in the present context is that Chi-an and Wu-yun are easily accessible by the regular river trade-route from Jao-chou and Ching-tê-chên where the jar was undoubtedly made. The Kan River on which Chi-an and Wu-yun stand was the main trade-route from the lower Yangtze to Canton. The 1496 vase in the Foundation was also presented by a native of Jao-chou Prefecture. There is a similarly decorated vessel in the Field Museum of Natural History, Chicago, although the dedicatory inscription of seventy-one characters is undated.

68. **1552** VASE with pear-shaped body, curved neck and wide flaring mouth. Lions playing with the streamers of brocaded balls decorate the central zone; while plantain leaves and beaded string motifs appear on the neck and streamers above the foot. Over the central zone two lines of Portuguese are written upside down in crudely formed letters. These were obviously inscribed by a Chinese artisan who was unfamiliar with the foreign language and who merely copied the text he was given. The date has been read as 1552 and part of the lines as 'O mandou fazer Jorge Alvrz' or freely translated 'Jorge Alvares ordered it to be made'. This Jorge Alvares has been identified as the second of two Portuguese seamen of that name who went to the Orient in the sixteenth century. Alvares was a close friend of the 'Apostle of the Indies', St. Francis Xavier, and their presence on the island of Samchuao (Sang-chuan), some thirty leagues from Canton, in the year 1552 has been recorded. On the base in a cash symbol are the characters reading: 'May endless blessings embrace your affairs.' Height 8 in (20.4 cm) *Walters Art Gallery, Baltimore*

69. **1552** BOTTLE with pear-shaped body and bell-shaped metal cover surmounted by a knob. Decorated on the body with an aquatic scene of ducks and water-plants. Above this is

an inscription, written upside-down, which appears to be incomplete but which states that the piece was made for Jorge Anrz (short for Anriques or Alvarez) in 1552. Height 9.5 in (24.1 cm) *Victoria and Albert Museum*

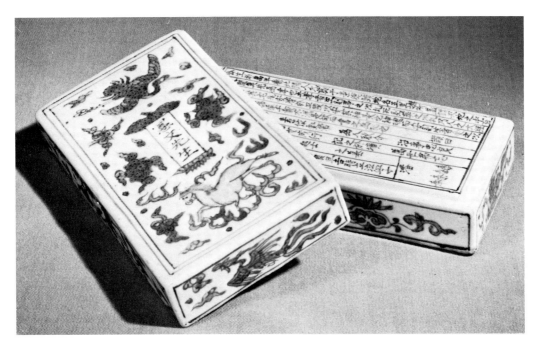

70. **1555** TOMB TABLET in the form of a rectangular box decorated round the straight sides with fungus scrolls, birds, flowers and fruit, insects, a phoenix and a lion. On the top is a small rectangular panel in which is the dead man's descriptive name; round this are clouds, a crane and a fiery horse. Inside the cover is written a record of the birth and death and burial; on the upper face of the lower half of the box is written the epitaph and eulogy, and on the base is the record of the reinterment and setting up of the tablet. The inscription reads: 'Our late father was born in the *wei* watch [1–3 a.m.] in the morning of the thirteenth day of the twelfth month of the *i-ssŭ* year [19 November 1485] and he died in the *hai* watch [9–11 p.m.] on the eighteenth day of the seventh month of the *i-ssŭ* year [24 August 1545] and now we reinter him in the *mao* watch [5–7 a.m.] on the twenty-fourth day of the tenth month of the *i-mao* year [7 November 1555] in this north-facing hill, with the mound orientated north and south. Here the Dragon appears.' On the upper face of the lower half: 'He was born in the district of Wan-nien and was a man of Pei-yu; he is buried at Ching-tê-chên in the cemetery of Wu-li as in the heart of the universe. Nothing comes before filial piety. Those who have filial piety serve the living according to the proper ceremonies, and the dead they bury in accordance with the rites; this is man's greatest duty. Now by divination we have found this place and the omens are auspicious. The coffin is interred in the mound in order to bring tranquillity to the spirit. When the spirit is at peace, the living inherit happiness, wealth and honours for as long as a thousand years and ten thousand generations. The reason

why we have written this is to keep the record. Our eulogy says: "Oh! Alas! Your goodness and virtue. You lived simply, in peace and prosperity. As a man you were resolute and straightforward. In all you did, you were loyal and good. You fostered respect for precedence between old and young, and your sons and daughters have flourished. We record this in the tomb for ten thousand generations that you may not be forgotten.' In the tomb of the retired scholar, the late P'an Chao-t'ang, of the Ming Dynasty, known as Hsienwên, his mourning sons set up this tablet at an auspicious hour on this good day, twentyfourth day, tenth month, in the winter of the thirty-fourth year [7 November 1555] of the Chia-ching period. P'an Tai, P'an Ch'un, P'an Ch'in, P'an Fêng.' On the base: 'His sons set up the tablet correctly in the tenth month of the thirty-fourth year of Chia-ching of the Great Ming Dynasty [November 1555].' Length 7.1 in (18 cm) *Percival David Foundation*

71. **1561** JAR of *kuan* shape, decorated with figures in a landscape; below a border of petal-shaped panels and above a floral scroll interspersed with playing lions. Round the neck is a brocade border with flowers and small panels containing characters reading: 'A hundred pots of delicious wine for official use', and 'Made in the fortieth year [1561] of the Chia-ching period.' Height 12.2 in (31 cm) *Private Collector*

Lung-ch'ing, son of Chia-ching, succeeded his father in 1567 and ruled for six years. It was an uneventful reign with the eunuchs once more all-powerful, and what had come to be expected as part of nature's counteraction to man's progression, floods and earthquakes. The decoration on blue and white porcelain in general continued in the Chia-ching tradition, although some designs are of a distinctly erotic nature, reflecting, it is said, the less reputable side of the Emperor's

72. **1564** SCROLL WEIGHT modelled in the form of a bell of oval octagonal section. Decorated with scrolling lotus and Buddhist emblems within formal borders. In two of the eight panels is an inscription reading: 'For the use of the family of Wu Chih-lun, made in the forty-third year [1564] of the Chia-ching period.' Height 3.5 in (8.9 cm) *Kiuan Wou*

73. **1566** BOWL with rounded sides and decorated on the exterior with pairs of birds perched in the branches of fruiting peach and prunus, the foot with an undulating scroll border and the interior with a peach spray enclosed by blue ground waves and scroll borders. On the base is an inscription reading: 'Made in the forty-fifth year [1566] of Chia-ching' within a double blue rectangular frame. Diameter 6 in (15.3 cm) *Private Collector*

character. There are very few pieces with the reign-mark of Lung-ch'ing, and no precisely dated examples are recorded.

Wan-li, son of Lung-ch'ing, succeeded his father in 1573 at the age of ten. His regime of forty-seven years (1573–1619) began well enough under an able prime minister, but before long the reins of government again reverted to the eunuchs. Now, however, in addition to domestic problems, they had to face the very real threat of invasion, primarily from an endless series of Manchu incursions, during one of which Japanese troops landed at Fusan, Korea. The year was 1592, and the general, the famous Hideyoshi, who successfully led his troops to victory at Seoul. There seems to have been no worthy successor, for after his death in 1598 the Japanese armies did not again invade China until the present century. The Spaniards were also active in the Pacific Ocean, and in the Philippines, which they finally conquered during this reign, and which remained in their possession almost consistently for some three centuries, as we saw in Chapter 1.

The potters at Ching-tê-chên were also having their troubles. The Ma An Mountains, which had been the original source of the fine clay in use since the beginning of the Ming Dynasty, were becoming exhausted. Another site, Wu-men T'o, although able to supply equally good material was double the distance from Ching-tê-chên, so that the time and expense involved in transporting the clay would only be justified for use for Imperial wares. The private potters had therefore to be content with the rather inferior clay which was to be found in the vicinity of their local kilns. A similar situation would have been created by the fast dwindling supply of 'Mohammedan' blue, had not the resourceful potters been able to develop an excellent colour from native cobalt. A trifle pale, admittedly, and of a somewhat silvery hue, but ideally suited to the pieces in the style of the Ch'êng-hua period which were then being made. Such a piece is the small incense burner, dated 1612, which includes the name of the maker and will appear in its appropriate chronological sequence (see page 102). This is but one of the many comparable examples decorated in the same delicate style which support the Chinese records that most of the pieces made in the last hundred years of the Ming Dynasty were the work of artist potters. Their standard was high and they elevated the rather derogatory term 'provincial' by imitating so well the masterpieces of the fifteenth century and creating new styles which were themselves to be a source of inspiration to their descendants in the succeeding centuries.

We are indebted to Father Ricci, the Italian Jesuit priest, for a contemporary account of the Chinese porcelain industry at the end of the sixteenth century. He had entered China through the port of Canton in 1582, and some eleven years later was received by the emperor in Peking, the capital, which he found to be as dissipated as the ancient city of Babylon.

The so-called provincial wares, which number amongst them all the precisely dated material here recorded, are represented by the following noteworthy pieces of the Wan-li period. (See also pages 122–5.)

74. **1580** Circular INK-PALETTE with rounded sides and decorated with debased classic scrolls in white against a pale greyish-blue ground. On the glazed base is an inscription reading: 'Made in the eighth year [1580] of Wan-li for an official of the T'ien shui chün.' Diameter 4.4 in (11.2 cm) *Percival David Foundation*

75. **1587** ALMS BOWL, unglazed on the base, which has no foot-ring, and unglazed inside except for a band on the inward inclined rim. Decorated outside with four flower sprays, the prunus, peony, chrysanthemum, and lotus. Round the rim runs an inscription reading: 'Made to order for the use of Ch'en Tung-shan on an auspicious day in the first summer month of the fifteenth year [1587] of the Wan-li period of the Great Ming Dynasty.' Diameter 6.2 in (15.7 cm) *Percival David Foundation*

76. **1592** ANCESTRAL SHRINE divided into three niches with Ts'ai P'ing-shan, the deceased,

99

sitting between his two wives. The first wife is on his right with honorific title *fu-ren*; on the left, the second wife or *kung-ren*. On either side are inscriptions: by *fu-ren*, 'Going west, the Queen Mother descends to the jade pond', and 'In the rain, bamboo leaves shed green tears'. By *kung-ren*, 'Coming east, purple clouds fill the Han Ku Gate', and 'When snow falls, prunus blossoms wear white crown'. On the back is an inscription reading: 'Mr Ts'ai P'ing-shan, whose given name was Li-ch'eng, enjoyed eighty-six years of life. He was a descendant of Lord Ch'eng-i. He served in the army of the Great Ming Country. In the twenty-sixth year [1548] of Chia-ching, an uncle, Ts'ai Chin, was given the office of Inspector of Rites. He was later killed by the rebel Prince of An-hua in the forty-eighth year [1570]. By the grace of His Majesty, Ts'ai P'ing-shan was allowed to retire to his land so that he might devote his time to farming, weaving and educating his children. The family prospered and four generations lived in the same house. At the age of eighteen he married a daughter of the Chin family who gave him four sons. At twenty-two he married a daughter of the Teng family who gave him five sons. He was born on the third day of the third month of the second year [1597] of Chêng-tê; he died on the eleventh day of the seventh month of the twentieth year [1592] of Wan-li. This shrine is made in reverent worship and for communication in generations to come. Dedicated with a hundred bows, in the Great Ming Dynasty on an auspicious day in the autumn month of the twentieth year of Wan-li by the reverently worshipping sons, Chuan, Lai, Shiu, Shun, Fu-ho, Te, T'ai, Lin, Pao; sons and granddaughters, nephews and nieces. Height 35.2 in (89.4 cm) *City Museum and Art Gallery, Hong Kong*

77. **1595** PAINT-PALETTE with short rounded sides and recessed base, decorated round the sides with two phoenix and two floral scrolls. On the wide flat base is an inscription reading: 'An auspicious day in the summer months of the twenty-third year of the Wan-li period [1595] of the Great Ming Dynasty; a vessel for the use of P'êng Mou-lin.' This is followed by a commendatory mark reading: 'Fine vessel for the Jade Hall.' Diameter 4.5 in (11.4 cm) *Percival David Foundation*

78. **1597** STOVE JAR with rounded sides and waisted neck below a straight-sided mouth-rim. The body of the vessel is decorated with figures in a garden, trees, rocks, and waves in the foreground, the sun and clouds overhead. In the centre of the neck on a raised band is an inscription reading: 'Dedicated by the Buddhist disciple Huang Hui-san when he was sixty-one years old in the spring of the twenty-fifth year [1597] of the Wan-li period of the Great Ming Dynasty.' Height 14 in (35.6 cm) *D. Bolton*

79. **1601** SAUCER with everted rim, decorated outside with two sprays of orchids, and in the central field inside with a hare among flowers and rocks. Round the border are peonies, rocks, orchids and a flowering shrub in which perches a bird. On the base is an inscription reading: 'Made in the Hsing-hsu year [1601] of Wan-li' within a double blue ring. Diameter 5.4 in (13.7 cm) *Percival David Foundation*

80. **1604** Miniature MORTAR of flattened circular form inscribed on the exterior in underglaze blue enclosed by double line borders 'Made in the thirty-first year [1604] of the Wan-li period of the Great Ming Dynasty'. The inside and the rounded unglazed base are burnt red around the edges. Diameter 2.3 in (5.8 cm) *Wellcome Trustees*

81. **1612** INCENSE BURNER with slightly curved sides and decorated with formalized scrolls at the base; flowers and leaves below the mouth. On the base is an inscription reading: 'Made at the Cheng-t'ao Kuan [Pottery Moulding Office] in the thirty-ninth year [1612] of Wan-li.' Diameter 3.6 in (9.2 cm) *British Museum, Riesco Collection*

82. **1612** INCENSE BURNER of cylindrical form with three animal-head masks round the base, and decorated with two four-clawed dragons in clouds pursuing pearls above a wave border. These face a cartouche within which is an inscription reading: 'Presented in the thirty-ninth year [1612] of Wan-li to Mr Ming Wang, devout Mohammedan, by his co-religionists of the Honai Department of the Huai-ch'ing prefectural district, Honan, on behalf of all dwellers in the valley along the river's edge.' Height 8.7 in (22.1 cm) *The late P. J. Donnelly*

83. **1617** INCENSE BURNER of rectangular form supported on corner feet, the steep, slightly rounded sides each with a panel recessed on a 'Y'-diaper ground reserved with *ju-i* and cash motifs. Decorating the longer sides are two groups of four of the Eight Immortals in a landscape, carrying attributes and accompanied by a crane, an inscription appearing on either side, reading respectively: 'Made in the forty-fifth year [1617] of Wan-li' and 'Beautiful vessel of Wang Shêng-yu'. On the shorter sides are Ho-ho Erh-hsien and Liu-hai with his toad talking to a young boy, in similar landscapes, the waisted neck with vignettes of cranes and *jui'i* heads on a florette cell-diaper ground below a key-fret border encircling the galleried rim, set on the shoulders with two 'S'-shaped handles; decorated on the recessed exterior with flower sprays and on the curved interior with clouds and trigrams. Height 11.8 in (30 cm) *Private Collector*

84. **1618** INCENSE BURNER decorated with phoenix round the shoulders; encircling the body are two dragons facing an incised cartouche between lotus leaves. The inscription includes a reference to a pair of incense burners and the date of the 'Forty-sixth year [16 April 1618] of Wan-li'. There are three apertures at the foot, two on the shoulders, and a pair of circular holes on the lip. Height 12 in (30.5 cm) *National Museum, Tokyo*

85. **1618** STOVE JAR with rounded sides and short waisted neck. Decorated with a dragon amongst clouds below fungus border-scrolls. In a panel on the body of the jar is a long inscription reading: 'The believer Chi Shang-hsin and his son Chi Wei-hsin in the district of Kao-p'ing in the prefecture of Tzu-chou, in the province of Shansi, made and presented a set of three porcelain stove jars for the Nine Emperors' Hall of the Ch'ing-chen Monastery to be preserved by the Taoist Li Hsuen-i and his friends. This is written in grateful memory of the gift. Made and fired on the sixteenth day of the intercalary fourth month of the forty-sixth year [1618] of Wan-li.' Height 14.5 in (36.8 cm) *The late Sir Harry Garner*

T'ai-ch'ang, eldest son of Wan-li, occupied the throne for one month, 28 August to 26 September 1620. The dowager empress, who was not his mother, is said to have poisoned him because she had hoped to put her own son by Wan-li on the throne. Instead her son banished her, and in time fathered a son—both used the title Prince of Fu—who proclaimed himself emperor at Nanking after the death in 1643 of Ch'ung-chêng, the last Ming ruler. Less than a year later he was captured and killed by the Manchus. We are fortunate in having a precisely dated piece from T'ai-ch'ang's brief reign.

86. **1620** BOWL decorated with figures in a garden, and with an inscription reading: 'Made in the *keng shen* year', which can only apply to the year of the very brief reign of T'ai-ch'ang in 1620. It thus marks the beginning of the transitional era. Diameter 5 in (12.7 cm) *City Museum and Art Gallery, Hong Kong*

T'ien-ch'i, eldest son of T'ai-ch'ang, succeeded his father in 1621, as we have seen. He was fifteen at the time and died in his twenty-second year. Again the destiny of the kingdom fell into the hands of the eunuchs, for this emperor was a dilettante and a carpenter, who preferred to devote himself to the ruler, the square and the chisel rather than to affairs of state. The Manchus continued to increase their territorial gains, and had already occupied Mukden. In 1623 the Dutch took the Pescadores and landed at Amoy, only to be driven out the following year, whereupon they crossed the straits and occupied Formosa. The Imperial kiln does not appear to have been in operation now or in the succeeding reign, and we have again to rely on the private potter for our precisely dated material, of which the following are worthy examples.

87. **1621** ALMS BOWL of squat form on a small foot, decorated with a winged dragon in clouds on the body, and with an inscription round the mouth reading: 'Made in the first year [1621] of the T'ien-ch'i period.' Diameter 5 in (12.7 cm) *Private Collector*

88. **1621** INCENSE BURNER, barrel-shaped, decorated round the body with a running flower scroll; above and below are raised bands. On the base is an inscription reading: 'Made in the first year [1621] of the T'ien-ch'i period.' Height 2.25 in (5.7 cm) *British Museum, Franks Collection*

89. **1625** KENDI decorated with phoenix among flowers on the body, interspersed with the eight precious objects, which also decorate the neck and spout; these also have butterflies mingled with the flowers. On the base is an inscription reading: 'Made in the fifth year [1625] of the T'ien-ch'i period.' Height 7.5 in (19 cm) *Wu Ying*

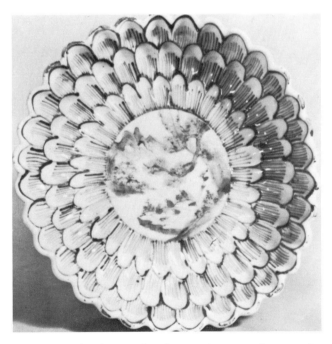

90. **1625** DISH modelled in the form of a chrysanthemum flower; three rows of petals surrounding a circular medallion decorated with landscape scenes, mountains, trees, and figures. On the base is an inscription reading: 'Made in the fifth year [1625] of the T'ien-ch'i period of the Great Ming Dynasty.' Diameter 10 in (25.4 cm) *Mr Senja Sato, Japan*

91. **1625** INCENSE BURNER of cylindrical form with three animal's head masks round the base. Decorated with two three-clawed dragons in clouds pursuing pearls above a wave border facing a cartouche, within which is an inscription reading: 'Presented in the fifth year [1625] of T'ien-ch'i to Mr Ming Wang, devout Muslim by his co-religionists of the Honai Department of the Huai-ch'ing prefectural district, Honan Province, on behalf of all dwellers in the valley along the river's edge.' Cf. incense burner dated 1612. Height 7.7 in (19.8 cm) *The late P. J. Donnelly*

92. **1627** INCENSE BURNER of archaic bronze form with the top partly covered, leaving only a flanged rectangular aperture. The two handles are ornamented with debased animal masks in relief. The vessel is undecorated except for an eight-character inscription in underglaze blue reading: 'Made in the seventh year [1627] of T'ien-ch'i of the Great Ming Dynasty', and a four-character mark reading 'Sacrificial vessel for the Confucian Temple'. Width 8.7 in (22.1 cm) *Percival David Foundation*

Ch'ung-chêng succeeded his brother T'ien-ch'i in 1628 and reigned for seventeen years. He struggled nobly against his own people who were now in open revolt, while in 1629 the ever-encroaching Manchus reached Peking but were forced to retreat before they could storm the gates of the capital. In 1637 they captured Korea, their leader having already assumed the role of emperor with Ta Ch'ing as the new dynastic title. In 1644, Ch'ung-chêng, now a broken man, hanged himself on Coal Hill in the palace grounds, as traitors threw open the gates of Peking. During this period the Imperial factory was virtually inactive, so that the mark of Ch'ung-chêng on porcelain is comparatively rare, but the following precisely dated pieces show that the private potter continued to distinguish himself.

 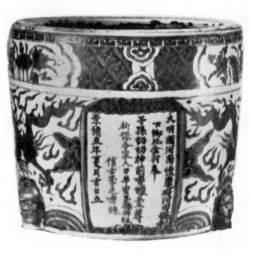

93. **1628** DISH with flattened foliated rim, the raised edge decorated with swirling floral scrolls; a front-faced dragon amidst clouds in the centre. The underside with grasses and butterflies. On the base is an inscription reading: 'Made in the first year [1628] of Ch'ung-chêng.' Diameter 7 in (17.8 cm) *Private Collector*

94. **1632** INCENSE BURNER, cylindrical and of stout construction. Decorated with dragons and waves, and supported on three feet moulded with monster masks. On one side of the vessel is an inscription reading: 'May His Majesty live a myriad years', and 'The hamlet of Pi-chien in the village of Li-hsien in the district of Ho-nei in the prefecture of Huai-ch'ing in the province of Honan in the great Ming state, has the honour to lay this incense burner before the Goddess of Prosperity. Presented by the true believer Li Chin-hsiu who prays that all members of his family be vouchsafed peace and happiness and that his descendants enjoy prosperity. Set up on the altar on a lucky day in the summer month of the fifth year [1632] of Ch'ung-chêng.' Height 7 in (17.8 cm) *Private Collector*

95. **1632** INK-STONE of rectangular form, decorated with various hatched designs on the sides and with an inscription on the base reading: 'Made in the fifth year [1632] of the Ch'ung-chêng period.' Length 7.3 in (18.5 cm) *Private Collector, Japan*

96. **1635** TEA WHISK of cylindrical form decorated with dancing figures, and with an inscription reading: 'Made in the eighth year [1635] of the Ch'ung-chêng period.' Height 3.5 in (8.9 cm) *Yamaguichi, Osaka, Japan*

97. **1636** VASE of uniform shape decorated on one side with the sun and clouds above a *chi-lin* in a landscape of rocks, prunus and bamboo, and on the other side with an inscription reading: 'Made in the ninth year [1636] of the Ch'ung-chêng period.' Height 5 in (12.7 cm) *British Museum*

98. **1637** INCENSE BURNER decorated with dragons pursuing a pearl in the lower zone and with an inscription of fourteen characters among clouds on the other side. This gives the date of the 'Tenth year [1637] of Ch'ung-chêng', and states that the vessel was dedicated with reverence by Wang Ta-yuan. It also comes from the same district, Huai-ch'ing Fu, as the two vessels dated 1612 and 1625, described earlier. Height 7.25 in (18.4 cm) *Private Collector*

99. **1638** VASE with straight sides, narrowing to a waisted neck with spreading mouth. Decorated with banana trees and rocks below a border of plantain leaves, and with an inscription in a single column reading: 'Made in the eleventh year [1638] of the Ch'ung-chêng period.' A wash of green enamel is brushed over the blue and white porcelain. Height 12 in (30.5 cm) *Richard de la Mare*

100. **1638** VASE of roll-wagon shape, the sides of the almost cylindrical body painted with the meeting of a lady, attended by three girls with a fan and auspicious gifts, and a bearded dignitary accompanied by a boy with a peacock, and a sage, in a landscape with rocks, trees, and cloud bands between engraved borders; the neck with pendent stiff leaves. Above the male figure is an inscription reading: 'Second autumn month of the eleventh year [1638] of the Ch'ung-chêng period', and is signed with the studio name 'Ts'ao-shih Chu'. Height 17.5 in (44.4 cm) *Mr and Mrs W. R. Bindley*

5

ENAMEL WARES

AFTER THE FINAL EXPULSION OF THE MONGOLS in 1368, a Chinese house—the Ming—was once again in power. The founder, a Buddhist monk and general, adopted the title of Hung-wu and reigned for thirty years. His capital, Nanking, was readily accessible to Ching-tê-chên, the area which had already developed as an important ceramic centre and where now Tuan T'ing-kuei, junior secretary of the ministry of works, was appointed superintendent in charge of the manufacture of porcelain destined for the court. Although there must have been a large quantity of wares made in the style we associate with early Ming, there are none, apparently, from Ching-tê-chên bearing the reign-mark of Hung-wu, that are reliably believed to be of the period, nor any of the succeeding reign of Chien-wên, the ill-fated emperor who ruled but three years. He was succeeded by his uncle, Yung-lo (1403–24), the most energetic of all the Ming emperors, as we saw in Chapter 1. It was now that the Imperial kilns at Ching-tê-chên, numbering over two hundred, really came into their own, and although surviving examples bearing the reign-mark of the period are few, those that exist bear testimony to the superb delicacy of the craft. This ascendancy survived the removal of the capital in 1421 back to Cambaluc, now renamed Peking, which Yung-lo decided should once more be worthy of the great nation he represented. Plans for the rebuilding of the palaces and city walls had begun in 1406, the fourth year of his reign, and were in feverish activity between 1417 and 1420. The general layout was based on the model of Nanking, only on a grander and more beautiful scale. Peking remains today almost as in Yung-lo's blueprint, and it is here in the Forbidden City, which lies in the immediate foreground, that many of the Imperial porcelains have remained in safe keeping for more than six hundred years.

It was in the reign of Yung-lo, too, that the outstanding ceramic monument, the Porcelain Pagoda, was erected in the grounds of the Pao En Ssu Monastery, outside the south gate of Nanking. This monastery, whose origin dates back to the Three Kingdoms period (220–80), was rebuilt by Yung-lo as a tribute to his father, Hung-wu, the founder of the dynasty.

113

The Porcelain Pagoda was one of the wonders of the world. It took nineteen years to build, the foundation stone, as it were, being laid in 1413. It was described by Captain Loch in 1842 as 'An octagonal building of nine stories, rising to a height of two hundred and sixty-one feet, bright with many coloured porcelain, which throws off a glittering light like the reflected rays of gems; it is in perfect preservation. The porcelain is fastened to the tower with mortar, as Dutch tiles are upon a stove, except the projecting cornices and bas-reliefs of grotesque monsters which are nailed. The various colours are white, yellow, red and green; the roofing tiles are all of the imperial yellow.' In describing the interior, the writer continues: 'The walls are all lined with square porcelain tiles, each separate, one embossed with a small device in the centre; those upon the ground floor are entirely covered with gilding. The others of the eight upper stories, differ, by having a black edging round the gilded device, which has a good effect.'

Although not precisely dated, the Pagoda establishes the fact that not only white, but yellow, red, black and green enamels were used in the Yung-lo period. In addition some of the tiles were gilded, a feature mentioned in the *Ko Ku Yao Lun* which says: 'There are also dark blue as well as black wares with gold decoration.'

Yung-lo's eldest son, Hung-hsi, inherited the throne when his father died in 1425 but he survived him for less than a year. This particular year, however, is not without significance in ceramic annals. For the first time the welfare of the potters was the subject of an official instruction which ordered the building of a temple inside the Imperial factory. Hung-hsi's successor, Hsüan-tê, reigned until 1435, as already described. Despite his youth the emperor kept his eunuchs under control, and his country comparatively peaceful and prosperous. Being himself an artist, with a preference for animal subjects, which he portrayed with lifelike detail, he had a connoisseur's judgement of painting. Though his reign of nine years is most celebrated in the world of art for its porcelain, vessels of bronze, cloisonné and especially lacquer were of more than considerable merit in their particular fields.

We cannot, unfortunately, draw on the Imperial factory for our earliest precisely dated enamelled piece, although it is an object of particular interest. It is furthermore a piece which may well have come from Shih Ma or another kiln situated close to the southern coastal region of Fukien, between Amoy and Chang-chou. It was at such a site that the so-called 'Swatow' ware was made and of which this could well be a forerunner. The decoration derives from a similar palette, and has the same spontaneity of drawing, although rather in the manner of the Sung bird and flower technique than in the bold interpretative design which we associate with this popular export porcelain.

It was in this year, too, that ten foreign ambassadors were received in state at the capital. Here in Peking, where these envoys remained for some three years, their arrival was celebrated with much colour and pageantry, the giraffes, the zebras, and the ostriches, which were among the many gifts they brought for Hsüan-tê, adding

101. **1433** BOWL with rounded sides, decorated in turquoise, brown, green, red, and yellow enamels, inside with a prunus tree and outside with birds on prunus branches under a crescent moon. On the base is an inscription reading: 'Made in the eighth-year [1433] of the Hsüan-tê period' within a double blue ring. Diameter 8.5 in (21.6 cm) *Percival David Foundation*

greatly to the splendour of the occasion. The choice of the reign name by this fifth Ming emperor is of significance, for it indicates his wish to make Peking rival the K'ai-fêng of Hui-tsung (1101–26) as a centre of artistic creation. Of the many reign-names of this Northern Sung emperor that of Hsüan-ho is associated with the zenith of aesthetic achievement, and the publication of the famous catalogue of his collection of paintings, entitled *Hsüan-ho hua p'u*.

Since the 'ceramic interregnum' of 1435–65 contributes nothing in the way of precisely dated pieces, we must wait until the tenth year of Ch'êng-hua, 1474, before continuing our chronology. The emperor who adopted this reign title ascended the throne in 1465 on the death of his father, T'ien-shun, as described in Chapter 1. He was then but a young man of seventeen, and guided by his strong-willed mother, and displaying an indifference to affairs of state, enabled the palace eunuchs to strengthen their own positions at court; for them he was an ideal ruler. He was thus left to follow his own devices, and indeed encouraged to do so, with the result that his reign has become identified with aesthetic achievements rather than with anything of major political significance; but during it such enterprises as the refortification of the Great Wall and the deepening of the Grand Canal were in fact accomplished.

Ch'êng-hua's consort, the beautiful and talented Wan Kuei-fei, influenced the emperor in affairs of state as she did in his private life. It was again a period of refinement in living, when scholar and artist emerged from retirement and held the attention of the dilettante emperor and the Lady Wan. It had become the custom now to send down to the Imperial factory paintings and sketch-books from which the artist could select the theme most suitable for adaptation by the potter. Since it is well known that a particular interest of Wan Kuei-fei was her love of porcelain, it is more than likely that she participated in the selection of such material and that it was due to her enthusiasm for the subject that the ceramic industry flourished. At any event, to our enlightened twentieth-century eye, the porcelain of this period may yet qualify as the finest ever to have emerged from the Imperial factory. Certainly in the opinion of many Western connoisseurs, the naive sophistication of Ch'êng-hua porcelain puts it in a class apart. Seldom was the hand of the Ming potter more controlled, or that of the Ming painter more inspired, for at their best the sensitively potted wares of this reign portray a greater delicacy and refinement than any others. The most characteristic features are the translucent porcelain with its mellow ivory-white glaze and the softness of the misty blue decoration. Ming writers who have waxed poetical in praise of Hsüan-tê blue and white, are equally impressed with Ch'êng-hua coloured wares. While those from the Imperial factory need no introduction and are of surpassing beauty, none are precisely dated. Luckily, there are three pieces of the period which meet the requirements of this study and are of equal importance, for once more they reveal the highly successful results achieved in a less exalted atmosphere.

102. **1474** FIGURE OF A LOHAN seated on a rock above white-crested waves. The body is stoneware and the enamels green and yellow with touches of aubergine. On the base is an inscription reading: 'In the first month of the tenth year [1474] of the Ch'êng-hua period, the Monk Chen Hsüan bestowed (this) to receive lofty and encompassing enlightenment.' Height 15.2 in (38.6 cm) *The Asian Art Museum of San Francisco, Avery Brundage Collection*

103. **1482** Tileworks RELIEF showing a deity standing with hands held in the attitude of prayer, his loose robes glazed in green, yellow and white, with long streamers falling from his shoulders, his feet supported on lotus pedestals and cloud scrolls flanking the mandorla behind his head; a canopied panel supported by a lotus flower. There is an inscription reading: 'Made by Ch'a P'ing-jên on the tenth day of the twelfth month of the eighteenth year [1482] of the Ch'êng-hua period.' Height 21 in (53.4 cm) *William Clayton*

104. **1484** FIGURE OF PU-T'AI with a fragmentary inscription giving the date of the 'twentieth year [1484] of the Ch'êng-hua period'. Height 46 in (117 cm) *British Museum*

Ch'êng-hua was succeeded in 1488 by his third son, Hung-chih, who like his father, being something of an artist, attracted to his court a number of important painters. Unlike his illustrious parent, however, who had been a weak ruler, Hung-chih with his strong character and unwavering determination continued the policy of his earlier predecessors whereby China was governed by a truly native form of constitution, as we saw in Chapter 4.

The reign-mark of Hung-chih is comparatively rare on porcelain, and the two following precisely dated pieces are the only examples of enamelled ware so far recorded.

105. **1497** Glazed pottery group of BUDDHA AND MOURNING DISCIPLES—Paranirvana— 'The Sleep of Buddha'. The faces are portrayed in clear glaze while the bodies are decorated in green, yellow and dark brown. On the back is an inscription reading: 'In the sixth month of the tenth year [1497] of the Hung-chih period on the Western Cliff of Mount P'an-t'ing, the holy monk Hui T'ai fulfilled his aspiration and made: One sleeping Buddha, one Sakyamuni, one Maitreya, one Kshitigarbha, one Avalokitesvara, and seven famous

monks.' On one side is written 'Good men who assist [in] Dharma', and on the other 'The Eastern Gate of this Hsien. The Tai-chao [rank of office, especially artist]; Ch'iao fecit.' Height 8.75 in (22.2 cm) *Purchase, 1925, Fletcher Fund, Metropolitan Museum of Art, New York*

106. **1499** FIGURE OF A DIGNITARY shown seated in dragon robes, wearing riding boots and court hat; the base moulded and carved with pierced rocks and with a basket of fruit. The whole figure is glazed in tones of turquoise, violet, yellow and green with some aubergine. On the back is an inscription reading: 'Made in the ninth month of the twelfth year [between September and October 1499] of the Hung-chih period.' Height 10.5 in (26.7 cm) *New York, Private Collector*

Hung-chih's eldest son, Chêng-tê (1506–21), following in the tradition of his forebears, learnt to wield the brush with considerable dexterity, and so once again attracted many painters to the Forbidden City. Peking had been the residence of Ming emperors since the early years of the fifteenth century, and in this somewhat rarified atmosphere they lived a life of seclusion, which gradually developed into a lack of contact with their subjects, to the detriment of the individual as much as to the country as a whole.

Chinese texts report that the Imperial factory was reopened in the early years of Chêng-tê and that control of the kilns remained in the hands of the eunuchs. The quality of the only three precisely dated pieces that have come to light, support the contention that the early sixteenth-century wares continued to uphold the traditions of the past, losing perhaps a degree of elegance, but certainly making their own contribution in the way of originality.

107. **1509** One of a pair of TEMPLE VASES of baluster form with two handles springing from animal masks on the neck. Decorated on a background of mottled blue in turquoise, yellow and pale aubergine with a design of peacocks among peonies. Above and below are petal and ogee panels with flowers and elaborately designed Buddhist emblems. Round the upright mouth is an inscription reading: 'In the fourth year [1509] of Chêng-tê, the faithful disciple Shao Chi-hsi, from the prefecture of Hui-chou [Anhwei Province], district of Hsiuning, Chung-hsiao village donated a pair of vases to be offered to Tai Mountain to pray for blessing in return.' Height 26.5 in (67.3 cm) *Formerly Norton Simon Foundation*

108. **1512** Tripod INCENSE BURNER with two handles. Of globular form with short straight neck, wide lip, and three feet projecting from the mouths of Foo dogs. Decorated with a deeply reticulated design of leaves and peonies in yellow and green glazes on a cream slip over a reddish clay. On one side of the body are two confronting sea dragons and a sacred jewel, while beneath the lip and on the sides of the handles are panels of *ju-i* motifs. Under each handle is an inscription reading: 'Made in the sixth month of the seventh year [1512] of the Chêng-tê period.' Height 19 in (48.3 cm) *Metropolitan Museum, New York, Gift of Mrs Harry Payne Bingham, 1962*

109. **1520** INCENSE BURNER with rounded body, straight deep mouth and slightly concave neck; on three feet joined to the body by animal masks. Two similar masks below the neck, above each an open rectangular hole. Decorated in turquoise, blue, green, ochre and cream with two five-clawed dragons below two phoenix. Under the mouth-rim is a long inscription dedicating the vessel to a temple in the 'Fourth month of the fifteenth year [1520] of the Chêng-tê period'. Height 11.25 in (28.6 cm) *Museum of Fine Arts, Boston*

Chia-ching, Chêng-tê's successor (see page 91), was more a poet than a painter. At Ching-tê-chên a new system of control of the Imperial factory was put into effect whereby positions of authority previously held by eunuchs were now assigned to the assistant prefects of the circuit on an annual rotation basis. The wares of this period could well be called the most colourful of all the Ming reigns with lavish use of turquoise, yellow, emerald, leaf green, aubergine, tomato red, sapphire blue, golden brown, and white glazes. They were used as monochromes or in a striking combination of colours such as designs in red on a yellow ground or vice versa, red and blue on a yellow ground, red on a blue ground, or red on a green ground. The latter became the most popular of export pieces, especially to the Near East, and many were further embellished with metal mounts. The three precisely dated examples illustrated here incorporate many of these colourful enamels and show how well the wares of the period upheld the noble traditions of the past.

110. **1524** Tileworks JARDINIÈRE of rectangular shape, glazed in green and yellow, the front decorated with a well-drawn dragon pursuing a flaming pearl in high relief, the sides with Taoist immortals in a landscape and the reverse with an inscription reading: 'Made in the third year [1524] of the Chia-ching period of the Great Ming Dynasty.' The vessel is supported on a pierced plinth with scroll feet. Height 11 in (28 cm) *Private Collector, Scotland*

111. **1564** INCENSE BURNER with two elephant-head handles and rounded sides decorated in iron-red, green and yellow with pairs of winged dragons confronting a flaming pearl above a border of breaking waves; the splayed foot-rim with a ring of green and red *ju-i* heads. Encircling the galleried rim between line borders is an inscription reading: 'This censer was dedicated to the temple of the God of the Northern Heavens in the forty-second year [1564] of the Chia-ching period of the Great Ming Dynasty.' Height 6.5 in (16.5 cm) *Private Collector*

Chia-ching's son, Lung-ch'ing (1567–72) has his reign-mark on many fine enamelled wares but unfortunately not on any precisely dated pieces. His son, Wan-li (1573–1619), was the longest ruling emperor of the Ming Dynasty, as we have seen. In the second half of his reign, at the beginning of the seventeenth century, there was a revival of interest in the work of ancient masters. The instigator of this was the Crown Prince's tutor, Tung Ch'i-ch'ang, painter, minister, collector and

112. **1566** FIGURE OF KUAN-YIN in green and yellow glazed pottery. On the back and sides of the hollow chimney behind the figure is an inscription reading: 'Set up by the benefactor Wu Shang-pin to secure merit for the Wu household. Made on a fortunate day of the fifth moon in the summer of the forty-fourth year [1566] in the Chia-ching reign of the Great Ming Dynasty. The craftsman Ch'iao Shih-kuei of T'ung [?] Temple, Yang-ch'eng hsien [Honan].' Height 14.9 in (38 cm) *British Museum*

connoisseur, whose active participation in this endeavour brought new life into every branch of the applied arts, including that of colour printing, which was being introduced for the first time. During this reign, too, Wu Shih-chu, so called because he was the nineteenth son of his father, is said to have excelled in the manufacture of several kinds of porcelain. His pseudonym was *Hu Yin tao jên*—the Taoist hidden in the Pot—and his wares were known as *Hu kung yao*. His nickname has been described as having a rather epigrammatic sense: the 'old man', as the clever maker styles himself, is concealed in the pot like the fairy Hu Kung was in his, and although invisible he himself (i.e. his inventive genius) is contained in it. Incidentally, Hu Kung was a supernatural being in Annam who always carried with him an empty pot, by entering which he could render himself invisible. A yellow-glazed screen in the Percival David Foundation decorated with cocks and peonies has an inscription reading: 'Harmonize your wares by making simple articles decorative. The dragon reclaims the unctuous pearl in his mouth in order to brighten the Eastern Wall. Made by Wu Wei in the Wan-li period.' Our three precisely dated pieces are colourful examples of the prolific output of this long reign.

113. **1577** SEATED FIGURE of a Bodhisattva wearing blue-lined, deep-sleeved, long flowing robes, his right knee raised, on a rock-work base. On the back is an inscription stating that the figure was made in the 'Fifth year [1577] of the Wan-li period by Ch'iao Shih-lan'. Height 18 in (45.7 cm) *Major and Lady Eileen Duberly*

114. **1577** SEATED FIGURE of a Bodhisattva in yellow robes, in the witness attitude, on a turquoise-blue base. On the back is an inscription stating that the figure was made in the 'Fifth year [1577] of the Wan-li period by Ch'iao Shih-lan'. Height 18 in (45.7 cm) *Major and Lady Eileen Duberly*

115. **1577** INCENSE BURNER with four feet and two handles; decorated in red, yellow, and black enamels with Shou Lao, his deer and his attendants. The inscription round the mouth reads: 'Made in the fifth year [1577] of the Wan-li period. May the winds be harmonious, the rains obedient, the country prosperous, and the people quiet.' Height 5.2 in (13.2 cm) *The late Sir Harry Garner*

T'ien-ch'i, Wan-li's grandson (1621–27), was an industrious young man who took more pleasure in working as a cabinet-maker than in ruling his country. Although the Imperial factory is said to have been inactive during his reign, the first of our two precisely dated pieces is certainly an example of very high quality.

116. **1623** COVERED JAR with scrolling lotus in underglaze blue and red, green and yellow enamels, the former outlined in blue, the yellow in brown. On the base is an inscription reading: 'Made by Mr T'ang in the third year [1623] of the T'ien-ch'i period of the Great Ming Dynasty.' Height 7.7 in (19.7 cm) *Mr Shigetoshi Hozumi, Tokyo*

117. **1623** STELE decorated in relief with eleven sages in two rows seated on lotus bud padmasans, wearing black deep-sleeved robes. The background is aubergine with a turquoise border, and there is an inscription which gives the date of the 'twelfth day, first month, third year [11 February 1623] of the T'ien-ch'i period'. Height 17 in (43.2 cm) *William Clayton*

The Imperial factory still remained inactive under Ch'ung-chêng (1628–44) (see page 109), and there are few marked pieces of the period, so our one precisely dated piece is quite a rarity.

118. **1638** Pottery FIGURE OF A SEATED LOHAN, in brown and green robes tied with a yellow girdle, holding a scroll in the right hand, the left resting on the right knee, against a mandorla of two yellow and green lotus leaves, the back with an inscription in relief in yellow within a green and yellow panel, reading: 'Made on the lucky day of the first autumn month of the eleventh year [August 1638] of the Ch'ung-chêng period.' Height 19 in (48.2 cm) *D. W. Rudorff*

II

Metalwork

6

BRONZE AND CLOISONNÉ

The dating of archaistic bronzes during the period covered by this book—T'ang to Ming—presents a number of difficulties. These problems have been created by the Chinese scholar's reverence for antiquity, especially ritual bronzes, and the copying of them. In his effort to preserve for posterity the glories of his past heritage, confusion has arisen as to whether such copies represent an imitation of the antique or an original in a purely archaistic spirit. From a study of the latter one can appreciate how the ancient decorative motif was adapted to current style and material, which included jade, ivory, rhinoceros horn and porcelain. But it was only when the finished product was in metal that the total effectiveness of the copy became apparent, for on this surface alone could an imitation of patina be successfully applied. A by-product of this artificial patination was the development of a technique to variegate the colour of the metal. One system for achieving this is advanced by a thirteenth-century descendant of the Sung Imperial family, Chao Hsi-ku, in his *Conspectus of Criticism of Antiques*. He writes: 'In imitating ancient bronze objects their method is to mix mercury with powdered tin, which is the preparation used at the present time to polish mirrors. First, this preparation is spread evenly on the new bronze. Then a solution of powdered ammonia in strong vinegar is applied with a brush. After waiting until the colour becomes that of wax tea (a rich brown) the bronze is plunged into freshly drawn water and soaked in it, whereupon the metal acquires this colour. If one waits for the surface to turn the colour of lacquer before soaking in fresh water, the metal then assumes this colour. If the treated metal is not placed in water, its colour turns to pure kingfisher blue.' It is interesting to see how this information compares with the following passage on 'Ancient Bronzes' from the *Ko Ku Yao Lun*: 'The colour of a bronze vessel which has been buried under the soil for a thousand years is pure turquoise, like the blue feathers of the kingfisher; when it has lain in water for a thousand years it is pure green like the skin of a melon. In either case, the colour is as mellow as that of jade. If it has not been buried for so long a period of time, it may also be turquoise or blue, but not mellow in tone. Areas on the surface get corroded by the earth to resemble in a natural way the wriggling strokes of seal-script. Some vessels show traces of the use of the chisel. These are fakes. Corrosion can penetrate only into one-third of the thickness of a stout vessel or reduce its weight by half, though the vessel remains heavy. If, however, the vessel is thin, it may be corroded through in places to a point where one cannot find the natural colour of the bronze, but only the turquoise or the green of the corrosion. Sometimes there may also be streaks of vermilion. A vessel which has not been buried but has passed from generation to generation is dark brown in colour with raised vermilion spots like small heaps of cinnabar. Vessels like those mentioned above are truly wonderful. Some of them are as dark as the powdered tea of Fukien or as black as lacquer.' In speaking of 'Faked Bronze Vessels' the *Ko Ku Yao Lun* says that: 'The method of faking is to apply evenly a mixture of thickened vinegar and fine sand over a new bronze vessel. When its colour has turned to a dark brown, like the powdered tea of Fukien, or black like lacquer, or green, the vessel is soaked in water and then held over a straw fire till it is covered with smoke. Afterwards, it should be polished with a piece of clean cloth, or brushed. Cinnabar lacquer spots may be painted on it. But all these operations can only affect the body of the vessel. They are easy to detect.'

The shapes and decoration of the original were reproduced with the same attention to precise detail as the fake patina had received. It was of course the copy of an inscription that appealed most to the scholar with his antiquarian instinct. Nevertheless, in the absence of the written word, he did take an appreciative interest in the form and ornament of the vessel. This may well have originated from the age-old tradition that the emperor should be the recipient of important excavated bronzes. The donor thereupon in turn established the precedent for the publication of catalogues to record the collections thus amassed. The first of these appeared in 1092. This was the *K'ao ku t'u (Pictures for the Study of Antiquity)* which described and illustrated not only vessels from the Imperial collection, but comparable material acquired privately by thirty-seven enthusiasts. The catalogue which became the most celebrated was the *Hsüan-ho po ku t'u lu (The Hsüan-ho Album of Antiquities)* being a record of the collection of the emperor Hui-tsung. This aesthetic emperor and great connoisseur, wishing to perpetuate the bronzes he had amassed, commissioned the work to be undertaken. The finished manuscript comprised thirty volumes and was completed in the twelfth century. The first edition of this book no longer survives in print, and the second edition is merely based on a manuscript copy of the original, two factors which have caused some doubt to be expressed about the reliability of the book. The wood-block illustrations, for instance, with their strange perspective are inclined to modify detail and thereby convey an impression rather more archaistic than archaic. One might even hazard a guess that the compilers occasionally resorted to substituting a contemporary fake for an original ancient, either because one was not available, or because they could not distinguish the new from the old.

Be that as it may, the catalogue enables us to see bronze vessels that Sung scholars saw, or as they imagined them to be. Although it is not a reliable guide to a study of ancient vessels, it is important for the picture of the situation at that time. Certainly these volumes assisted the copyist in his work for when the ancient original was unavailable, the picture-book was always to hand. With the fall of the Northern Sung Dynasty in 1127, and consequent retreat southwards of the heir and his faithful followers, the great Imperial collection was dispersed. Once the court had established itself in Hangchou, there began the manufacture of imitations of ancient vessels, a project designed to perpetuate the archaistic tradition.

The absence of bronzes precisely dated to the Southern Sung Dynasty presents a problem in assigning to this period pieces which must have then existed, for it had become a compelling desire to replace the lost collections of the north. Thus motivated, the creation of other works of art soon followed, especially in porcelain, their shapes conforming to the elegant outline of late Chou or Han rather than the sophisticated style of the Shang Dynasty. This was probably because the splendour of the inlaid bronze with its restrained technique had greater appeal than the vigorous cast bronze of the earlier epoch. It could also be that the Confucian scholar selected these objects to copy because he considered them to be of Shang date, for it was not generally realized in the Southern Sung period that inlay of precious metal on bronze did not go back earlier than to approximately the end of the Chou Dynasty (c. 1030–256 B.C.). This is a point substantiated by Chao Hsi-ku who wrote in the thirteenth century that inlaid bronze was erroneously accepted as of Shang date.

The *Ko Ku Yao Lun* describes 'Factory Vessels': 'From the T'ien-pao period [742–55] of the T'ang Dynasty to the reign of the last king of the Southern T'ang Dynasty, an official factory for casting bronzes had been in existence at Chu-jung Hsien. Their products often bear the seal of the Superintendent of the Factory. Their products are thin and light in weight, and their decoration fine and a delight to the eyes. These are not ancient. Some of them have blue or green patches as well as vermilion spots, but the corrosion neither penetrates nor is it mellow.'

The *Ko Ku Yao Lun* describes 'New Bronzes' as 'Vessels cast at Chu-jung and T'ai-chou during the Sung Dynasty'. These are decorated in the main with small 'thunder' patterns. It seems likely therefore that the official factory at Chu-jung was still in operation at least until the twelfth century. It is a matter of interesting speculation as to what forms these vessels finally took. The Sung stylists certainly developed their own individuality, but many of the inherent characteristics reverted to ancient times. Shapes changed, and a new definition of 'classical' emerged. There was more variety in the treatment of the inlay with wider lines of the precious metal alternating with thread-like ribbons to give greater effect to the general design.

The *Ko Ku Yao Lun* concludes the description of 'New Bronzes' by saying that 'In the Yüan Dynasty, Chiang Niang-tzu of Hangchou and Wang Chi of P'ing-chiang were both famous for their bronze pieces. Chiang's are better than those of Wang, but the designs on both are coarse, and they are not very valuable.' Unluckily, there are no precisely dated bronzes of the Yüan period, although many vessels must have been made in order to give credence to this statement in the *Ko Ku Yao Lun*. They were probably of original design for there would be no reverting to the lost collections of the Northern Sung emperors, and so we should look for a different stylistic tendency.

The position alters favourably for our chronology in the succeeding Ming Dynasty. A bronze figure is included here though its importance in the development of sculpture at this period is discussed later (page 181).

119. **1396** STANDING FIGURE OF BUDDHA, gilt bronze, on a lotus petal, with right hand in varada mudra, the left now broken, possibly in abhaya mudra. Unusual is the fine chain which supports Buddha's robes round his neck. The swastika in relief is placed now on his chest, very close to the straight-line upper hem of his under-garment. These, plus the rather tight and timid treatment of the draperies, especially the sleeves, are almost sufficient to verify the early Ming date in the inscription on the back fold of the right sleeve. This reads: 'On an auspicious day of the fourth month of the twenty-eighth year of Hung-wu [1396] Chu Fu made forty-eight identical sacred images to repay the four debts of gratitude.' Height 9 in (22.9 cm) *British Museum*

An example of the Yung-lo period in a private collection, which is unavailable for reproduction, is a bronze tablet, the upright plaque mounted on the back of a tortoise, the top of the plaque with dragons pursuing pearls in relief, black patination with green encrustation giving a mottled effect, the inscription, an 'Imperial Decree' telling of the erection of a stone tablet put up in memory of Chu Yuan-chang by his fourth son Chu Ti (Yung-lo), and dated to the 'First year [1403] of Yung-lo'. Height 18 in (45.7 cm).

It is in the reign of Hsüan-tê, however, that bronze vessels really come into their own, and when according to the *Ching pi-ts'ang* 'they are very refined'. The passage goes on to say that 'the inscriptions are in short characters, beautifully written. The vessels can be found in red, gold and gold-spotted red, or in brown, blue, or green, black lacquer or mercury. This is why good pieces made in Hsüan-tê are as costly as those of the Ch'in or Han Dynasties. Those made in the T'ien-pao period of T'ang are not their equal, and those made by Chiang Niang-tzu of Yüan are even more inferior.'

Hsüan-tê's reign also introduced fresh ideas on the question of form and variety in colour of the finished vessel. This reign became renowned for the manufacture of bronze vessels, although it is more widely known for the excellence of its blue and white, its monochrome glazed porcelain and its carved lacquer. Every piece in fact of this diversified group became so much admired that it was the subject of imitation throughout succeeding generations, and of course poses the usual problems of attribution. Such a piece is described below. It is one of several recorded Islamic bronze vessels, but the shape, calligraphic style and colour are significant, and point to an authentic example of the Hsüan-tê period. Arabic inscriptions appear frequently on objects made in the reign of Hung-chih (1488–1505) and Chêng-tê (1506–21), especially the emperor of the latter period, who studied the language and is rumoured to have embraced the Muslim religion.

120. **1430** CENSER of deep reddish brown colour on three short feet with bowl-shaped body and two 'heaven-soaring' handles; an Arabic inscription within a cartouche above each

foot. On the base within a square frame is a sixteen-seal character inscription reading: 'Made by Wu Pang-tzo, Superintendent of the Board of Works in the fifth year [1430] of the Hsüan-tê period.' Height 4.5 in (11.4 cm) *Mrs T. B. Blackstone Expedition, Berthold Laufer Collection, 1908–10, Field Museum, Chicago*

121. **1431** Another vessel from the same workshop is this CENSER of deep reddish brown colour on three short feet with bowl-shaped body and two 'heaven-soaring' handles, each decorated with a dragon in relief among clouds. There are two similar five-clawed dragons disputing a pearl above clouds and waves on either side of the vessel. On the base within a square frame is a sixteen-seal character inscription reading: 'Made by Wu Pang-tzo, Superintendent of the Board of Works in the sixth year [1431] of the Hsüan-tê period.' Height 3.8 in (9.7 cm) *Mrs T. B. Blackstone Expedition, Berthold Laufer Collection, 1908–10, Field Museum, Chicago*

Many bronze vessels exist with an acceptable Hsüan-tê period mark, written in seal script or the square hand. The best quality are those with the two characters 'Hsüan-tê', the second with the four characters 'Hsüan-tê nien chih', and the third with the usual six-character mark of the period, of which the following is a fine example, although in this case, precisely dated (Plate 122).

Although the considerable quantity of bronze vessels manufactured in this reign cannot compare numerically with the porcelain, especially blue and white, there was certainly enough metal in the country to make good the deficiency. This came about in 1427 when according to the contemporary publication *Illustrated Catalogue of the Ritual Vessels of the Hsüan-tê Period*, some 39,000 catties of copper were received by

122. **1431** INCENSE BURNER of deep brown colour on three short feet with bowl-shaped body. Coiling dragons decorate the sides of the vessel and form the upright handles. The cover is pierced and is decorated with dragons amongst clouds with a dragon finial in the centre. On the base is a six-character mark contained within a circle, which also encloses two dragons and which reads: 'Made in the sixth year [1431] of the Hsüan-tê period.' Height 6 in (15.2 cm) *O. B. Johnston, Los Angeles*

the emperor as tribute from the king of Siam. The following year an Imperial edict was issued whereby the palace workshops on instructions from the Board of Rites and the Board of Works, were ordered to fashion from the metal appropriate vessels for the Imperial altars and for the palace itself. The artisans were instructed to base their models on the illustrations in the *Pictures for the Study of Antiquity* and the *Hsüan-ho Album of Antiquities*, but despite these directives few of the pieces imitate ancient bronzes. The majority reproduce instead the porcelain copies of the ritual vessels made in the Imperial factory in the Southern Sung Dynasty. Six shapes from this repertoire were selected for copying in bronze and the colour effects achieved were deep yellow, wax tea (a rich brown) and ripe crab-apple red. The last appeared as a monochrome for ritual use in conjunction with contemporary porcelain and lacquer vessels of a similar shade, or when splashed with gold contributed to the array of special colour effects to which great attention was given. Some of the different styles of censer which are listed, are gilded on the upper half of the body, others on the lower section, the area clearly indicated by a wavy line at the appropriate line of demarcation.

Towards the end of the fifteenth century and some fifty years after the publication of the Hsüan-tê catalogue we have this archaistic type of vessel with a precisely dated inscription (Plate 123).

Another bronze of this reign, although not precisely dated, is in the Cernuschi Museum, Paris. It is a fine vessel of archaistic Ting form with inlaid decoration in silver wire, and with a similarly applied inscription reading: 'Made in the Ch'êng-hua period by the Wan Family.'

123. **1481** Tripod INCENSE BURNER, the rounded body surmounted by two curved handles; a row of ornamental bosses decorate the neck. Below this is an inscription of twelve characters which includes the date of the 'Fifteenth year [1481] of Ch'ênghua'. Height 23.8 in (60.5 cm) *Ethnographic Museum, Stockholm*

124. **1499** An unusual example of a Ming gilt bronze is this attractive BELL decorated in archaistic style with various motifs, including the *pa kua*. The knop is surmounted by a dragon handle, and the inscription gives particulars of the dedication ceremony which includes the date of the 'Twelfth year [1499] of the Hung-chih period'. Height 9.5 in (24.1 cm) *Sumitomo Collection, Osaka*

Some thirty years elapse before another dated piece comes to light. It is a magnificent object of exceptionally good casting and documentation.

125. **1532** BELL of monumental form decorated in archaistic style with a long dedicatory inscription giving details of the ceremony and the names of the participants; one, the eunuch Li-tuan, and the others, one hundred and seventy of his colleagues. The inscription ends with the date of the 'Eleventh year [1532] of the Chia-ching period.' *Ethnographic Museum, Stockholm*

It is interesting, yet strange, that the technique of cloisonné enamelling was not developed by the Chinese until the Yüan Dynasty. The *Ko Ku Yao Lun* published less than twenty years after the fall of the dynasty, refers to it as 'Ta-shih (Muslim) Ware' and says: 'The base of this ware is of copper, and the designs on it are in five colours, made with chemicals and fired. It is similar to Fo-lang-k'an (enamel ware). I have seen pieces such as incense burners, flower vases, boxes, and cups, which are appropriate for use only in a woman's apartment, and would be quite out of place in a scholar's studio. It is also known as Ware from the Devil's Country. [A] In the present day, a number of Yunnan people in the Capital [Peking] make wine cups [of this ware], commonly known as inlaid work of the Devil's country. The objects made in the Imperial Palace are fine, lustrous, and [therefore] delightful.'

There is no doubt that these colourful metal vessels were introduced at this time because their gaiety appealed to the Mongols, just as it had with the flamboyant wares of Tz'u-chou and Ching-tê-chên a few decades earlier.

The Chinese term for cloisonné was *fa lang*, a transliteration of their name for Byzantium; it was also known as *ta shih yao*, Arabian ware. Both are Chinese interpretations of foreign terms, and signify the period of its inception. What is original to the country of its manufacture is the term Ching-t'ai, denoting the reign-period of the emperor who ruled from 1450 to 1457. A number of examples exist bearing the four- or six-character mark of the period which seem to justify the claim that this was the classical period of its production. It is the view, however, of Sir Harry Garner that no piece of Ming cloisonné has yet been found which possesses a contemporary Ching-t'ai mark, although some pieces with the mark probably date from the fifteenth century. I am convinced that some pieces with the mark that I have examined are in fact of the Ching-t'ai period and others may well be of fifteenth-century date whether their marks were genuine or not. Unfortunately for our study, there are no precisely dated pieces of cloisonné until a century later, when the following pair are the only recorded examples.

126. **1557** Pair of cloisonné LIONS. The male with a brocaded ball, the female with a cub. Each on an ornamental base. Dark green is the dominant colour, with red, lapis blue, and dull greyish white. On the front of each pedestal above a lotus flower is inscribed in gold: 'Made in the sixth year [1557] of Chia-ching of the Great Ming Dynasty.' On the back of the pedestals is an inscription in four gold characters reading: 'Presented to Chang Chu-cheng.' It is quite likely that they were made for the scholar and official of that name, born in 1525, who took his *chin shih* in 1547. Height 12.5 in (31.7 cm) *Collection of the Birger Sandzen Memorial Gallery, Gift of Mr and Mrs Charles Pelham Greenough, Nelson Atkins Art Gallery, Kansas City*

127. **1564** We return to the general subject of bronzes with this important FIGURE REPRESENTING A WARRIOR, possibly intended for Kuan-ti the God of War. Seated, wearing scale armour below a flowing surcoat, belted round the chest, his head facing to the front and wearing a high hat with flowing ribbons; his heavy boots cast with rams' heads at the top. On the back is an inscription referring to Shang Shan of Nanking and giving the date of the casting in the 'forty-second year [1564] of Chia-ching'. Height 24 in (61 cm) *Private Collector*

The technique of silver-wire inlay is one of the varieties of decoration mentioned in the *Illustrated Catalogue of the Ritual Vessels of the Hsüan-tê Period*. This attractive embellishment to an otherwise sombre vessel was another archaistic theme developed to enhance the new ritual vessels then being made. So effective was this technique that it continued with great success throughout the sixteenth century, culminating in the accomplished products of Hu Wen-ming. This master craftsman was active between 1583 and 1613, and became celebrated for his bronze ritual vessels. For these he developed a subtle sense of style, avoiding the obvious and concentrating on fine casting of relief decoration accentuated by parcel gilding. His signature and the earliest precise date of his active period are inscribed in silver on the following piece.

128. **1583** Gilt bronze KUEI, lavishly inlaid with silver and gold and decorated with degenerated *t'ao tieh* masks between bands of animal heads alternating between whorl circles and quatrefoil above, and below confronted dragons separated by the character *wang* (king); two handles surmounted by monster heads. Inside is an inscription in seal characters reading: 'Made in the chrysanthemum month (ninth) of the tenth year [1583] of Wan-li, by order of Hu Wen-ming from Yun-chien.' Apart from the outlines of the main features, the dots and scrolls are the remnants of the *t'ao tieh's* anatomy; so too is the decoration of the handles. Yun-chien is the former name for Sung-chiang, Kiangsu, and a famous centre for bronzes. Height 9.5 in (24.2 cm) *Private Collector*

A second piece bearing the same signature, and the precise date of the last year of his period of activity, is in another private collection but unavailable for reproduction. It is a bronze kuei inscribed in silver with the characters recording that it was: 'Made in the autumn of the fortieth year [1613] of Wan-li by Hu Wen-ming for the use of the Shih Yu Chai [Studio of the Conversation of Stones].'

7

IRON

IRON IS THE SECOND MOST IMPORTANT mineral in China. In its natural state it is to be found in most parts of the country, but it can only be worked to advantage in those provinces where large quantities of coal are available, such as Shansi and Shensi in the north, and Kiangsi and Kuangtung in the south.

In 1951–5, tombs of the late Chou Dynasty were excavated near Hui-hsien in central Honan. These were found to contain a variety of iron tools, including spade blades made wholly of the metal, the edges for wooden spades, and a number of agricultural implements. The high cost and scarcity of bronze had necessitated the use of wooden tools by the peasant farmers, but the evidence for skilful casting given by the Hui-hsien finds makes it clear that iron was at that point coming more into general use.

Evidence for the artistic use of iron—for belt hooks—has been established by the excavation of graves datable to the fourth and third centuries B.C. During the Han Dynasty (206 B.C.–A.D. 220) the mineral continued to be employed, and it was worked additionally in the manufacture of vessels for ritual and domestic purposes. In the T'ang Dynasty, Buddhist images cast in iron were added to the multifarious uses of this versatile product, although until mediaeval times such products lacked the necessary refinement for classification as works of art.

The *Ko Ku Yao Lun* [A] has some interesting remarks to make on the subject of 'Iron Tallies', and describes first 'Gold Character Iron Tally': 'Kao Tsu of the Han Dynasty having unified the Empire, split tallies and invested his meritorious ministers with grants of land, some of them becoming Princes, others Marquises. In the Twelfth year, after the Marquis of Huai-yin had been pardoned, he again invested 143 persons with grants of land and Marquisates—a major grant consisting of not more than ten thousand households, a minor of but five or six hundred. The credentials of the Marquises were written in vermilion and the oath of allegiance taken with a white horse as ceremonial sacrifice, both being manifestations of trust and loyalty. He also inaugurated the institution of the Iron Tally [*t'ieh chüan*].

141

Characters were inscribed on the Tally and filled in with gold. Thus it became known as the Gold Character Iron Tally. Among the oaths of allegiance at enfeoffment ceremonies, one was "Until the Yellow River becomes a belt and the T'ai Mountain a whetstone, the Empire will live forever and its bounty be shared by future generations." The Emperor deposited the Tallies in a gold box, and the box was placed in a stone room in the Ancestral Temple.'

The *Ko Ku Yao Lun* continues by commenting on 'the occasion of Ch'ien Yün-yi's Returning to T'ien-t'ai', of which it says: 'In the eighth month of the second year after the Emperor [Hung-wu's] accession [1369], the Marshal of the Army led a successful campaign to pacify the Prefectures to the north-west of the ancient capital of Yen. Thus China became once more unified, and in the winter of the following year, it was decided that the Emperor would report his military achievements to Heaven and to Earth in a great ceremony outside the Capital. He also contemplated the taking of the oath of the "River-belt and the Mountain-whetstone" by issuing Iron Tallies to the Ministers who had rendered great services in founding the Empire. Since His Majesty's instructions of the previous month, the officials of the Board of Rites had been discussing an adequate system of doing this. Meanwhile, an official reported that a tally had been given to Prince Wu-su, Ch'ien Liu, during the reign of T'ang Chao Tsung [889–905] and that the tally was still being kept by Ch'ien Shang-tê, a fifteenth-generation descendant of the Prince. The Emperor at once sent an official to the Ch'ien home, and soon after the tally and the portraits of five Princes of the family were presented to His Majesty.

'The Emperor was greatly pleased. He examined the tally and the other things with chief Minister Hsüan-tê, a meritorious official, Shan-ch'ang, the President of the Board of Rites Liang, and the Vice-President of the Board Shu. A banquet was given at the Office of the Board of Rites in honour of Shang-tê.

'Later, Shang-tê decided to depart for his home in the east. On the day he bade farewell to the Emperor, he was given back the tally and the portraits, and was sent off with due ceremony. I was then holding an office in the Capital. Shang-tê knew I was familiar with the history of the iron tally; he therefore asked me to write this as well as a poem to commemorate the event.

'The Ch'ien family have kept the tally for five centuries. During the Ch'un-hua reign-period [990–4] of the Sung Dynasty, the Prefect of Hangchou presented it with the family's Jade Book [*yü-ts'ê*] to the Emperor. They were again presented to the Emperor in the fifth year of the Yüan-fêng reign-period [1082]. The tally was lost in the Kuan-wei River in the upheavals at the end of the Southern Sung Dynasty, and fifty-six years later, in the second year of the Chih-shun reign-period of the Yüan Dynasty [1331], it was discovered by a fisherman and was sold to Shang-tê's father, Shih-kuei. Now, in this virtuous dynasty, Shang-tê has again presented it to the Emperor. In all, it has received three Imperial audiences. In its long history of distinction and oblivion, the tally has been protected by the care of the gods and its owners. The family's long possession of it also manifests their worthy tradition. Shang-tê's style is Yun-yi, and he is a native of T'ien-t'ai.

'T'ang Chao Tsung enfeoffed Ch'ien Liu, Prince of P'êng-ch'êng, with a grant of land and presented him with a Gold Character Iron Tally.

'Chuang Tsung of the Later T'ang Dynasty enfeoffed Ch'ien Liu, the Prince of Wu-Yüeh, and presented him with a Jade Book and a Gold Seal.'

The *Ko Ku Yao Lun*, in describing the 'Researches on the Presentation of an Iron Tally to Prince Wu-su, Ch'ien Liu, of Wu-Yüeh', gives these interesting details: 'The tally was in the shape of a roof tile, about a foot *(ch'ih)* long and two feet wide. The characters were carved in *intaglio* and filled in with gold. In one corner there was a mark made by an axe.

'The Oath on the tally and the Imperial Patent read: "On this, the fourth day of the eighth month of the fourth year of the Ch'ien-ning reign-period [4 September 897], the Emperor solemnly states to Ch'ien Liu, Commander of the Chên-ting Army, Military Inspector of the Eastern and Western Circuits of Chekiang, the Officer in charge of the garrison troops and at the same time in charge of the distribution of the salt and iron of Chekiang, the Military Governor having a Secretariat in the same manner as a President in the Court, and with the title of Chief Minister, Commissioner in charge of the military affairs of the Prefectures of Min and Yüeh and as their Military Governor, and the Most Meritorious Prince of P'êng-ch'êng, that he is hereby enfeoffed with a hundred households, together with the collection of taxes from five thousand households.

' "I have heard that the merits of Têng Chih are recorded in the documents of the Han Dynasty, and those of K'ung K'uei in the *Spring and Autumn Annals*. Excellent deeds were then praised as indeed they are now.

' "Previously, Tung Ch'ang rebelled and usurpingly claimed the throne in Tung-hun. His rebellion was supported by a host of others and caused the people of Ch'i untold sufferings. Yet you challenged the evil bandits and pacified the coastal areas. Your loyalty has been the safeguard of the destiny of the dynasty, and your benevolence enjoyed by the people. It is your genius that has made the harassed areas content and the weary people happy. It was you who saved the people of Yüeh, and your army showed impeccable discipline, and it was you who strengthened the defences of Chekiang, so that your policy bore fruit. You deserve the highest Imperial praise, and your merit would surpass that of any other lord. All this should be recorded in history, so that it may forever be remembered. However, no inscription, not even that of the Cauldron of Chung Yu, or that of the Tablet of Tou Hsien on Mount Yen-jan, can adequately praise your achievement. Therefore I give you this gold-inscribed iron tally, on which I inscribe my oath. The Yellow River may one day become a belt, and the T'ai Mountain a mere whetstone, but my own and my descendant's memory of your merit will never wane. You and your offspring shall forever receive favour and respect and enjoy distinction and wealth, as you do now. You shall also receive nine pardons from death penalties, and your sons and grandsons three each. No official in the whole of this Empire can ever impose any other punishment on you or on them. I solemnly swear this, and order that this event be recorded in history and made known to the whole Empire." '

The *Ko Ku Yao Lun* then continues with 'Ch'ien Liu's Memorial to the Emperor to Express His Thanks' and concludes the section on 'Iron Tallies' thus: 'Your Majesty's benevolent grant of the iron tally and nine pardons from death penalties to me and three to each of my sons and grandsons is an expression of your great regard. My inconsiderable work has been rewarded with your Mountain-River Oath, which is inscribed and filled in with gold and taken in the presence of the Sun. The Oath is now known to the Gods, and it touches my heart.

'I often recall my modest origin and my career with the Army. What contribution have I made to deserve such great favour? To think of this makes me more modest. I dare not take undue pride. I am fully aware that excessive enjoyment can be the cause of disaster. I shall do my best to be careful, as I have done so far. Yet your Majesty, by your kindness, has even considered that my distinction may invite danger, nor is my cautiousness fool-proof. Hence it is now extended to protect me and my family by the pardons from death and the exemption from other punishment. Emperors and parents often grant their favours with forgiveness and tolerance, but Ministers and children should not carelessly hurt the feelings of the benevolent.

'I shall become increasingly cautious and leave a warning to my sons and grandsons. We shall not, because of your favour, become ungrateful, nor shall we deliberately court our own undoing. I have only one thought, which is to wish my saintly Lord a long life.'

Despite the number of graves that have been excavated, a precisely dated example of iron is not recorded until towards the end of the fifteenth century, nearly a hundred years after the beginning of the Ming Dynasty. It had been during the reign of Yung-lo (1403–24) that an iron foundry was established for the casting of the numerous bells required by the emperor, who was an ardent Buddhist, when he was rebuilding the city. At the entrance to the foundry was erected a stone wall, carved with dragons on either side, to prevent evil spirits from approaching. Gradually the intense smoke from the furnaces blackened the wall until it resembled the colour of iron, when it was appropriately called 'Iron Shadow Wall'.

The sixteenth century is much more rewarding, and the following seven precisely dated examples of iron give us an idea of some of the varied uses of this increasingly popular metal (Plates 130–136).

The Field Museum of Natural History in Chicago has a most interesting group of precisely dated iron objects. Two are the work of the metal-founder Li Kai-tsu, while the third records the name of another artisan, Hu Ying-shi, and that of his son, Hu Tien.

129. **1489** PAIR OF FIGURES of dignitaries in cast iron, each standing dressed in long robes with hands clasped, intended probably to hold sceptres; pendent ornaments encircle their necks, while their exalted rank is portrayed in the serene expression on their faces. Each figure is supported on a semi-circular base with bracket feet and each bears an inscription recording that it was cast by a Buddhist in the 'Second year [1489] of the Hung-chih period'. Height 53 in (134.7 cm) *Private Collector, London*

130. **1524** SEATED FIGURE OF A LOHAN in cast iron, supported on a base with bracket feet. On the base is a cast inscription reading: 'Made in the third year [1524] of the Chia-ching period for the T'ien Ning-ssu [Temple of Heavenly Repose], Peking, at the command of the Monk Chen Tz'u, the Monk Ta Yüeh, and the Donor Chin Wei.' Height 32 in (81.3 cm) *Royal Ontario Museum of Archaeology, Toronto*

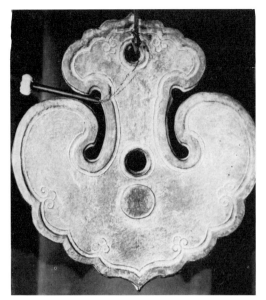

131. **1527** Buddhist TEMPLE GONG of cast iron. Of foliated outline with a prominent hand round the rim, and with fungus scrolls at the top and along the base. A circular hole in the middle and below, a boss in strong relief, where the gong is struck. On the back is a cast inscription which is dated to the 'Twenty-seventh year [1527] of the Chia-ching period'. Height 39.5 in (100.4 cm) *Museum für Völkerkunde Ostasiatische, Berlin*

132. **1553** GONG of cast iron, bowl-shaped with globular body and rounded base. On one side is a long dedicatory inscription to the Temple of the Seven Sages, preceded by the date, which is the 'Thirty-first year [1553] of the Chia-ching period'. Height 25 in (63.5 cm) *Adler Collection, London*

133. **1590** PLAQUE of cast iron with foliated top and decorated with the seated figure of Yu-huang, chief god of the Taoist Triad, in high relief. His flowing robes reveal his clasped hands and fall in graceful folds about his feet which rest on a low pedestal. A cast inscription on the right reads: 'Made on the sixth day of the third month of the eighteenth year [1590] of Wan-li', while the inscription on the left records that it is the work of the 'Metal-founder Li Kai-tsu'. Width 13 in (33 cm) *Mrs T. B. Blackstone Expedition, Berthold Laufer Collection, 1908–10, Field Museum, Chicago*

134. **1591** TEMPLE GONG of cast iron. Bowl-shaped with freely executed design of floral emblems below a border of swirling waves in low relief. In one of the panels is a cast inscription reading: 'Made in the nineteenth year [1591] of Wan-li.' Height 21 in (53.4 cm) *Mrs T. B. Blackstone Expedition, Berthold Laufer Collection, 1908–10, Field Museum, Chicago*

135. **1595** Buddhist TEMPLE BELL of cast iron, resting on six bracket feet, above which a gently curving line, in low relief and running parallel to them, displays the hand of an accomplished craftsman. The body is divided into three horizontal zones in which inscriptions alternate with floral emblems. The former includes the information that the bell was 'Made in P'u-chou, P'ing Yang Fu, Shansi, for the Temple of San-Kuan Lao Yu, donated by the Li Family, in the twenty-third year [1595] of Wan-li'. Height 38 in

(96.5 cm) *Mrs T. B. Blackstone Expedition, Berthold Laufer Collection, 1908–10, Field Museum, Chicago*

136. **1599** TEMPLE BELL of cast iron, resting on six bracket feet, above which run three

parallel lines in petal formation. The body is divided into a similar number of panels, two of which are decorated with floral designs in relief; while the third contains an inscription running in a horizontal line from right to left and reading: 'Made in the twenty-seventh year [1599] of Wan-li'. Height 16.5 in (41.9 cm) *Mrs T. B. Blackstone Expedition, Berthold Laufer Collection, 1908–10, Field Museum, Chicago*

In the seventeenth century we have an example of the work of Chang Ao-ch'un, who is on record as having specialized in the making of iron *ju-i* sceptres, inlaid with gold and silver. One of his principal customers was the grand censor, Chao Nan-hsing, for whom the following example was made.

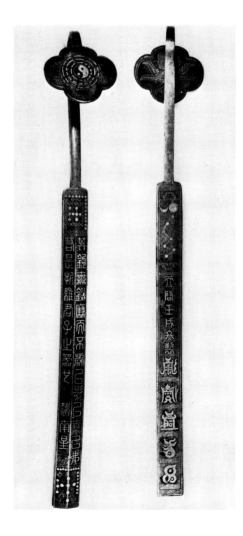

137. **1622** Iron *ju-i* SCEPTRE the head decorated with the Eight Trigrams inlaid with silver around a gold *yin yang*, the flat shaft with the symbols of the constellations represented by dots at either end of a long inscription in archaic characters. This records that it was 'Made in the second year [1622] of T'ien-chi by Chang Ao-ch'un', and continues 'Its hook has no barb; catches no fish. Be honest without injuring others. With song and dance. Considering negative as if it were positive. This is the implement of a gentleman.' The inscription is said to have been supplied by Chao Nan-hsing, and the sceptre is to be 'held and used' by one Sun Shen-hsing. Length 20 in (50.8 cm) *Royal Ontario Museum of Archaeology, Toronto*

8

SILVER

Fʀᴏᴍ ᴇxɪsᴛɪɴɢ ᴅᴏᴄᴜᴍᴇɴᴛᴀᴛɪᴏɴ, it appears that silver played an insignificant role in the manufacture of artistic or ritual objects up to the fifth century B.C. At about this time a method was evolved for controlling the desired amount of lead and copper that silver should contain, by adding to or subtracting from its original ingredients. In the succeeding century, silver was inlaid on bronze in the same manner as gold has been since earlier in the Chou Dynasty (1030–256 B.C.). The smooth perfection of the finished product clearly demonstrates that the required inlay was cut to precise specifications before insertion, so that no additional hammering was necessary. The decorative motifs were usually of a geometric design, a style that became gradually less severe and in the Han Dynasty (206 B.C.–A.D. 220) was already being overshadowed by realistic landscape and figure subjects. At the same time, cast silver was used for the reproduction of small bronze-form ornaments, vessels for the table, and belt hooks, which were then often quite elaborately embellished with gold and turquoise.

Several centuries were to elapse before the T'ang Dynasty (618–906), when the Chinese produced their finest silverwork. In the intervening years, old styles were copied and elaborated upon, new ideas on shape and decoration naturally developed, and these in turn became the inspiration for the ceramic form—or perhaps the incentive was derived from an already well-known type. Apart from the aesthetic merit of such pieces, many of them are undoubtedly influenced by craftsmen from Sassanian Persia, who fled before the advancing hordes of Islam to the T'ang capital of Ch'ang-an. The Chinese empire was now expanding well into Central Asia, and by 659 the area of their control extended to the Oxus, Ferghana, Samarkand, and Tashkent, and the facilities available within this enlarged empire must have contributed to the variety of styles which are readily apparent in T'ang silverwork. These would have evolved gradually and since the earlier styles continued in use alongside the newest creations it is, as usual, difficult to assign any of them to a specific period. It is only with pieces that can be precisely dated, either from internal evidence or from historical documentation, and from tombs so dated, that the relevant material can be authenticated. The Shoso-in Repository at Nara in Japan (see page 159) furnishes the nearest approximation to a definite date with the inventory record of a deposit in 767 of a silver Buddhist bowl decorated with a hunting landscape showing clear elements of Persian style and shape.

On the subject of silver, the *Ko Ku Yao Lun* makes the following interesting comments: 'Silver. This is produced in the mountains of Hsin [-chou] and Ch'u [-chou]. The finest is made into sycee, the best of which should have gold sparkles, the next best, green sparkles, and the third, black. Hence the name *hua-yin*, sparkling silver. There are bee-hive holes [in sparkling silver] with lustrous outflows. This kind of silver does not change its colour in the fire. There is an inferior variety [of silver] to which litharge has been applied, specimens of which have artificial gold sparkles. If there are black spots, and not enough lustre, there must be lead in it. When [such specimens] are burnt in the fire, a piece of ninety per cent fineness develops a dead white colour, while its edges turn grey.

[A] '"Gold-flower" silver is the finest. Another very fine variety shows lines at both ends when the piece is cut in two; these lines are called "thick lines". If a piece contains only eighty-five per cent silver, its surface lacks [brilliant] whiteness. An inferior variety shows lines at only one end [when bisected], and there are no *kuo* (beehive holes). This variety contains no more than eighty per cent silver, and shows only four or five lines. A piece of seventy to eighty per cent fineness normally falls apart when cut in two or three *fen* [1/10 of an inch] deep into it. Fifty or sixty per cent fine silver has *intaglio* lines. This is of the lowest variety and produces a yellow liquid like the juice of liquorice root, when rubbed [in water].

'A good ingot should have lines and a smooth surface and no beehive holes. Fine ingots are [brilliantly] white [in colour] when they emerge out of the mould after being put on a fire. Inferior ingots are grey in colour, while [varieties] still more inferior are black after being put on a fire.

'An ingot breaks into pieces when cut, if there is an excess of lead in it. This variety is commonly described as "wet". With fifty or sixty per cent silver in it, an ingot does not turn red when rubbed. But when there is too much copper in it, an ingot becomes very hard and turns red when burnt in the fire. The lowest variety also turns red when burnt, but it can be broken into small pieces. An old proverb goes: "When burnt black, it [silver] is still genuine; when burnt red, it [silver] is merely copper."

'*Imitation Silver*: The "tripod" silver [*ting-yin*] simply turns into smoke in the fire. Mercury, however, contains sixty per cent silver. Other varieties of imitation silver should be carefully examined. Fine silver is soft, but becomes hard when there is copper mixed with it. Furthermore, a copper mixture turns red when rubbed. The way to test a piece of imitation silver is by rubbing and firing. Yet some good imitation silver needs four firings before its quality can be ascertained.'

According to the *T'ien kung k'ai wu*, an outstanding treatise on the sciences of ancient China, published in 1637 by Sung Ying-hsing: 'China is very rich in silver, especially from the mines of Ch'u Hsiung, Yung Ch'ang, and Ta Li in Yunnan, which had a yield of more than double that of Kiangsi, Honan, Szechuan, and Fukien.'

T'ang silverware is perhaps the foremost artistic accomplishment of this period, displaying as it does high standards of workmanship and great aesthetic appeal. Many beautiful objects were indeed produced, and many would have appeared amongst the paraphernalia of the emperor's apartments, and added significantly to the splendour of the T'ang court. The craftsmen were not only highly qualified to produce articles of unrivalled beauty, but were able to dissociate themselves from earlier prototypes and develop fresh ideas with a character all their own.

Silver, like porcelain, had now gone through important technical and aesthetic developments, although the intrinsic value of the metal has left far fewer objects for us to study and admire. Even so, although little precisely dated material appears to exist, we have been able to assign to a specific period a number of pieces excavated from tomb sites or similar well-concealed hiding places. An exception to these somewhat vague attributions is compensated for by the silver bowl dated 767, according to the inventory, in the Shoso-in Repository at Nara, Japan, and again more than a century later by a group of silver vessels found at Pei Huang Shan, near Sian, Shensi Province. One of the vessels bears an inscription reading: 'Made to the order of the great officer Wang in the fourth year of Ch'ien Fu [877] Weight according to the standard of the public office of the municipality, $2\frac{1}{2}$ ozs.' There are three pieces from this group in the British Museum. One, a bowl, decorated with two parakeets flying among flowers, recalls the Yüeh ware of Shang-lin Hu.

The T'ang period witnessed the introduction of an extended use of chasing and decoration, and tracing—techniques developed from Near Eastern silversmiths but executed with the refinement of the more accomplished artisans. The Chinese even devised a method of thermostatic control of hot liquids when placed in a bowl, so that they would be cool to the touch, by placing inside the vessel an exactly fitting inner lining.

We are less fortunate in the next phase of our chronology, for the material is only datable by the death of a sovereign, Wang Chien (901–18), ruler of the state of former Shu, modern Szechuan. Inside the tomb were lacquered boxes inlaid with silver openwork panels decorated with phoenixes and lions among flowering plants. Another silver object from this tomb is a bowl with a design in gold foil of flowers and birds; the outer surface being strengthened with lead and then lacquered. In addition, there were two other lacquer pieces, a dish on a silver-pewter foundation and a mirror box, measuring 10.6 sq. in (27 sq. cm), embellished with *p'ing-t'uo* 'flat cut-out' designs and with its original mirror. The box, of red lacquer, is decorated on the lid with two lions playing with a ball, against a background of flowers; the borders are inlaid with silver. The sides of the box display flowering plants and auspicious birds between two silver borders.

P'ing-t'uo is a method of applying an inlaid design so that it is flush with the background. First, the gold or silver designs, in small pieces, are stuck on a smooth-surfaced foundation; the surrounding background is then filled in with lacquer. Finally, the surface is burnished to ensure that the designs and lacquer form a level plane. The designs are not necessarily in gold or silver: jade or other precious stones can be used.

The *p'ing-t'uo* technique was invented in the T'ang Dynasty when, it is said, according to Tuan Ch'êng-shih in his *Jottings of Yu-yang*, 'General An Lu-shan received many favours from the Emperor as well as many gifts. Among the gifts there were spoons and chopsticks decorated with gold *p'ing-t'uo* rhinoceros heads, a dish for holding meat pellets decorated with gold *p'ing-t'uo* designs, a foot rest with gold *p'ing-t'uo* designs, a bottle with silver *p'ing-t'uo* designs and a salver with silver *p'ing-t'uo* designs.' According to the *Tzŭ-chih T'ung-chien*, in the tenth year of the T'ien-pao period (751), 'The Emperor ordered a residence to be built for An Lu-shan. Luxury, not its cost, was to be the consideration.' Amongst the furnishings were 'Silver *p'ing-t'uo* screens, measuring sixteen feet'. An informal biography of Yang Kuei-fei, supplementary wife of the emperor [Ming-huang], by Yüeh Shih in his *Yang T'ai-chên Wai-chuan* says that the lady 'Gave [An] Lu-shan a jade bowl with gold *p'ing-t'uo* designs and an iron bowl with gold *p'ing-t'uo* decorations'. These gifts were recorded because *p'ing-t'uo* objects were regarded as extremely valuable in the T'ang Dynasty. Indeed, they were considered such a great luxury that when finances became strained, the making of them was forbidden. In the *New History of the T'ang Dynasty*, it says: 'in the second year of the Chih-tê reign-period [757] in the twelfth month, pearls, inlaid ware, jades, *p'ing-t'uo* ware, gold-sprayed ware, and embroidery were prohibited.'

More than a century and a half elapse before our next documented find, but now at least we have a precisely dated piece to substantiate the discovery. This occurred in the north-western province of Kansu, where a remarkable hoard of some one hundred and seventeen pieces of silver were found in an iron tower in Kan Lo-ssu Temple in Chin Kiang City. Among them was an upright rectangular box decorated and inscribed on the base with the date of the 'First year of Yüan-fêng [1078]'.

In the *History of the Sung Dynasty*, the private life of the aesthetic emperor, Hui-tsung, is described in detail (see page 30). In this voluminous work, the entry for 21 March to April 1102, records that: 'In the spring, third month, Ch'ung-ning first year, Hui-tsung ordered the eunuch T'ung Kuan to set up a Bureau in Soochou and in Hangchou, which was responsible for making various objects for the Palace.' It manufactured wares of ivory, rhinoceros horn, jade, gold, silver, bamboo and rattan. It also dealt with the mounting of paintings, lacquer works, carving and embroidery. These works were executed with great skill, the raw materials coming to the Bureau as a kind of levy. 'In the second month of Ch'ung-ning third year [28 February to 17 March 1104] the Emperor issued an order that the gold and silver produced in the Empire should henceforth be sent to the Imperial Treasury. In the eleventh month of Ch'ung-ning fourth year [9 December 1105 to 6 January 1106] Chu Mien was given charge of Supplies in Soochou and in Hangchou.'

The emperor Hui-tsung was extremely talented. He could compose impromptu poems, paint in Hsueh Ch'i's calligraphic style, understand the tracts of all three religions, and retail very well the allusive stories of the nine professions. He had many palaces, and the Wan-shui Shan (Longevity Mountain) built and filled with rare flowers, strange animals, unusual rockeries and uncommon birds. The pillars were painted and the beams carved. There were innumerable lofty towers and secluded chambers. Hui-tsung changed his reign-title six times during the twenty-six years he occupied the dragon throne, from Chien-chung-ching-kuo, to Ch'ung-ning, Ta-kuan, Chêng-ho, Chung-ho, and finally to Hsüan-ho.

A second tomb has been excavated in the state of former Shu, modern Szechuan. This was at Tê Yang, and is dated by coins to the early decades of the twelfth century, some two hundred years after that of Wang Chien. In the later tomb were found many silver vessels and boxes of unfamiliar shapes. The former, while differing in style and shape from earlier metal forms, where akin in their general appearance to contemporary porcelain wares. The boxes were round with foliated edges and two were decorated with phoenixes amidst flowers. Some of the finds were inscribed with the names of women for whom the pieces were made, while others designated the actual craftsman, frequently a member of the Chou or P'ang families, who were working at Hsiao Ch'üan, a town near Tê Yang. In the phrase 'ten parts', meaning pure silver, comprised part of the inscription, the work would certainly have been by the hand of a Chou silversmith.

Two more centuries elapse without the appearance of any dated or datable material. This brings us to the Yüan Dynasty (1260–1368) which was a period of transition, not only between two ruling dynasties, but also between two cultures, the native Chinese Sung and the Central Asiatic Mongolian. The conquering Mongols introduced into China much that was alien to that country and its way of life. The hard-riding, plundering nomads could find little to admire in that most characteristic material of Chinese arts and crafts—porcelain—and yet the shapes of such wares certainly inspired most of the metal forms which the Mongols held in the greatest esteem. The dining tables of the Great Khan, Marco Polo tells us, glittered with massive vessels of gold and silver. Their manufacture therefore became the main occupation of Chinese craftsmen. These precious vessels of the period have almost entirely disappeared, as one would expect, and today little survives.

By a lucky chance, however, three important fourteenth-century hoards have recently been discovered, and these pieces are impressive examples of the Yüan interpretation of T'ang traditional styles as they emerged after the intervening periods of Liao and Chin influence.

The earliest of these finds is dated to 1304, according to the funerary inscription, and is the tomb of Lu Shih-meng in Wu Hsien, Kiangsi. The tomb contained four silver boxes, one moulded in octagonal form with pointed foliations, the lid decorated with a pair of phoenixes flying in a circle. Amongst other attractive pieces was a persimmon-shaped water-dropper, surmounted by a four-petalled lid on which is delicately modelled a stalk and leaves.

The second find was another tomb, also excavated in Wu Hsien, Kiangsi, and again dated by the funerary inscription, this time to the year 1315. The tomb contained numerous silver vessels, and the first example of an assay mark on a plain gold bowl (see page 160).

The third and most important discovery, because it contained precisely dated material, was at Ho Fei, Anhwei Province. The hoard was composed of one hundred and two pieces of gold and silver which were found buried in an earthenware pot and displayed a rich repertory of shapes and designs. The find comprised the following vessels: six gold plates, four gold cups, nine silver plates, six silver cups, a large silver fruit box, the sides divided into ten foliations, with a lid and interior tray, nine bottle gourd-shaped silver flasks, four with covers, a long-handled silver ladle, and fifty-five pairs of silver chopsticks. Three of the six gold dishes have the four-character mark reading 'Made by Chang Chung-ying', and the same mark appears on the four gold cups; one silver platter is also similarly inscribed, and gives the additional information that it is 'nine parts' silver. One of the flasks has the four-character mark: 'Fourth year of Chih-shun [1333] reign-title of the Emperor Wen-tsung.' Four of the flasks marked 'Chang Chung-ying' have a longer inscription, of which some characters are too worn to decipher, but those that can be read give the additional information; 'Weight 14 ounces'. Four of the silver cups have on the inside of the foot the four-character inscription 'Lu-chou Ting-p'u'—'No. 4 shop' at Lu-chou. So within the group, eleven are marked as the work of Chang Chung-ying, i.e. three gold dishes, four gold cups, and four silver flasks. One silver flask bears an era mark corresponding to the year 1333; and four of the six silver cups mention the place of manufacture—Ting-p'u (market-place or district of Lu-chou), the modern Ho Fei, Anhwei Province.

The majority of the pieces in all three finds show a marked preference for the plain surface of beaten silver which was characteristic of the early Yüan period and was soon to give way to the elaborate and more sophisticated technique of chiselling.

Outstanding ancient silversmiths did not command the same esteem among their contemporaries as ancient painters and calligraphers, and so their lives were not carefully recorded. A notable exception, for he became well known in his own lifetime, was the great Yüan silversmith, Chu Pi-shan, who might be called the Benvenuto Cellini of China, and who is the only silversmith of this dynasty whose name has been found inscribed on surviving pieces. He used the names of Hua Yü, Chê Chih Hsiu Shui Jen, and Wu Tang Jen.

The piece described below is a different phenomenon from the other works in precious metal. It is an innovation in structure comparable to that of the literary man's style that evolved in the Yüan Dynasty. Its obvious delight in gnarled surfaces and in the 'aged' effect is a part of the traditional Chinese scholar's fascination with old trees, rocks, and semi-precious stones.

138. **1345** WINE CUP, silver, repoussé and chased, in the form of a hollow boat-shaped tree-trunk in which sits Chang Ch'ien, the famous traveller, with silver beard and clad in

garments of archaic cut; an inscribed prop-stone in his right hand. On the scars of the realistically gnarled tree-trunk are four inscriptions. The first, a poem, is followed by the artist's seal 'Pi-shan'; second, the name of the vessel 'raft-cup'; third, the date—fifth year (1345) of Chih-chêng—and fourth, another seal 'made by Chu Hua-yü'. Height 6.5 in (16.5 cm), Length 8.5 in (21.6 cm) *Formerly David Collection*

This cup was cast by the *cire perdue* process and thereafter carefully finished with the chisel. The figure seated in the hollow tree-trunk represents Chang Ch'ien, a minister of the Han emperor Wu Ti, who lived in the second century B.C. He was sent by the emperor to Hsu Yü (Turkestan), as an envoy to the Getae, and to the kingdom of Ta Yüan (Fergana), the land of the blood-sweating steeds, whence he is popularly said to have brought back the grape as well as the art of wine-making to China. He is also reputed to have explored the source of the Yellow River, which was believed to be a continuation of the Milky Way. One legend tells how Chang Ch'ien, sailing up the stream for many days, reached a city where he found a girl weaving and a young man leading an ox to the water to drink. When Chang Ch'ien inquired the name of the city, the girl gave him the stone which was propping up the loom, telling him to take it back with him and to show it to the star-gazer Yen Chün-p'ing, who would know from it where he had been. When this was done, it was found that on the very day and hour of Chang Ch'ien's visit a wandering star had been observed to intrude itself between Chi Nü (the Weaving Damsel, à Lyra) and Ch'ien Niu (the young man, b Aquila), so it became apparent that the voyager had actually sailed upon the bosom of the Milky Way. The long inscription on the base of the cup has been rendered:

Whoso wishes to reach the Milky Way is obstructed by the sky.
Once there was a man, restless and valiant, who penetrated into the Silver sea.
Alas! Why did he not seek for some embroidery from the Celestial Loom?
He only brought back in his hand a slab of the stone which was used for propping up the Loom!

The other inscriptions read: '*Ch'a pei* [log-raft cup] made by Chu Hua-yü in the fifth year [1345] of Chih-chêng', and on the object which the figure holds in his hand '*Chih chu shih*' (stone for propping up the loom).

The cup is enclosed in its old black-wood box, the exterior of which is almost entirely covered with inscriptions, their characters numbering several hundred. These are from the compositions of Sung Wan, a seventeenth-century poet, Chu I-tsun (1626–1709), the famous archaeologist, and the Hanlin academician and great art connoisseur and collector, Kao Shih-ch'i (1645–1704), all three members of a literary coterie. They tell us that the vessel was made by Chu Pi-shan as a Sconcing Cup for the Hall of Literary Competitions, and that in the fourth month of the summer of 1686, the cup was brought to Kao Shih-ch'i by a fisherman who had dredged it up from the West River. 'There is no equal to this small antique raft with its branching stem and hollow trunk', says Kao Shih-ch'i. 'What a delightful object this is to handle! How could any common workman have wrought it so finely with the chisel? Read the tiny seal characters, drawn to perfection, not a fraction amiss. Verily, this is fit to be treasured with the sacrificial vessels of the Hsia, Shang, and Chou dynasties.' From Kao Shih-ch'i, who was a close friend of the Emperor K'ang-hsi, the cup seems to have passed through K'ang-hsi into the Imperial collection, and so descended to the Emperor Ch'ien-lung, at whose command the box was engraved with these inscriptions in the autumn of the year 1777.

In the anonymous world of Chinese silversmiths, Chu Pi-shan stands out as the most famous and the best recorded artist, leaving a corpus of 'crab-cups' and 'shrimp-cups' and other equally fanciful designs from the forty years of his productive period, that is, about 1328 to 1368. Among his creations, the most unique and important is the 'raft-cup' of which he is recorded to have made five; three in 1345, one in 1361 and the last in 1362. The first three found their way into the Imperial collection of the Emperor Ch'ien-lung, while the present example was formerly in the Yuan Ming Yuan.

It is not until the middle of the sixteenth century—two hundred years later—that any precisely dated or otherwise datable material has so far been found. We are again indebted to the Chinese for making available, by recent excavations, two important discoveries of Ming silver.

In a tomb dated to 1553, excavated in Ch'i Ch'un Hsien, Hupei, numerous silver vessels were found, including a wine-ewer and a bronze-form ritual vessel.

In a tomb dated to 1589, excavated near Shanghai, numerous silver vessels were found, including a box of melon shape surmounted by a knop composed of a branching stem and hanging leaves.

9

GOLD

GOLD IS FOUND IN THE SAND in the southern and western Barbarian regions, Yunnan and Korea, according to the *Ko Ku Yao Lun*, which describes the precious metal in the following informative terms: 'When it is in small pieces, like melon seeds or wheat husks, it represents the unprocessed state. There is also processed gold, like the gold leaf from Yunnan and Muslim coins from the Western Barbarian Regions. Gold is soft and heavy and its colour red. The finest has patterns like pepper blossoms, phoenix tails, or the surface of sunset clouds. When silver is mixed with it, the gold is even softer, leaves a bluish mark on a lydian stone (touch-stone), and does not turn black in the fire. When ch'i-tzu (that is hung-t'ung [copper] also called chang-hung and shên-tzǔ) copper is mixed with it, the gold makes a sound [when struck], leaves small grains on a lydian stone, turns black in the fire, and is hard [in texture] and red in colour. The ancient saying goes: "Gold fears the touch-stone, and silver the fire." The colour of gold of 70 per cent fineness is of a bluish hue; 80 per cent, a yellowish hue; 90 per cent, a purplish hue; and 100 per cent fineness, a reddish hue. The last is the finest.

'[A] Nanking goldsmiths beat the gold into foil, sometimes called gold leaf. This kind of gold often contains sandy particles, and the goldsmiths agree to melt the foil into ingots to get rid of the particles only after the business transaction has been completed. One should carefully wash the foil in water. The gold is heated and washed alternately three times, and then quenched in vinegar in a pottery or wooden vessel. If the gold be of the finest quality, its colour should be yellow, if blended with copper, the colour will turn black.' Under the heading 'Brown Gold', the *Ko Ku Yao Lun* [O] says: 'The ancients said that the half-tael coins were made of "brown gold". People of today manufacture brown gold by blending copper with yellow gold. In fact, there has never been genuine tzu (purple) gold.'

The *T'ien kung k'ai wu*, a seventeenth-century handbook, makes the interesting observation that gold has the pliancy of a 'willow-branch', and refers to the 'purity' of its colour as judged by a streak on a lydian stone; a green hue resulting from seven parts purity, yellow from eight parts, purple from nine parts, and red (pure gold) from ten parts. It describes the customary way of making gold leaf, which is by beating the well-flattened foil between layers of the inner skin of certain bamboo trees, their outer surface being burnished black from the smoke of heated bean-oil. When the gold leaf was used to gild an object the foil would be stuck to the surface with a lacquer substance.

There is no positive evidence for dating goldwork earlier than the Han Dynasty, even by association with objects excavated from a datable tomb. An example of this was recently brought to light by the discovery of a tomb at Ho Fei, Anhwei. Amongst the treasures was a small gold bell, 0.9 in (2.3 cm) high, inscribed with three characters in filigree, reading: 'May you have children and grandchildren.' The outer surface revealed a design suggesting a cloud and dragon motif, carried out in granulated lines attached by the same method as practised in the West, from where the technique had arrived in China via the regular trade routes. Other tombs of the third to the sixth centuries have yielded granulation work of equally decorative little objects, such as earrings and other trinkets, mythological human beings and animals.

Remarkably fine as this early goldwork undoubtedly was, it falls short of the magnificent and numerous vessels produced in the eighth century for Emperor Ming-huang and his court. Especially appreciated were the beautiful gold mirrors, of such superb craftsmanship as to be worthy birthday gifts for the emperor and his favourite concubine, the talented Yang Kuei-fei. A newcomer to the Imperial court, General An Lu-shan, favoured the *p'ing-t'uo* technique, by which the gold sheet was 'flat cut-out' in the *ajouré* method, engraved and then inserted into a lacquer plaque. This highly skilled art form was so expensive to produce that it was discontinued under the sumptuary laws of Emperor Su-tsung, Ming-huang's successor. Many of these treasures found their way to the Shoso-in Repository at Nara in Japan, built by Chinese workmen and dedicated in 756 by the widowed empress. Having been preserved from the harsh sunlight and the vagaries of temperature, they remain as fresh as ever and reproduce for living memory the household effects of an emperor who died more than twelve hundred years ago.

Certainly the majority of T'ang metal vessels appear to have been made of silver, but this is conjecture at present because surviving examples of silver outnumber those of gold. Quite possibly as many of the latter were originally made and, judging by existing examples, the workmanship of earlier times was surpassed; many of the smaller objects display the exotic note which dominates the work of the T'ang goldsmith. Cast gold was seldom employed, but the precious metal was used to decorate Buddhist images and shrines and to fashion filigree plaques on which birds and flowers appear on a granulated ground as fine as gold dust.

There are no precisely dated examples of the goldsmith's craft from the T'ang Dynasty or, for that matter, from any succeeding reign. This account has been included here because a number of dated tombs have been excavated over the past decade or so which have contained gold objects and have revealed certain interesting facts which could well at a later date be the means of establishing more positive data.

In a tomb in Anhwei, dated to the Five Dynasties period, were found some gold hairpins composed of jade pendants hanging from filigree butterflies, which had the charming effect of swaying as the head moved. The tomb is datable to the 'Third year [946] of K'ai-yun'.

From this time up to the fourteenth century there are few pieces which can contribute anything—other than on stylistic grounds—to an authentic dating of the goldsmith's art. This is too nebulous a principle on which to base positive facts, and we hope future excavations will prove more helpful. For the present we can therefore only attribute to the T'ang Dynasty such pieces as are decorated in the miniature-like style of the period, while those that follow the artistic grace of the Sung Dynasty, although occupying a later place in history, may one day perhaps be accorded a higher status in the aesthetic world. We are more fortunate with the Yüan Dynasty, however, for recent excavations have brought to light the following two important finds.

In a tomb at Wu Hsien, Kiangsu, dated to the 'Second year [1315] of Yen-yu' of the Yüan Dynasty, was found, amongst other treasures, a plain gold bowl inscribed: 'Excise of the Yüan Government; gold of sufficient colour.' This is of particular significance because it is the earliest recorded example of an assay mark. There were also five gold belt-plaques, one decorated with human and animal figures, the others with flowers, fruits, and ducks, all in high relief and showing a new trend in decoration, a tendency to relax the formal Sung approach to design for something less conventional.

Another and much more important find was the tomb dated to the 'First year [1333] of Yüan-t'ung' of the Yüan Dynasty. The tomb contained a silver vessel bearing this precise date mark. It also numbered amongst its treasures, six gold plates and four gold cups. Three of the six gold dishes, and all the cups have the four-character mark reading: 'Made by Chang Chung-ying.' Four of the six silver cups also mention the place of manufacture (see page 154).

In the Ming Dynasty, the goldsmith's art seems to have assumed a mantle of gaudiness in direct contrast to the refined taste of their ceramics and lacquer. The only positive dating, however, that we have is furnished by the treasures taken from the tomb of Hsüan-tê (see pages 42 and 88), which for sheer opulence were a fitting tribute to a great emperor. The vessels themselves are of familiar shapes, a simple basin, a covered vase, and a ewer. There were also two dress ornaments in the form of openwork plaques for attaching to the front and back of the emperor's robe. All the vessels are made of heavy beaten gold with traced ornament of five-clawed dragons, cloud scrolls and stylized leaves, typically Chinese motifs of the period. It is only the further embellishment of pearls and uncut precious stones, roughly set in gilt foil and scattered at random over the surface, that introduces a foreign and rather barbaric element into an otherwise beautiful subject. Perhaps it was done hurriedly, and simply for burial purposes, and is therefore inconsistent with accepted methods of decoration. Let us hope that future excavations will reveal that objects made of the precious metal were intended to remain unadorned—except for a traced design of familiar motifs—and that the goldsmith's art upheld in every detail the high standards of this period.

More than a century later there is the tomb of Chu Hou-yeh, a member of the Imperial family who died in the 'Fifteenth year [1547] of Chia-ching' and who was buried in Nan Ch'eng Hsien, Kiangsu. Except for a head-dress of plaited gold wire, set with uncut stones in the manner of the Hsüan-tê find, though here arranged with obvious symmetry, the articles are only of passing interest.

The last tomb to be excavated which falls within our period is that of Wan-li (1573–1619). Here, too, there is a head-dress of gold wire, and in addition a couple of the emperor's personal vessels, a ewer and a goblet on a dish, all set with roughly cut stones, again contributing little to a serious study of the subject.

It is indeed strange that the quality of the goldsmith's art should have fallen so far below that of porcelain and, as we shall see, lacquer and woodwork of contemporary date. Perhaps the grave robbers in the intervening years were discriminating in their choice of loot and took only the best.

III

Stone

10

JADE

THE AESTHETIC CHINESE IS FAR MORE ACUTELY SENSITIVE to the appeal of tactile values than the Western connoisseur. This is especially true of jade, that material of surpassing beauty and indestructibility, valued since ancient times for its pure and noble qualities. It can only be worked by grinding with abrasive sand, as the surface is too hard to be penetrated by metal.

The art of jade carving has been practised with consummate skill since the second millennium B.C. Shang-Yin Dynasty sites have yielded vast quantities of small jades displaying decorative features that are so similar in the designs on First Phase bronzes that we can assign them definitely to an era about 900 B.C. Equally convincing evidence has enabled us to date many more jades as a result of excavations of Warring States and Han Dynasty sites. During this period the repertoire of the jade carver had graduated from simple ritual objects to the more ambitious sword and scabbard fittings, belt-hooks and clasps, and even to purely practical objects such as plates and bowls for the table.

Further support for these attributions was forthcoming in 1968 with the discovery of the burial site at Man-ch'eng in Hopei of Prince Liu Sheng, who died in 113 B.C., and his wife Tou Wan, who survived him by several years. The Prince was the ninth son of Emperor Ching-ti, by whom he was created King of Chung-shan—a large domain situated to the south-west of Peking—and a brother of the famous Han emperor Wu-ti. Even more interesting that the historical background of this cave-tomb is the artistic importance of the flexible burial suits which completely encased each of the royal personages. These were exquisitely made of jade plaques linked with gold thread, twisted from twelve filaments; the heads of the reclining figures were supported on fine gilt-bronze rests ornamented with animal heads and inlaid with jade. Close to their hands were flat crescent-shaped jades and, alongside the bodies, each in their separate burial chambers, were found objects of gold, silver, bronze and ceramic ware. These included jewellery, pierced jade disks, lamps with movable sides and a ceremonial dagger. That the armaments should be confined to one simple defensive weapon was in pursuance of the life-time role of the deceased, that of a peace-loving man with an obvious preference for the pen rather than for the sword. The burial suits are a development from an earlier custom where only the head of the corpse was encased in a fitted covering composed of similar plaques. Sometimes just a small piece of jade, in the form of a cicada or a seal, was placed on the eyes or in the mouth of the dead, who were thus accompanied into the grave by the simple emblem of faith that they had worn in life as a charm against evil. In the present case, the fact that the burial suits were entirely of jade illustrates the tremendous importance of jade to the Chinese and their belief in the strength of the material as a life-giving power and agent to prevent putrefaction of the deceased. Incidentally, another tomb over two thousand years old was recently discovered in Hupei, Central China. The tomb was that of Mr Sui, whose name was inscribed on a jade seal found in his mouth.

It is the dating of jades after the Han period and before the tenth century that has been virtually impossible due to a scarcity of dated or datable archaeological evidence. This hiatus unfortunately includes the T'ang Dynasty, for even the Shoso-in Repository, which has furnished us with several precisely dated pieces, refers but briefly to a jade cup in the inventory.

Our study of jades in the T'ang Dynasty is therefore confined to a comparison with other material which is dated or datable. Such pieces tend to display in their stylistic characteristics the qualities of vitality and exuberant energy so typical of T'ang Dynasty art in general.

Luckily, the early years of the tenth century have provided revealing information on jades of Imperial quality, as a result of the excavation in 1942 of the Royal Tomb of Wang Chien. This former military commander and self-styled emperor, conformed to T'ang tradition and continued to hold the seat of government at Chêng Tu, the capital of Szechuan, from 907 to 918, after the collapse of the dynasty a year earlier. It is evident that his tomb was looted soon after burial, but the remaining contents are particularly rewarding in the quality of the material they reveal. Amongst many other treasures, there were two lacquered wooden boxes each containing a jade book made up of fifty-three jade leaves, delicately bound together with silver wire. Each leaf is inscribed with gilded characters, and the two outer plaques, which form a cover, are embellished with the figure of a warrior painted in gold and colours. The subject of the books is a eulogistic essay and an essay offering a posthumous title, both of them being engraved in *k'ai-shu* script and filled in with gold.

There were also in the coffin eight jade plaques, all decorated in relief with dragons and balls. Seven of them were square, the eighth oblong and bearing an inscription referring to the year 915 when a lump of jade was snatched out of a fire and was believed to have been destroyed. But it was treasured by the emperor, who believed that the supernatural material could never suffer damage. He ordered it to be sawn open and from the clear white centre was fashioned a broad belt with three-inch square plaques and a six-and-a-half-inch long tail. In the tomb there was also a stone statue of Wang Chien wearing a belt of a design similar to the jade plaques found in it, and from the oblong one, which is dated 915, we have contemporary evidence for this being the belt in question. Two other jade objects were also found in the tomb, a jade ring-disk with an incised design of phoenix and dragons, and a jade seal engraved with animals and bearing the posthumous title and surmounted by a crouching tiger which serves as a handle.

So, for the first quarter of the tenth century, we have this important find of superior quality white jade displaying a variety of decorative devices, carving in relief, engraving, polychrome painting, gilding, and very fine calligraphy—such as would embellish the everyday accoutrements of a high-ranking official.

A second important find was made in 1950, when the tomb of another Five Dynasties ruler, Li Pien, was excavated. In the Mausoleum were found twenty-three engraved jade tablets datable to 943. Their colour was a pale greenish-white, and there were traces of the gold which had originally filled in the characters of the eulogy. These were the only jades of importance and they were of less artistic merit than the pieces found in the tomb of Wang Chien.

Although both these tombs are of the Five Dynasties period, the stylistic trend of the material they revealed points rather more to a T'ang date. Certainly the large jade plaques in the earlier tomb retain much of the spirit of T'ang design, although the smaller pieces are already beginning to reflect the more refined style of the Sung Dynasty. The change was of course gradual, but it began with the introduction of a new form of government by the first Sung emperor who, although himself a general, abolished rule by the military and established in its place a bureaucratic system of authority. This change brought about a period of withdrawal from foreign influence and the creation of a small but powerful state with the subsequent rising status of the official and merchant classes. Within this atmosphere of social stability there was a time for reflection on past achievements. That manifested itself in a revival of antiquarian interest in literary studies and in the applied arts, such as bronze, pottery and jade. Although this virtual renaissance indicated a loyalty to ancient forms, the reserved elegance of Sung styles gradually tempered the vitality of the earlier motives. There was a period, however, when the decoration of the carving embodied a combination of the original vitality with a form of Sung archaism, creating a somewhat baroque effect. It is well exemplified by the rhyton cups, by the vessels in ritualistic shape, in human and animal form, and by the myriad plaques and belt-hooks. While none of the jade carvers has been identified by name and nothing is known about the location of any particular workshop, it is certain that they were established within the metropolitan precincts so that they could supply the court and wealthy patrons. This situation continued, in all probability, throughout the tenth and eleventh centuries, judging from the quantity of related objects which have survived—but which can only be assigned to this period on stylistic grounds and their relationship to other dated material.

We are more fortunate, however, in the early years of the twelfth century, for towards the end of the Northern Sung Dynasty, we have some precisely dated jades of superb texture. They are all of the same high quality, and since one includes the name of the 'Jade Workshop of the Hsiu Nei Ssu' in its inscription, one might reasonably suppose that they all emanated from the same source. This at least gives us an indication of the class of jade being used by the Imperial household in the reign of Hui-tsung which is well illustrated by the following pieces.

139. **III9** BELL of light mutton-fat jade. It has a flat top, straight base and the body is octagonal in section. The top and base are oval, and the former is surmounted by a flat rectangular loop with rounded corners. The bell is plain except for a Buddhist sutra and the date, 'The first year [1119] of Hsüan-ho of the Great Sung Dynasty', which are inscribed in minute characters with double contour lines on the flat sides and are so lightly engraved as to be hardly visible. Height 3 in (7.6 cm) *Art Institute, Chicago, Russell Tyson Collection*

140. **II2I** BRACELET of light mutton-fat jade, of low barrel form. The inner and outer surfaces of the band are slightly convex, the two edges being concave. On the outer surface are engraved in minute characters with double contour lines thirteen poems (part of the set of the nineteen famous poems) and an inscription which includes the date, 'The third year [1121] of Hsüan-ho of the Great Sung Dynasty'. These cover the entire bracelet and are so

lightly engraved as to be hardly visible. Diameter 3 in (7.6 cm) *Art Institute, Chicago, Russell Tyson Collection*

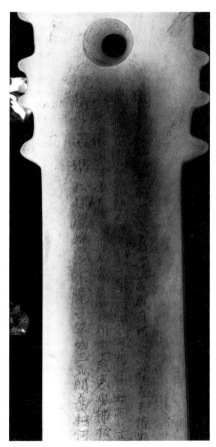

141. **1121** KNIFE of light mutton-fat jade engraved in minute characters with double contour lines, eight complete poems entitled *Miscellaneous Thoughts* by T'ao Yuan-ming (365–427), and with an inscription reading: 'Respectfully made by the Jade Works of the Palace Work Bureau, on an auspicious day in the twelfth month of the winter, in the third year [1121] of Hsüan-ho of the Imperial Sung Dynasty.' Length 9.5 in (24.2 cm) *The Cleveland Museum of Art, Gift of Mrs John Lyon Collyer in memory of her mother, Mrs G. M. G. Forman*

There is no doubt that in following the archaistic trend of design, the craftsmen were inspired by the reproductions of vessels appearing in the *Hsüan-ho po ku t'u lu*, an illustrated catalogue of bronzes in the Hsüan-ho palace. This was republished in the Chih-ta period (1308–11) from a manuscript copy of the original twelfth-century edition which was not available at the time. Even so, the reproductions modified some aspects of the original, and magnified others, thus creating a *tour de force* impossible to ascribe to a positive date. We are constantly faced by this problem with the Chinese craftsman, who with his innate feeling for antiquity and his inherent desire to improve on the original, however slightly, often gave way to his creative imagination with the result that his designs were composite and quite problematical to date on stylistic grounds alone.

The *Ko Ku Yao Lun* in describing jades says: 'Jades are to be found in Yu-t'ien (Khotan) in the Western Regions. They come in five colours. Even a sharp knife does not leave a mark on them. Warm and mellow, one can feel when one fingers them, as if some unearthly stream is flowing into one's hand.

'On examining jades, one should regard those as white in colour as the best, though yellow and blue jades are not without value. The pieces that are finely carved are especially precious. Those which have flaws or veins of stone, with the wrong shade of colour or with insufficient warmth or mellowness, are less valuable.' Then follows a description of the various colours of jade. These are:

'White Jades: The most valuable stones are of mutton-fat colour. Those with the colour of ice or rice-porridge, or of the colour of fat or of snowflakes are next in quality.

'Yellow Jade: Stones with the colour of the chestnut kernel, known also as pure (literally "sweet") yellow, are the most valuable. The smoky yellow is next in quality.

'Dark Green Jade: Those coloured like indigo are the most valuable, while those with small black spots or of a lighter shade of green are of less value.

'Ink Black Jade: This is lac black [in colour] and is known as "ink jade". It is usually quite cheap and is found [among other places] in Sze-chuan.

'Red Jade: This is red like a cock's comb. Good pieces are hard to come by.

'Green Jade: Deep green coloured stones are good, while those of a lighter shade [of green] are less good.

'Pure Blue Jades: The colour [of these stones] is a light blue with a yellowish tinge.

'Spinach Jades: The colour [of these stones] is neither blue nor green, but rather like that of vegetable leaves. Such jades are the least valuable.'

The *Ko Ku Yao Lun* in describing 'Ancient Jades' says: 'Among ancient jades, the white jades with blood-red stains called "blood ancient" or "corpse ancient" [jades] are the best. Among the jasper pieces, there are "ancient black lacquer" jades, "ancient rabbit", and "muted ancient" jades. They are, however, cheaper. I once saw a pair of linked rings of spinach jade on which there was a layer of yellow clay which could not be washed out.'

In describing 'Sandy Jades', the *Ko Ku Yao Lun* says: 'These are pink and unctuous, and as rare as white jades. They are generally small and are used for decorating sword handles or for making rings. There are few big pieces.' The last category is Jar Jades, of which the *Ko Ku Yao Lun* says: 'Snow-white jar jades were made in the north by heating some chemicals in a jar. Those without air-bubbles look like real jades. But when compared with real jades, they are much less lustrous and have a few "fly-claws" in them. They are exceedingly brittle.'

The *Ko Ku Yao Lun* has thus given us an excellent idea of the different types of jade known to exist before the end of the Yüan Dynasty, but of which we have few authenticated specimens. Alas, the situation does not much improve in the fifteenth century which has rewarded us so richly in the field of ceramics and lacquer, and in a variety of the minor arts. While it is believed that most of the jade-stone reaching China at this time would have come from Khoton and Yarkand and could have been in pieces of modest size, there are references to a 'mountain' of jade, a 'pointed gong', and a 'large wine bowl', an example of which some five feet wide is still preserved in the T'üan Ch'êng Pavilion in Peking.

The sixteenth century passes with little additional information, and it is not until we reach well into the reign of Wan-li that the curtain lifts in a foreign land on a unique case of documentation. Had it not been for the magnificent donation by Shah ʿAbbas the Great to the shrine of his ancestor, the Sheikh Safi, in 1611, the Ming Dynasty would have revealed very little positive evidence on the subject of jade. The gift comprised carpets, manuscripts, porcelain, and two jade cups, one oval in shape, the other circular, both with handles in the form of a dragon. One cup bears the seal of Shah ʿAbbas, engraved at the time of the donation, and the names of Behbud and Sultan Ibraham; the other that of Behbud alone.

Our last reference to jade before the Ch'ing Dynasty occurs in the *T'ien kung k'ai wu*, published in 1637 by Sung Ying-hsing. The book, which is divided into eighteen chapters, is an outstanding treatise on the sciences of ancient China, and gives a comprehensive account of the agricultural and industrial techniques of the Ming Dynasty. It also discusses such varied topics as metals, pottery manufacture, coal mining, inks, pearl diving and weapons of warfare. The last chapter includes a section on the mining of jade which is described by the author as coming from Sinkiang.

11

SCULPTURE

THE RENDERING OF THE HUMAN FORM in sculpture as a vital living force was inspired by the introduction of Buddhism into China in the first century of our era.

In the Shang Dynasty (c. 1550–c. 1030 B.C.), sculpture fashioned from blocks of marble or limestone displayed the same vigour of construction as contemporary bronzes, which set the pattern of decoration. The human form is seldom represented in bronze, and it is rather more in the imaginative field of animal and bird motifs that they have a common interest, although the familiar tiger, bear, ram and even elephant, when carved in the round in sculpture, have been reproduced with much more powerful realism than when confined to the limitations of a bronze vessel.

Similar bronze objects continued to be produced throughout the succeeding Chou Dynasty (c. 1030–256 B.C.), although there appears to be a distinct regression in other forms of material civilization, including stone sculpture, which seems to have virtually disappeared until the Han Dynasty. All that we have in the way of sculpture is the figures from Hui-hsien in Central Honan. These illustrate with charming simplicity the graceful movement of the individual, but have as little aesthetic appeal as the rather doll-like figures from Ch'ang-sha in Northern Honan, which were evidently made as burial substitutes so that the deceased could continue a familiar existence.

The image of an animal in the round is featured on the lids of bronze vessels of the Warring States period (481–221 B.C.). A more spontaneous representation of such creatures flourished during the Han Dynasty (206 B.C.–A.D. 220) when they appeared in a similar position or formed the entire object. The latter category, including human figures, are represented in a variety of forms and materials, clay models being the most numerous. The majority of these were made for burials and reproduced the entourage of the deceased so that they could serve or entertain him in the spirit world: the scholar-official with a model of his tower house and gateway, his ladies, his horses with their grooms, his musicians, and his servants; the farmer with his barnyard, his granary, his wagon, and his animals. These burial figures, many of them covered with the newly introduced lead-glaze, stained green, yellow and brown, have a certain artistic merit and subjects modelled in the round were beginning to take their place as a creative force. From these somewhat modest innovations developed a school of sculpture which was to identify for posterity this formative period of Chinese history. The earliest evidence of this is the series of reliefs on stone shrines at Hsiao-t'ang-shan (the Hill of the Hall of Filial Piety) near Fei-ch'eng in Shantung, datable to the first century B.C., which portray with dynamic strength a tableau of warriors and animals engaged in lively pursuit of the chase. Later in date, but even more important, is the so-called Wu-liang-tz'u series which decorate the funerary stones of the Wu family shrines near Chia-hsing in south-western Shantung, depicting scenes from history and legend—and again contributing to the great pictorial art of the Han Dynasty, for they are dated by their inscriptions to between A.D. 145 and 168. Some of the designs were carried out in line-engraving, often filled in with white clay, others in *intaglio* with bevelled edges, while the most lively style seems to have been achieved by cutting away the background so as to leave the subject in relief.

After four hundred years, the Han Dynasty finally collapsed, mainly due to economic confusion and palace intrigue. From then until the early years of the fifth century, the country was to experience a bewildering succession of dynastic changes, inevitably bringing about a conflict of religious thought. Buddhism, however, survived these years of confusion in spite of persecution by Confucians and Taoists alike, for it was an inspired religion, offering salvation to its followers.

The Chinese responded to the teaching of the two main schools of Buddhism, the Mahayana and the Hinayana. The former became the most popular and inspired the creation of religious art, maintaining that the dedication of sculpture and paintings could bring beneficence to the maker as well as to the donor. Under such encouragement sculpture flourished, and two of the noblest monuments of the fifth century are to be found at the cave temples of Yun-kang in Shansi and Lung-mên in Honan. Cut into the rock face of the former are the most famous group of Buddhist figures, some over sixty feet (eighteen metres) high, while the surface of the latter cliff is covered with grottoes, each with its group of smaller-scale figures. A more elegant type of image was produced in gilt bronze. Many of these images are precisely dated, and therefore provide an authentification of the approximate time of change from the ponderous figures wearing robes with regular folds to those with softer more flowing garments, which adorned both large-scale and miniature figures of Buddha and Bodhisattvas during the late Six Dynasties and on through the Sui Dynasty (A.D. 590–618).

Buddhism was becoming the most widely accepted religion, and sculpture the most important of the arts, with Amitabha, the Buddha of the Western Paradise, being repeatedly portrayed in stone and bronze. So, too, was the Bodhisattva Avalokitesvara (Kuan-yin) who now becomes less austere and more human with naturalistically draped garments, elaborately ornamented.

Extravagance and corruption brought the Sui Dynasty to an end after twenty-nine years of rule. In 618, Li Shih-min became the first emperor of the T'ang Dynasty, which lasted nearly three hundred years, as we have seen. It is the most brilliant period in Chinese history, with the cosmopolitan capital of Ch'ang-an attracting officials and merchants from the Central Asian countries, as well as Buddhist priests and Nestorian Christians.

The movement of Chinese pilgrims to the Holy Land of Buddhism and the corresponding influx of Buddhist missionaries from India had now increased considerably, and there was a very close relationship between the religious art of the two countries. During the T'ang Dynasty, Buddhist sculpture in China reached a high peak, and the examples of the classical Gupta period in India had a stimulating effect on the native craftsmen; but the Chinese interpretations were somewhat restrained and showed less of the sensuous exuberance of the original and more of the qualities of realism and nobility which were to distinguish the one from the other.

In the year 629 the great Chinese monk Hsüan Tsang went overland to India to study the Sanskrit canonical texts, and he has left us a most interesting account of the Buddhist holy places he visited in his *Record of Western Countries*. This is the year, too, which commemorates the first precisely dated piece to come within our present sphere, that of a Lohan, a follower of Buddha who was half-saint and half-recluse, living in mountain solitude.

142. **629** Dark grey stone FIGURE OF A LOHAN carved in relief. It shows a profile of his face with bulging forehead, round protruding eyes, open mouth, and wide round halo. Seated, with left knee raised, right hand thrust into his robe; his left hand holds a rosary. Inscriptions on either side. The right reads: 'Twenty-sixth day, third year [629] of Chêng-kuan of the Great T'ang Dynasty.' The left inscription reads: 'Chen Hai Ssu [temple]'—one missing character and then—'Monk Pi Ch'iu [Cultivator of Virtue]'. The Lohan or Arhat depicted is Nakula (sometimes written Vakula), the fifth of the group of fifteen Great Arhats. Height 17 in (43.2 cm) *Honolulu Academy of Arts*

Perhaps the most significant of the many seventh-century sculptural finds is the sarcophagus of the Emperor Kao-tsung, who died in 683. This is located at Ch'ien-chou in Shensi, and the animals decorating the tomb were a winged horse or unicorn and several guardian lions, all of colossal dimensions and sculptured fully in the round. Of equal consequence is the group of cave temple figures at T'ien-lung-shan, central Shansi. These, too, are carved fully in the round, and although they display some of the Indian voluptuousness, a feeling of movement is clearly discernible. The most important of the seventh-century sculptural finds, however, is a group located at Feng-hsien-ssu, Honan, which form part of the cave temple complex at Lung-mên. The work was begun in 679 by Imperial order, and the majority of these figures are modelled in the round and stand apart from the surrounding wall, a substantial achievement in construction, for they are much more artistic than the earlier examples which had merely a frontal aspect. Here at last are true statues, and the most popular subject was Avalokitesvara, the Bodhisattva whom the Chinese worshipped as Kuan-yin, Goddess of Mercy, the universal saviour of all living beings, especially from the peril of the sea. Our earliest precisely dated statue of Kuan-yin is of the first decade of the eighth century, by which time the Bodhisattva had become a fully developed type of figure. Undoubtedly the majority of these images were made to be placed in temples, but others found a niche in an artificial grotto which effectively reproduced the rocky shore of the Bodhisattva's legendary home on a mountain off southern India. While still emphasizing the noble attributes of earlier representations the divinity is now characterized by a more graceful form, with soft flowing lines, and a full round face (Plate 143).

Contemporary with this dynamic statue are the innumerable tomb offerings in the form of human and animal figures which illustrate so lucidly the contemporary way of life and customary mode of attire. The passion for horses, shared by nobles and common folk alike, made the animal the most frequently represented, and polo the favourite sport—an amusement thoroughly enjoyed by the beautiful Yang Kuei-fei, supplementary wife of the Emperor Ming-huang. Important, too, are the guardian figures of this period, who are portrayed as possessing superhuman energy and project their role as defenders of the Buddhist church against its enemies. Often accompanied by lions and dragons, they serve together as symbols of the vital spirit which made T'ang Buddhism such a powerful religion.

The vast T'ang empire survived in all its glory for nearly three centuries, but gradually and inescapably the conquered kingdoms broke away or were absorbed by Arab and Mongolian invaders. There followed the epoch of the Five Dynasties, which has been described as the darkest period in the history of the empire, with military governors and powerful magistrates assuming territorial command and subjecting the people to a period of tyrannical misrule. When the emperor died in 959 his heir was only six years old, so Chao K'uang-yin, a prominent official, became regent, and the following year seized absolute power; although sixteen years elapsed before he was in control of all the states except for Wu Yüeh in Chekiang and the

143. **706** Limestone FIGURE OF KUAN-YIN fashioned from a resonant stone which rings when tapped. The figure is draped in long richly jewelled robes and wears a high head-dress on the front of which is the image of Amitabha Buddha, whose manifestation the Bodhisattva is believed to be. The back is inscribed with the date of the 'Second year of Shên-lung [706] of the Great T'ang Dynasty', and the name of the carver 'Cheng Tao'. Height 36 in (91.5 cm) *University Museum, Philadelphia*

northern Han in Shansi, which did not yield for another twenty years.

We now enter the highly civilized Sung Dynasty (960–1279), with its capital at K'ai-fêng becoming the centre of cultural life and artists and philosophers flourishing under Imperial patronage. There were no territorial additions of any significance, for valiant as her troops undoubtedly were, they did not succeed for more than a hundred years in breaking the ring of hostile forces surrounding the Imperial boundaries, mainly due to a shortage of horses and a consequent lack of mobility against the opposing cavalry. The Sung Dynasty is divided into two periods, the Northern lasting from 960 to 1126, when the Jurchên raided K'ang-fêng, captured the emperor, his father and three thousand courtiers, and forced a young prince and the remaining officials to flee across the Yangtze to Hangchou. Here was established the Southern Sung Dynasty which lasted until 1279 when it was finally overthrown by the Mongols—who now occupied the whole of China. Our first precisely dated Sung piece is of the Northern Sung Dynasty and is another image of Kuan-yin.

144. **1091** Stone carving of KUAN-YIN seated on a lotus throne supported on the back of a dragon and flanked by two attendants, one holding the flaming pearl. The Bodhisattva wears flowing robes and richly jewelled necklace and head ornament. On one of the narrow sides of the base are the names of eighteen donors from Shan-yang village. On the back of the figure, in the centre, are the three large characters 'The Great Sung Dynasty'. Beneath these is an inscription which can be rendered: 'Wisdom is the ultimate source and compassion the basis of the actions of Bodhisattvas. Their wisdom embraces all things and all sentient beings. They avert the dangers of the "Eight Calamities" and the "Three Evil Paths". Consequently, all sentient beings in myriad ways make manifest their gratitude by their unlimited donations.

'At this spot the views of the mountain appear with clarity, as on Mt. K'ung and Mt. T'ung. Above is the aspect of precipitous slopes, while below is the view of the sources of pools. When Buddhists pass through the area, they often visit the groves and streams and are moved to declare this is a truly scenic spot, worthy to be the abode of a wonderful image.

'Now in this village there is one Sire Mu, whose sobriquet is Tzü-pai, who has good karma from previous existence and who finds great happiness in Buddhism. His creative mind brought forth the suggestion, and he gathered together a few people who collectively had made one beneficial image of Kuan-yin peacefully seated within a niche, to be the object of eternal offerings and devotion. This would constitute merit to endure for a thousand years and bring about happiness to endless generations.

'This image was erected on the *wu-tzu* day, approaching the first day of the second month of autumn, the sixth year of Yüan-yu [19 September 1091] of the Great Sung Dynasty.

'Director of Meditation Liu Cheng, Yüan Kuei, and Mu-jung Ch'ing of Shan-yang Village. Composed and written by Wang Tao, Commoner of Lung-ch'üan. Carved by Yang Shih-ching of Chung-shan. Mu-jung Ch'üan, who is called T'ien-chung.' Height 52.5 in (133.3 cm) *Freer Gallery of Art, Washington, D.C.*

Even at the height of their supremacy over nearly all China, the ruling house of the Sung Dynasty preferred to fall back on their own traditions rather than cultivate the contacts with the outside world that had become an essential way of life during the T'ang period. A contributing factor to this withdrawal was the gradual disappearance of Buddhism in India, which severed the most effective means of communication between the two countries, for as a result of these religious contacts there had emerged a widening scope for commercial and diversified interests. The other deterrent to overseas expansion was the constant threat from the Tartars in the north, coupled with internal dissension between rivalling factions. Out of this retirement from foreign association emerged an epoch brilliant in all the arts, inspired by the scholar and generously patronized by each reigning emperor.

Buddhist sculpture in the Northern Sung period continued in the T'ang tradition, and concentrated on the subject of Kuan-yin, the Goddess of Mercy, who now usually appears as a woman. She is frequently portrayed as a majestic figure wearing long rich robes, necklaces, and a tiara, but there is about her an air of tranquillity and a sweetness of expression which makes her almost human and thus combines informality with her dignified role of a deity. Unfortunately there are no precisely dated pieces of the Northern Sung Dynasty showing Kuan-yin in this particular interpretation of her diversified character, and none of the Southern Sung Dynasty either, although from this period we do have an accurately documented figure of a Lohan, or disciple of Buddha (Plate 145).

From existing data Buddhist statuary of the Sung period is better represented by the Tartar dynasties that ruled from Peking than by the Chinese dynasty of that name. This is certainly evident in the Chin Dynasty (1115–1234) which represents a kind of renaissance in the arts generally and of religious sculpture in particular, as witnessed by the statues in white marble from Hopei, and related stones, and in painted wood (see page 229).

Early in the thirteenth century Genghis Khan, to become one of the greatest conquerors in history, mustered together into a formidable army all the Mongol tribes of the northern steppes. They swept across Central Asia to beyond the Caspian, and across the Great Wall into China, where they conquered the Chin Tartars, and broke through the last Sung fortification. In 1262 his grandson, Kubilai Khan, was proclaimed emperor of China in Peking, the newly established capital,

145. **1180** Marble FIGURE OF A LOHAN, dressed in monastic robes, and standing on a lotus pedestal, the right leg brought forward, the right hand holding prayer beads; the left hand is raised with the palm outward. The head, slightly turned to the right, is rendered realistically with large deep-set eyes whose pupils are painted black; high cheekbones, and wrinkled forehead, curled brows, moustache, and beard. The muscular neck and part of the bony chest are bare. A twenty-one-character inscription giving the date of the 'Seventh year of Shun-hsi [1180] of the Great Sung Dynasty' is engraved on the front of the square base. Height 43.6 in (110.8 cm) *Asian Art Museum of San Francisco, Avery Brundage Collection*

which he had transferred from Karakoram in Mongolia. The Chinese, with their customary resilience, tolerated their barbarian conquerors, for the wise Kubilai made it abundantly clear that he respected their culture and admired their scholarship. He demonstrated his concern by encouraging them in the pursuit of agriculture, and in the building of canals and highways. Foreign trade flourished, and Peking became a most beautiful city, second only to Hangchou in the eyes of that celebrated traveller, Marco Polo. The Mongols had by this time become Sinicized, and recognizing as wholly their fault the damage inflicted on temples and monasteries, set about the restoration of these religious establishments. Yüan Buddhist sculptures, which are happily identifiable by dated examples, appear more elegant, with a newly conceived vigour, although the basic structure is in reality a T'ang revival. A carved wood figure of Kuan-yin (see page 229), one of the main themes of Buddhist statuary, provides a most graceful expression of this new sculptural style. It is also the earliest dated example, having been carved only three years after the foundation of the Yüan Dynasty.

From the scarcity of dated material it is obvious that Yüan sculpture is rare, although at Hangchou, Marco Polo's Quinsai, are examples that can be positively assigned to this period, and of which he writes: 'There in that most noble and magnificent city, for its excellence, importance and beauty, is called Quinsai, the greatest city may be found in the world, silhouetted in water of lagoons'—which he naturally likens to Venice—'there by its famous west lake stands a hill, one of many, known as Fei-lai Fêng—the hill that came flying over.' It is so called because it is said to resemble in its contours Mount Vulture, the sacred Buddhist mountain in central India. Tradition has it that an Indian Buddhist monk having noted its resemblance to Mount Vulture, remarked that this mountain must have come over on wings from India to Hangchou. In the sides of the Fei-lai Fêng are four grottoes, in each of which appear a number of Buddhist figures and images carved out of the living rock. They range in date from the tenth to the fourteenth century. The Yüan sculptures are concentrated in the Lung-mên grotto. Over part of the doorway is an inscription dated to the year 1289, and over another part of the same entrance the inscription states that the colouring of the carvings was renewed in 1310. These sculptures have distinctly Lamaistic tendencies of style. Kubilai was known to be attracted to and greatly influenced by Lamaistic aspects of Buddhism and was in communication with the High Lama in Tibet. Thus it was that the great Tibetan reformer Pagspa promulgated the short-lived Pagspa script, as described earlier, which was named after him. It seems likely that Marco Polo himself visited some of these Buddhist temples and grottoes, for in speaking of the west lake at Hangchou, he says: 'And all round this lake are built many beautiful and great palaces, and many abbeys and many monasteries.'

The marble relief sculpture from the Cloud Terrace of the Chü-yung Kuan Gate north of Peking, dated 1342–5, helps to establish a more positive Yüan attribution, on a stylistic basis at least, for a group of objects in a variety of materials including jade, stone and lacquer. So many of the decorative features are familiar—the cusped cloud, the dragon and phoenix, the lotus, the peony, and the chrysanthemum, to say nothing of the ferocious-looking temple guardians, and the Buddha and Bodhisattva images. Some gilt-bronze representations of such Buddhist deities have been found with what are now obvious Yüan traits, though they had previously been described as T'ang, from which they derived their inspiration. Only a few seem to have survived the looter or the melting pot, frequently used for the minting of coinage.

After Kubilai there were no Mongol emperors of ability, and the foreign invaders gradually lost control of the country. Minor revolts broke out in the south, and in a more serious rebellion led by Chü Yuan-chang, a monk turned politician, Nanking was seized in 1356. As a result of this successful beginning came the expulsion of the last Mongol emperor from Peking and the establishment of the Ming Dynasty in 1368 by Chü Yuan-chang, who took the reign-title of Hung-wu. The capital remained at Nanking during his reign and that of his successor, Chien-wên.

The new Ming Dynasty rivalled the T'ang in wealth and enterprise. Architecture, painting and the decorative arts flourished. Sculpture seems to have been the exception since few dated examples have survived. There is, however, a well-integrated group of gilt bronze esoteric Buddhist images that are brought together by a precisely dated example in the reign of the first Ming emperor, and yet observe certain Yüan traits (see chapter on Bronzes, page 132).

Hung-wu's brother became the third Ming emperor and under the reign-title of Yung-lo occupied the throne from 1403–24. He proved to be a most far-sighted ruler, and he was the instigator of several naval expeditions. The first of these was in 1405, a century before the Portuguese discovered the sea route to the Far East. Quantities of Chinese works of art were carried in their vessels and, later, in Dutch and English ships.

Yung-lo moved the capital to Peking in 1409, the rebuilding of the city having been begun three years earlier, as I have mentioned (see page 113). It consisted of the Imperial City and within it the Forbidden City, which was filled with audience halls, courts, terraces, shrines, gardens and lakes. Outside the Imperial City and south-east of the Chinese City, Yung-lo built the Altar of Heaven, a circular temple resting on three marble terraces, and a masterpiece of Chinese architecture. North of Peking, the tombs of the Ming emperors are situated in a landscape enclosure and are approached by an avenue lined with great statues of dignitaries and animals. One of the most magnificent tombs is that of Yung-lo, and this, the gateways, temple and altar are the work of his grandson, Hsüan-tê, who became the fifth emperor, following the death of his father, Hung-hsi, after only ten months on the throne.

Hsüan-tê died in 1435, and until the succession of Ch'êng-hua thirty years later there are turbulence and strife alternating with interludes of uneasy peace. But even during these troubled years, the Ming craftsmen continued to carry on their successful projects of the past, including the copying of ancient bronze forms, the elevation of the minor arts to a high plane, and the bringing of education to a wider public by the mastering of the technique of book-printing. One can therefore call this an era of artistic enterprise in every field, except perhaps that of sculpture. The monumental statues of the past, now seem to have been replaced by ivory and porcelain figures, which are dealt with in the appropriate chapters.

12

INK-STONES

THE 'FOUR PRECIOUS THINGS OF THE LIBRARY'—the brush, the paper, the ink-stick and the ink-stone—represent the essential accoutrements of the scholar's studio, and great care was taken in selecting each of the treasures because they form an integral part of his aesthetic life. The choice of the ink-stone deserved particular attention, for unlike the other three 'precious things' whose span of life was necessarily limited, the virtually imperishable ink-stone was to be cherished as an heirloom for the delectation of future generations.

On the subject of the brush, the *Ko Ku Yao Lun* [A] says: 'In P'an-yü (Canton) and other prefectures of Kuang-tung, people use the hair of black goats, or cock feathers, or those of hens or ducks for the writing brush. Sometimes they also use the feather from a pheasant's tail for this purpose, and this is delightfully colourful. Apart from these, fox and wild-cat hairs, weasel whiskers, goat, musk-deer and civet hairs, goat beard, and a stillborn baby's hairs are also used to make it. But hare's fur is the best.

'A brush should have four qualifications: [it should be] well-pointed, even, strong, and durable. Most of the brushes available to-day have long points, which are soon worn to stumps.

'Chu-ko K'ao of Hsüan-chou and Hsü Yin of Ch'ang-chou make the best water rat dishevelled-hair brushes and long-pointed brushes.

'In the present dynasty, Lu Chi-wêng and Wang Ku-yung are both famous brush-makers. They are natives of Hu-chou, but live in Chin-ling (Nanking).

'At the beginning of the Yung-lo reign-period [1403–24], Chêng Po'ch'ing of Chi-shui used pig's bristle to make brushes. They had long points and were very strong.

'Before putting his brushes away, Su Tung-p'o used to make a paste with boiled aloe water and powder, dip his brushes into it, and wait until they were dry. Huang Shan-ku, on the other hand, used Szechuan pepper for the boiled solution, to which he added ground pine-wood charcoal. This mixture prevented pests from damaging his brushes.'

On 'Washing a Brush', the *Ko Ku Yao Lun* says: 'Put the brush in a bowl of warm water and let it stand in it for about the time needed for taking a meal. Then stir it gently. Afterwards, rinse it in cold water.'

We are now concerned with the interesting details of paper as they are referred to in the *Ko Ku Yao Lun* [A]: 'There was no paper in ancient times. Bamboo strips were then in use. The plaques were baked to make them "sweat", or dry out. In this way, the green could be got rid of, so as to make writing easier.

'During the reign of Ho Ti of the Han Dynasty [89–104], Ts'ai Lun invented paper, and was created Marquis of Lung T'ing. Ts'ai Lun's old residence stands to the north of Lai-yang hsien. West of the residence there is a stone mortar believed to be the one used for making paper by Ts'ai Lun himself.

'Szechuan Writing Paper. According to the *Nan Pu Hsin Shu*, early in the Yüan-ho period [806–20] of the T'ang Dynasty, Hsüeh T'ao, a courtesan in Shu (Szechuan), made small sheets of paper in ten different colours for writing letters; these were known as Hsüeh T'ao's Writing Paper. She made a career for herself out of this.

'Paper of Hsieh. Hsin-an of the T'ang Dynasty was Hsieh-chou of the Sung, and is Hsieh Hsien of Hui-chou in Southern Chihli of the present day. There, papers known as "blue hue", "white and smooth", "frozen wings", and "crystallized frost" were produced.

'Ch'êng-hsin T'ang Paper. "The Hall of Untroubled Thought" paper was used by most of the famous men of letters of the Sung Dynasty for writing, and also by Li Po-shih for painting.'

The ink-stick will be fully discussed later, so we shall continue now with the interesting comments the *Ko Ku Yao Lun* [O] has to make on the subject of Tuan-hsi ink-stones, which are certainly the best: 'Stones from the Old Pit of the Lower Cliff in Tuan-hsi. Such stones came from Tuan-hsi in Chao-ch'ing Prefecture. The oval-shaped stones from the Old Pit in the Lower Cliff are as black as lacquer and as smooth as jade, with "eyes" that have iridescent centres. Sometimes six or seven "eyes" arranged like a constellation appear on a single stone. This pit was exhausted [of its stone] in the Ch'ing-li reign-period [1041–9].

'There is another kind of oval-shaped stone which should have its crust removed [before it is made into an ink-slab]. Its colour is a bluish black and is as smooth as jade, with blue spots on it about the size of the head of a chop-stick, rich green like the green stone, or with white spots like millet seeds arranged like constellations, which are visible only when the stone is wetted. The stone emits no sound when struck or rubbed with a stick of ink. These two kinds are the most valuable.

'Stones from the Old Pit and New Pit of the Middle Cliff in Tuan-hsi. The stones from the Old Pit of the Middle Cliff in Tuan-hsi are also oval-shaped. Their colour is purple like tender liver, and they are as smooth as jade. The "eyes" on them are as small as green beans; in some, there are green or white stripes. The "eyes" are round and vertical, while the stripes are long and horizontal. These stones make no sound when struck or when an ink-stick is rubbed on them. This pit became depleted in the Northern Sung Dynasty.

'The stones from the New Pit of the Middle Cliff are light purple with "eyes" like thrush eyes with iridescent centres. A new piece does not emit any sound when struck, but it makes a faint sound when an ink-stick is rubbed on it. After long use it shows wear. There are two kinds of stone [from this pit]—the dry and the damp. The latter is rather difficult to come by. Nevertheless, it is three grades lower than the stones from the Lower Cliff.

'Stones from the Old and the New Pits of the Upper Cliff in Tuan-hsi. Stones from both the Old and the New Pits of the Upper Cliff are greyish purple in colour and coarse with "eyes" as large as the eyes of a cock. They emit a sound when struck, or when an ink-stick is rubbed on them. After long use, they become as burnished as mirrors. The Old Pit stones are slightly better than those of the New Pit.

'Only the Tuan stones have "eyes". It is said: "A stone cannot be a Tuan [stone] if it has no eyes". There are lively "eyes", tearful "eyes" and dead "eyes". The first are better than the second, the second better than the third. It has also been said: "Too many 'eyes' make a stone faulty."'

The *Ko Ku Yao Lun* then goes on to describe stones from the Old and New Pits from the Lung-wei River in Hsieh-hsien, Anhwei. 'Those produced in the Old Pit are oval-shaped, in a light blue-black colour without veins, and as smooth as jade. They turn slightly purple and show faint white lines that look like mountains, rivers, and constellations, but when they dry, these disappear. The large ones are no more than four or five inches in length, and are often cut into moon-shaped ink-slabs in accordance with their natural forms.

'Four kinds of ink-stones are produced in the Old Pit. They are bluish-black [in colour] with fine veins, and as smooth as jade. The "mesh veins" are like fine gauze; the "brushed threads" are as fine and as dense as hair; the "gold and silver brushed threads" are also fine and dense; and the "small eyebrows" are like the marks made by finger-nails and can sometimes be as large as silkworms.

'These four kinds are also to be found in the New Pit, but they are coarse and dry. Their veins are thicker. The "eyebrows" may be as long as two or three inches; there are intervals of one or two tenths of inch between the "brushed threads". The "mesh-veins", however, are similar [to those produced in the Old Pit]. The large ones can be two or three feet long.

'The "Gold Star" stones from the Old and New Pits. They are light blue [in colour] and coarse and dry [in texture]. The large stones are about a foot long. After long use, they become burnished.

'The "Silver Star" stones from the Old and New Pits. They are also coarse and dry [in texture] and of a light bluish-black colour. The stone cannot withstand the rubbing of an ink-stick where there are silver stars. Thus it has to be cut sideways [in order to avoid the stars], to make ink-slabs. But [even so], these slabs become burnished like a mirror after long use. Large ones can be about a foot long.

'The "Gold Star" stones of Wan-chou. "Gold Star" stones from the perpendicular cliffs of Wan-chou are not as good as those of the Lower Cliff of Tuan-hsi. Their colour is lac black and their texture as smooth as jade. Gold Stars appear on them when they are wetted. They produce abundant ink when an ink-stick is rubbed on them. They do not wear with long use. They should not be confused with Hsieh-hsi stones.

'The green stones from the T'iao River [in Kansu] which are of a blue colour almost as dark as the dye of indigo plant, and as smooth as jade. Their ink-producing quality is comparable to that of Tuan-hsi stones of the Lower Cliff.'

The *Ko Ku Yao Lun* concludes its long discourse on ink-slabs by referring to those which come from 'The Roof-tiles of the Bronze Bird Terrace, situated on the south-west outskirts of Lin-chang in Honan. The tiles having been buried under water for a great number of years [have a damp quality] thus producing ink richly and profusely. The same can be said of the Roof-tiles of the Wei-yang Palace which was situated ten li north-west of Ch'ang-an, but of these it was also claimed "Antique lovers use them as ink-slabs."'

The following passage is taken from the late Dr. Van Gulik's excellent translation of Mi Fu's *Yen Shih (Account of Inkstones)*. 'The ordinary ink-slab is divided into an upper and lower part. The upper part is called *yen t'ou*, and here is a cavity filled with pure water for moistening the stone before rubbing the ink. The depression is called *yen ch'ih* or *shui ch'ih*. The lower part of the stone is formed by the flat surface on which the ink is to be rubbed. This place is called *mo ch'ih* or *mo ch'u*; also *yen ch'ih* just like the upper part. When one is rubbing the ink many things may happen. For instance one feels the stick of ink slip—it does not grip the stone; then the stone is called *hua* "slippery". This will occur when the stone has become rubbed too much and has become "tired" *fa*; or when the stone has been rubbed with greasy fingers; or simply because the stone is naturally very hard and smooth. In this case, it will take more time than usual before the three constituents of good ink, viz. water, ink, and the fine dust ground off the stone by rubbing, mix to "produce the ink", *fa mo*. Then the stone is called "slow" *man*, in contradistinction to "quick" *k'uai* stones, which produces ink in a short time. Some stones "repel" the ink, *chü mo chê*, that is to say, the ink mixes with the water, but not with the stone itself, with the result that the ink becomes "shallow" *tan*. The opposite of *chü mo chê* is *cho mo chê*, and is said of those stones that "grip" the ink. When the ink is rubbed, some very porous stones will absorb the ink, so that it soon dries up. This is a bad quality in an ink-stone, a fault that is called "absorbing" *shên*. In judging an ink-stone attention is also given to the colour and sound. The sound of a stone is tested by suspending it on a hook and rapping it with the knuckle of the finger. Very important, finally, is the *shih li*, the grain or texture of the stone. When the grain is too hard, the place where the ink is rubbed will after being used for some time become uneven, and chips will be knocked off the stick of ink. Stones with a good grain will, on the contrary, facilitate the movement of rubbing. Important also are the "markings", the pattern of the stone. These markings are called *wên* when they run parallel to one another, and *lo wên* when they run criss-cross.'

The *Ko Ku Yao Lun* [A] says that 'An ink-slab must be washed every day. It does not give the same lustre to the ink if it has not been washed for two or three days. The water on it should be changed at least every day, even if a day-to-day cleaning is not possible. During the warmer seasons of spring and summer, it is absolutely necessary to wash it daily, in order to get rid of the ink glue that settles on the slab.

'Hot water should not be used for washing an ink-slab, nor felt, nor paper. The best things for washing slabs are dried lotus-seeds or charcoal. A kind of slab-washing stone is produced at Tuan-hsi.'

I have so far been able to locate only five precisely dated ink-stones, although I have seen two others. Unluckily, their present whereabouts cannot be ascertained. They were both of rectangular shape; one was dated to the 'Second year [1089] of Yüan-fu', and the other of the 'Tenth year [1140] of Shao-hsing'. An interesting specimen in the Palace Museum, Taiwan, is described as coming from the 'Hall of Meditation' and having an inscription by the Ming calligrapher and painter, Tung Ch'i-ch'ang.

146. **1337** Tuan-hsi INK-STONE decorated with a finely carved design of Hsiang Lung Luo Han (a dragon suppressing Buddha) with his tamed dragon, which represents a teacher of Ch'an (Buddhism). The T'ang style characters on the upper part were written and engraved on the 'Fifteenth day of an autumn month in the third year [1337] of Chih-yüan by Master Kuo Chiu Ssu', a famous painter of the Yüan Dynasty. On the base of the ink-stone is written and engraved a poem composed by Lu Liu Liang, who was a scholar and violent anti-Manchu leader whose teachings and preachings all advocated the overthrowing of the Manchu Government. Height 9.5 in (24 cm) *S. Lee, Tokyo*

147. **1344** INK-STONE of rectangular shape decorated on the upper surface with a toad emerging from a small pond surrounded by fungus scrolls. These symbols of longevity are appropriate embellishments for the wish that the ink-stone give a myriad years of service to the owner and his heirs. On the base is inscribed a couplet dated to the 'Fourth year [1344] of Chih-chêng. Length 6 in (15.3 cm) *Formerly David Collection*

148. **1371** INK-STONE of rectangular shape, the well carved with two monkeys under a pine tree, a crane in clouds and a deer in the foreground. On the reverse is an inscription of fifty-five characters with the terminal phrase 'Made by Sung Lien on a happy day in the third year [1371] of Hung-wu.' Length 10.2 in (26 cm) *Chait Collection, New York*

Sung Lien (1310–81) a native of Chin-hua, Chekiang, went to Nanking in 1367 as tutor to the heir apparent. Two years after, he was appointed to edit the history of the Yüan Dynasty, and later became president of the Han-lin Academy. In 1380, because of his grandson's involvement in the conspiracy of Hu Wei-yung he was banished to Szechuan and died on his way there.

149a, b. **1426** INK-STONE of rectangular shape with a circular depression for grinding the ink. Above is a poem 'In praise of Lai-weng', extolling its qualities and antiquity, and its matchless origin from the Shih-ch'u pavilion (used for storing books in the Han Dynasty), and saying that now its fief has changed to that of ink, the nobles of the orchid tower (i.e. calligraphers) should treasure it, as it brings the scent of writing. On the under-side is inscribed the title 'Tile from the Shih-ch'u Pavilion', and the date 'First year [1426] of Hsüan-tê, converted [that is, for use as an ink-stone]' with two small seals, Hsüan and Tê. Length 5.7 in (14.5 cm) *Formerly David Collection*

150. **1546** INK-STONE of rectangular shape; the under-surface supported on four cylindrical pillars. The upper-side has a depression for holding water which surrounds the area on which the ink-cake will be moistened. On the left side is an inscription dated to the 'Twenty-fourth year [1546] of Chia-ching.' Length 8.2 in (20.9 cm) *British Museum*

Ink-Cakes

THE MOST SIGNIFICANT DIFFERENCE between Western ink and Chinese ink is that the former, in its liquid form, remains undistinguished, whereas the latter, in its solid state, can be moulded into graceful shapes, with the black monotony relieved by engraving in gilt and colourful ornamentation.

The history of Chinese ink is obscure, but existing evidence favours a date well before the Chou Dynasty (c. 1030–256 B.C.), when the chief ingredient was lacquer, the writing surface slips of bamboo or other wood, and the writing instrument a stylus. By the second century B.C., the composition of the substance had changed and the main item was lampblack, which is made by placing a dome-shaped lid of iron over a vessel filled with oil into which have been placed several well-lighted wicks. The resulting combustion covers the inside of the lid with black soot, which is then removed and mixed well with a solution of gum and other ingredients to advance its cohesive and indelible properties. Further changes were experienced at the end of the Han Dynasty (206 B.C.–A.D. 220) when paper began to replace bamboo, as we saw in the last chapter, and when the use of ink both for writing and printing came into more general use, as a result of the efforts of the first authenticated ink-maker, Wei Tan, who served at the court of Emperor Hsien-ti and died in 251. At this time, too, it was found that the best soot was made from specially selected pine trees, a fact referred to in a poem by Ts'ao Chih (192–224) which reads: 'Ink is derived from the soot of black pine.' Later it was discovered that the best ink is obtained from the burning of particular vegetable oils, like sesamum seed or China wood-oil, to which is added a sort of isinglass made from fish-maws, and a blending of aromatic musk or camphor to conceal unpleasant odours. The materials thus prepared are then put into wooded moulds and dried, which takes as long as twenty days, even in fine weather. When removed, they are in the form of solid ink-sticks or ink-cakes, and when required to be used for writing will be rubbed in water on an ink-yielding slab and examined for sheen and tone of colour—purple black is best, pure black next, and so on through blue black to dull grey black. In its composition it is quite unlike Western ink, so it does not lose its colour when exposed to light, which is one of the many reasons why there are in existence a number of examples going back at least twelve centuries. Our point of departure is thus again the Shoso-in Repository at Nara in Japan, the middle section of which numbers among its many treasures fourteen ink-sticks which are certainly of T'ang date. Twelve are oblong, and two are cylindrical. There are two with inscriptions in relief reading: 'Hsin Shiragi [i.e. Korea] House of Wu. Excellent Ink', and 'Shiragi House of Yang. Excellent Ink', indicating perhaps that they were made in the Shiragi (Silla) Dynasty (57 B.C.–A.D. 952) and were of Korean origin.

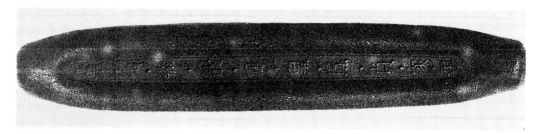

151. **716** In the Shoso-in there is a third INK-STICK of oblong form with an inscription reading: 'Flower mist flying dragon and phoenix Sovereign Chu House Ink', and on the back in red lacquer: 'Made in the autumn of the fourth year [716] of K'ai-yüan.' Length 6.5 in (16.5 cm) *Shoso-in, Nara, Japan*

Fragments of another ink-stick bear a label with the title 'Tempyo Treasure' indicating its probable use at the inauguration service of the Great Buddha in 952. A second 'eye-opening' ceremony was attended by the Emperor Goshira-kawa in 1185 when the new head of the Great Buddha was formally installed.

According to the *Ko Ku Yao Lun* [A]: 'A General Commentary on the Ink-stick. At the end of the T'ang Dynasty, the ink-stick maker Li Ch'ao and his son, T'ing-kuei, crossed the Yi River to take up residence in Hsieh-chou. Their family name had originally been Hsi and the name, Li, was given to them by the ruler, Li, of the Southern T'ang Dynasty. As a result, there were the Hsi T'ing-kuei as well as the Li T'ing-kuei ink-sticks.

'Connoisseurs of today regard Li T'ing-kuei's inks as the best; next came the sticks made by Chang Yü of the Yi River.

'There are two grades of Li T'ing-kuei's ink-sticks; the top grade having a dragon pattern with two ridges, the second with one ridge. Chang Yü's sticks can also be classified into two grades; first tributary ink-sticks from the Yi River, the second those presented to the Board of [Rites]. In recent times Ch'ên Lang of Yen-chou was also an excellent ink-stick maker and his products could be considered as next best.

'Other makers of renown at the end of the T'ang or in the Five Dynasties era were Wang Chün-tê, Ch'ai Hsün and Chu Chün-tê. The latter two were famous for their small ink-sticks.

'Famous Ink-sticks of Various Places. Pan Yün-ku's ink-sticks were made in Ch'ing-chiang hsien, Lin-chiang Prefecture in Kiangsi in the Yüan Dynasty.

'Cha Wên-t'ung's ink-sticks were made near the Great Eastern Gate of the old city in Fêng-yang Prefecture of [Southern] Chihli; in the present dynasty [there are] Lung Chung-ti's ink-sticks at T'ai-ho Hsien, Chi-an Prefecture in Kiangsi, on them four characters are inscribed: ("Forgers will be condemned to death by Heaven").

The reputation of Li Ch'ao as an ink-maker is indeed well deserved, for the celebrated scholar Hsü Hsüan (916–91) claims to have used one such stick in the writing of several thousand characters each day for more than ten years!

In the Palace Museum, Taiwan, there is an excellent ink-stick signed by Li T'ing-kuei, who is said, incidentally, to have included powdered rhinoceros horn among the twelve ingredients he used for his inks. In the same collection are several ink-sticks attributed to the Sung Dynasty, when it was the custom to use both musk and camphor to flavour them. None of these has been specifically attributed to P'an Ku, whose work was greatly admired by the famous poet, Su Tung-po, who was himself an accomplished ink-maker, a distinction he shared with many of his contemporaries, among them the philosopher Chu Hsi.

The *Ko Ku Yao Lun* [A] goes on to describe the 'Storing of Ink-sticks. The sticks should be stored with processed artemisia. During the wet months they should be kept in lime, to prevent them from getting damp. [Wang Tso] often used stove ash, and was quite satisfied with the results. Thick sticks can be stored for a considerable length of time, but not if they are thin. Old and thin sticks usually break into pieces when rubbed for ink, no matter how carefully they are preserved.'

Although the shapes of pre-Sung inks were generally confined to the conventional outlines of circular and rectangular, those that were made later adopted novel and more graceful forms, often decorated with finely engraved designs, or carefully inscribed calligraphy, both ornamental themes being further embellished with gold and colours to relieve the monotony of the black surface. At this stage, they can certainly be called works of art, which indeed they are, and as one of the 'four precious things of the study'—pen, paper, ink, and ink-stone—are perhaps the most deserving of recognition in this category.

There are, unfortunately, no further precisely dated ink-sticks until the second half of the sixteenth century, of which the following is of particular interest.

It was during the reign of Wan-li (1573–1619) that Ch'êng Chün-fang and his pupil Fang Yü-lu became celebrated ink-makers. Ch'êng Chün-fang, an ambitious

152. **1576** INK-CAKE, circular, decorated on one side with a design of five pine trees in relief, and on the other with an inscription reading: 'The ink-cake of the soot of the blue green pine, made in the fourth year [1576] of Wan-li' followed by the seal of the maker, Ch'êng Yü-po. On the rim is another inscription reading: 'Treasured in the Collection of the Hsüan-ho Palace.' Diameter 5.2 in (13.2 cm) *Formerly David Collection*

153. This INK-CAKE is illustrated in the *Ch'êng shih mo yuan*, a book of designs for impressing on ink-cakes, with illustrations by many well-known artists among them Ting Yün-p'êng (active between 1585 and 1625), some of the reproductions appearing as colour-woodblocks. Compiled and published by Ch'êng Chün-fang, the illustration is taken from an incomplete copy of this rare work, the first published in the Far East with fine-colour printing, which may be earlier in date than the 1605 edition in twenty-four volumes containing only black and white reproductions. *Percival David Foundation Library*

man, who was both scholar and connoisseur, and as one of the Imperial conductors of ceremonies at the court of Wan-li, had ample opportunity for introducing his inks to the emperor, by whom they were highly praised and readily accepted for his personal use; a distinction indeed!

Fang Yü-lu, as ambitious as his master, and realizing he could only acquire the fame he sought by working on his own, parted company with Ch'êng. Fang, too, published a book of ink designs entitled the *Fang shih mo p'u*, with illustrations by Ting Yün-p'êng and other leading painters, and with inscriptions by noted calligraphers.

Ch'êng Chün-fang and Fang Yü-lu were both so accomplished in the manufacture of ink-cakes that they turned an object of utility into a medium of artistic design. Nothing was too fanciful or too complicated to be transferred from the drawing board to the surface of the ink-cake, but while many unusual shapes were employed for quite practical purposes, some were so irregular that they were clearly marked 'not to be ground'. The following ink-cake is the work of Ch'êng Chün-fang, although of quite conventional shape.

154. **1621** INK-CAKE, circular, decorated on one side with a design of the 'hundred birds', and on the other with an inscription reading: 'Made in the first year [1621] of T'ien-chi by Ch'êng Chün-fang.' Diameter 5.2 in (13.3 cm) *His late Majesty, King Gustaf VI Adolf of Sweden*

The following are two more examples of the T'ien-chi period and complete our group of precisely dated ink-cakes.

155. **1621** INK-CAKE, octagonal, decorated on one side with a dragon-horse carrying on its back the *pa-kua* (which combines the *yin yang* symbol with the Eight Trigrams) as he trots over the waves. Above is a poem describing Taoist principles of philosophy. The reverse side is decorated with the *yin yang*, symbolizing the male and female elements of nature. These are surrounded by the Eight Trigrams, each with its name, which are interpreted by the legendary Fu Hsi and taken as the basis of philosophy by the Taoists. On the edge is inscribed: 'The first year [1621] of T'ien-chi.' Width 5.3 in (13.5 cm) *British Museum*

156. **1624** INK-CAKE, square, decorated with a dragon and a phoenix disputing the flaming pearl. On the edge is inscribed: 'Made in the fourth year [1624] of T'ien-chi.' Width 4 in (10.2 cm) *British Museum*

IV

*Lacquer, Mother-of-Pearl
and Wood*

13

LACQUER AND MOTHER-OF-PEARL

Aʀᴄʜᴀᴇᴏʟᴏɢɪᴄᴀʟ ᴇxᴄᴀᴠᴀᴛɪᴏɴs ᴀᴛ Aɴʏᴀɴɢ in Honan, the Shang Dynasty (c. 1550–c. 1030 B.C.) capital, have clearly shown that lacquer ware is one of China's most ancient crafts. Naturally few pieces have survived from this early site, and for purposes of study the tombs of the Warring States period (481–221 B.C.) have proved much more rewarding. These are located in the area of Ch'ang-sha in Hunan, and the refinement of the decoration and the elegant forms of the excavated articles presupposes a long period of development.

By the Han Dynasty (206 B.C.–A.D. 220), the technique had progressed beyond the manufacture of purely utilitarian objects, such as weapons and furniture, to the beautiful and more sophisticated toilet boxes and winged drinking cups. Sometimes both the inside and the exterior were red, sometimes black, but most frequently these were interchanged, so that a piece that was black inside used the alternative colour on the outside, and vice versa. The ornamentation employed a similar contrast: on a red background it was usually green and yellow; on a black surface, red and yellow; while both were further embellished with traces of gold. The majority of pieces was decorated either with a geometric design of birds and dragons amongst clouds, or with abstract forms and human figures. On others appeared elaborate landscape or hunting scenes, resplendent with chariots and mounted archers. Several of the pieces excavated at Lo-yang, the Chinese colony in Korea, bear inscriptions giving precise date-marks, and some even include the name of the founder of the factory as well as the departmental chiefs involved in the production of the particular vessel, which is also recorded in complete detail. These finds are remarkable for the fresh colour of the lacquer, for their skilfully carved designs, and for the gold and silver inlay which decorate many of the pieces.

The preparation of lacquer begins with the cutting of horizontal incisions into the bark of the *Rhus verniciflua* tree, which is indigenous to China and is to be found in most of the central and southern provinces. From the incisions exudes a transparent substance, which with exposure to air gradually changes in colour from white through grey to black. The liquid is subsequently drained into wooden containers, then boiled and stirred, and finally skimmed and strained through hemp cloth to remove all impurities. Thus prepared, lacquer assumes qualities of firmness and resistance to acids, and so provides a smooth and lasting surface for carved, painted or inlaid decoration. It is to be found in a wide range of colours, and can be applied to almost any material. The core of the vessel was usually wood, covered with ramie cloth, over which several layers of lacquer were then applied.

In the first century of our era at least a dozen Imperial lacquer factories are known to have been established in Szechuan, and although there is no documentary evidence in support of a continuation of the Han style, there is every likelihood that a similar technique was employed during the Chin and Sui Dynasties. Fortunately for the present treatise we do have a precisely dated example from the T'ang Dynasty. Our source is once more the Shoso-in Repository at Nara in Japan, which houses the collection given to the Todaiji Monastery by the widow of Emperor Shomu after his death in 756, and comprises a remarkable assembly of lacquered wares, including musical instruments. Anticipating this gift by some thirty years is the following item, a precisely dated piece of great importance (Plate 157).

Chiu-lung was in Szechuan Province. Both the surface and the back of this zither are covered with crackled lines, about which the *Ko Ku Yao Lun* has made the following observations: 'Crackle on Zithers. Crackle on the surface of a zither is proof of its antiquity. Unless it be several hundred years old, a zither's surface does not have crackle. There are different kinds of crackle. The "snake belly" crackle cuts across the surface of the instrument at intervals of from one to one and a half inches. Fine crackle has hundreds and thousands of hair-thin lines. Sometimes crackle occurs on both the face and the back of a zither. There is also the "Prunus Blossom" crackle in patterns of prunus buds, which is a sign of great antiquity. But an ancient zither may not be valuable in spite of its crackle, if its tone is not resonant, or if it has other defects. Faked Crackle. [Crackle can be produced] by allowing [the zither] to bask in winter sunshine, or by warming it near a fierce fire before covering it with snow. In this way the lacquer will crackle, but its colour will still be new.'

The *Ko Ku Yao Lun* continues with a discussion of the different types of zither and allied subjects. These are listed under the appropriate heading and add considerable interest to an object which has always been of great significance to the Chinese: 'Colour of an Ancient Zither. The brilliance of the lacquer of an ancient zither disappears, leaving a [dull black] colour like that of ebony. An instrument [with such an appearance] is usually exceptionally rare.

'Zithers of the T'ang and Sung Dynasties. In the T'ang Dynasty, Lei Wen and Chang Yüeh were two famous zither-makers. On their instruments, the space between the First Hole and the Second Hole is hollowed out, so that the sound does not quickly disperse. In the Sung Dynasty, an official factory was set up for the manufacture of zithers. All the instruments made there followed a given pattern, so

157. **724** ZITHER with seven strings, covered with lacquer. On the under-side there is an inscription reading: 'Made in Chiu-lung Hsien on the fifth day of the fifth month of the twelfth year [31 May 724] of K'ai-yüan.' Length 65 in (165.1 cm) *National Museum, Tokyo*

that they were identical in size and were known as "Factory Zithers". Consequently, a zither [made in that period] which does not conform to this pattern is of "unconventional make". There are many faked official Zithers which should be distinguished [from those that are genuine.] [The first hole is called the "dragon pool", the second, the "phoenix pond".]

'The Yin and the Yang Wood for Ancient Zithers. The wood of a *t'ung* tree which is often shone upon by the sun is *yang*, and that of the shady side is *yin*. When it is put in water, a piece of *yang* wood, whether old or new, floats, while a piece of the *yin* sinks to the bottom. There is no exception to this rule. A zither of *yang* wood sounds muffled in the morning and clear in the evening, muted when it is fine and resonant when it rains. A zither made of *yin* wood is just the reverse. This can be tested. [A] "Some people say that wood taken from *t'ung* trees near Buddhist or Taoist temples is good because it has been influenced by the tolling of [temple] bells in the morning and the beating of [temple] drums in the evening."

[O] 'Pure Yang [Wood] Zithers. When both the face and back of a zither of this kind are made of *t'ung* wood, it is called a pure *yang* Zither. Such a type is, however, not ancient. Since they have only been made recently, the tone of zithers of this type is not muted when played in the night, or on a rainy day. But their sound does not carry, so that its tone is not true.

'Ancient Zither Types. There were only two [zither styles] in ancient times, that of Confucius and that of Lieh-tzŭ. Neither the primeval type which consists of a single piece of wood, not the various patterns of cloud-harmony type which came into being recently, is of ancient manufacture.

'Zither Tables. The zither table should be made of the Wei-mo style. It stands two feet and eight inches high, and has enough room to allow the knees to go under it. It should be wide enough to carry three zithers and longer than the zither by about one foot. The top of the best tables is made of *Kuo-kung* bricks, agate, Nanyang stone, or Yung [-chou] stone. If it is made of wood, the timber should be hard and more than an inch thick. It should be lacquered over with two or three thickened coats of lacquer and finished with another of glossy black lacquer.

[A] 'Method of Making Zithers. The method includes the choice of matching *yin* and *yang* wood in order to produce harmony. The *t'ung* wood is *yang*, and is used for the face of the instrument; the *tzŭ* wood is *yin*, and is used for its base. The face is convex, symbolizing heaven, while the base is flat, symbolizing earth. The length of a zither should be three feet, six inches, symbolizing the 360 days of the year, while the thirteen studs correspond to both *lü* [fourth tone] and *lü* [third tone] symbolizing the twelve months, with the middle stop as their "sovereign", representing the intercalary month of a lunar year. According to the *Ti Wang Shih Chi* (Records of Emperors and Kings), the Emperor Yen (Shên-nung) designed the five-stringed zither to produce five notes. The *Shih-chi* records that the great Shun designed the five-stringed zither and played the Song of the South Wind on it. Huan T'an's *Hsin*

Lun (New Discourse) says that Shên-nung invented the zither by using the *t'ung* wood and silk for its strings. It also says that King Wên and King Wu of the Chou Dynasty each added a string to make the seven-stringed zither, and the added strings are known as the *wên* (civil) and the *wu* (martial) strings.

'"Scorched-tail" Zithers. In the Han Dynasty Ts'ai Jung happened to have passed by a man who was burning the *t'ung* wood for cooking. From the crackling noise Ts'ai knew that the wood was excellent, and therefore asked for a piece of it to make into a zither. It had indeed a beautiful tone, and from its scorched tail the name of "scorched-tail" zither was derived.

'The Five Abstentions. Abstain from playing the zither when there is a high wind, or heavy rain, or in a market place, or when common folk are present, or when the player is not properly seated, or not properly dressed and hatted. [A following note says:] The above five abstentions are intended to show reverence for the way of the sages and to observe the principles embodied in the instrument.

'Methods of Preserving Zithers. When it is cold and muffled in tone, an ancient zither should be put in a sack of warm sand. The sand should be renewed several times, in order to maintain a constant temperature. Another method of dealing with this condition is to steam the zither in a container on a windy day. The instrument is taken out to dry in the wind when it appears to "sweat" in the container. [When it is completely dry], its resonance will be restored.

'It is advisable to place a zither, be it old or new, on one's bed. It is even better to put it under the bed-cover, so that it remains close to the human spirit.

'The way to restore the tone of an old string is to fasten it at one end and rub it with mulberry leaves.

'A connoisseur should not leave his zither at the mercy of the wind and dew, nor expose it to the sun. He will observe this rule in the summer as well as in the winter. He will keep the instrument in a place that is dark, warm, and free from both wind and dew.'

The tomb of Wang Chien, former commander and self-styled emperor, who died in 918 at Chêng Tu, capital of Szechuan, supplies the next evidence of datable material in our lacquer chronology. In the tomb were found two lacquered wooden boxes each containing a jade book, and a five-lobed dish with a circular base and foot-rim, 7.5 in (19 cm) in diameter. The foundation contained two layers, the inner silver, the outer pewter, making a total thickness of a millimetre. The surface of the outer foundation is rough where the lacquer has flaked off. The inner foundation of silver, which is not lacquered, forms the surface for a design, inlaid with gold, of two phoenix among branches. In the centre, each of the five lobes is decorated with lotus flowers. What little remains of the lacquer shows that it was red in colour, but whether it was carved or not is now impossible to determine. The *Hsiu Shih Lu* says: 'The ones with carved designs on lacquer were not lacquered over on the inside.' The inside of this is not lacquered and the part which is lacquered is made of pewter in order to strengthen the dish. It has been held that carved red lacquer began to be made in Sung times; in fact it may well have begun in the T'ang Dynasty. The former Shu Kingdom was founded in the early part of the Five Dynasties period and this piece from the tomb of Wang Chien should help to establish the point that at the end of T'ang the making of carved red lacquer was known.

The Sung lacquerers followed the same simplicity of form as that of the contemporary potter, who specialized in flower-form bowls and dishes, and in petal-shaped cups with stands. Such a piece is this precisely dated example.

158. **1082** Black lacquer high-footed BOWL with foliated rim. The inscription, written in red lacquer, runs along the inside of the mouth-rim. This gives the date of the 'Fifth year [1082] of Yüan-fêng', and names the 'Ma Family of Chih-chou'. Found at Chu-lu Hsien. Diameter 6 in (15.3 cm) *Tenri Museum, Japan*

159. **1099** A fine example of the 'dry' lacquer technique is this FIGURE OF A SEATED ABBOT. The legs are crossed and almost hidden by drapery, the eyes appear to be closed, the head is shaven, and the lobes of the ears long. His robe crosses his breast from left to right, ending in folds on the right leg. A band over the left shoulder supports a ring from which hangs a tassel. His hands lie on his lap, the right held in the left palm. Loose sleeves cover all but his hands. An inscription gives the date of the 'Second year [1099] of Yüan-yu', and the signature 'Liu Yun'. Height 18 in (45.7 cm) *Honolulu Academy of Arts*

Nearly one hundred and fifty years elapse before any more reliably authenticated material has so far been recorded. This brings us to the Yüan Dynasty (1260–1368) which supplies one precisely dated piece and two significant items of documentation, the earliest being the Chu-yung Kuan Gate of 1342–5 located north of Peking. This edifice reveals in its rich sculptural decoration many of the motifs— dragons, birds, flowers, human figures, and garden scenes—that formed part of the designer's repertory in the fourteenth century. The second is but a few years later and supports at least a mid-fourteenth century date for carved red lacquer as a result of the scientific data revealed on a site near Shanghai where the Chinese recently excavated a tomb of a member of the Jen family who died in 1351. Fortunately, for our purpose, one of the items in the tomb was a small circular carved lacquer box, the sides decorated with a fret border and the lid with the customary pastoral scene of a scholar with his attendant by a river bank, while rocks, trees, and shrubs complete a picture familiar on Ming Dynasty lacquers, but for which we can now give a Yüan attribution.

The precisely dated piece is earlier than the foregoing, and introduces the reader to the very attractive technique of *chiang chin* (by which a piece is hair-line engraved and filled in with gold). An almost contemporary source of information on this subject is the *Cho-Kêng* by T'ao Tsung-li, a descendant of the famous painter Chao Mêng-fu. According to this Yüan Dynasty publication (1366) there were two lacquer techniques, those with incised decoration of plants and animals, the engraved lines being inlaid with gold, and the 'shiny black' or chestnut coloured wares. It is interesting that both techniques are incorporated in the following piece.

160. **1315** SUTRA BOX of rectangular shape covered with 'shiny black' lacquer, and decorated on the lid, front and back with a peacock and a peahen in an ornamental cartouche surrounded by flowers. The sides are similarly decorated with two flying parrots. The entire design is executed in *chiang chin* technique—hair line engraved and filled in with gold. Inside on the red lacquered base is an inscription in black lacquer giving the date of the 'Second year [1315] of Yen-yu'. Length 15.75 in (40 cm) *Segan-ji Temple, Fukuoka, Japan*

On the subject of gold inlay, the following observations are made by the *Ko Ku Yao Lun*: 'Gold Inlay. The best pieces have solid lacquer with skilfully inlaid patterns in gold dust. At the beginning of the Yüan Dynasty P'êng Chun-pao of Hsi-t'ang in Chia-hsing was fairly well known for his consummate inlays of landscapes, human figures, pavilions, flowers, trees, birds, and animals.

[A] 'There are lacquer pieces painted in gold outline in Ning-kuo fu (Nanking) palace. Now craftsmen in the two capitals often make them.

[O] 'Pierced Hsi-p'i. Most pieces of this kind were made in the Sung Dynasty with gold-inlaid human scenes. Spaces between the patterns are pierced through, hence their name.

'Ancient Hsi-p'i. Among ancient carved wares, the most valuable is "burnished purple"; the most valuable pieces have burnished ground and show a reddish black colour. The bottom [of the incision] is like an inverted roof-tile, and [the wares] are lustrous, solid and thin.

'Less valuable are pieces where the colour is similar to that of the jujube and thence known as *tsao-erh-hsi*; less valuable still when the carving is deep.

'The pieces which used to be made at Fu-chou have a burnished yellow ground and circular patterns. They are known as Fu-hsi. They are solid but thin and are also difficult to come by.

'Those recently made by Yang Hui, in Hsieh-t'ang in Chia-hsing, though heavier by several taels and deeply carved are seldom strong.'

The *Ko Ku Yao Lun* continues with a discussion on 'Carved Red [Cinnabar] [T'i-hung]. Carved red wares, whether old or new, must be judged according to the thickness of the vermilion [lacquer], the fresh red colour and its strength and weight. Those carved with patterns of sword-rings and spiral scrolls are particularly fine. The pieces with a yellow ground on which are carved landscapes, human figures, flowers and trees or birds and animals, although the workmanship is of the finest, are liable to flake off. The thin vermilion [lacquered] red wares are cheap.

'Many of the lacquered pieces of the Sung Imperial Court were done in unadorned gold or silver.

'At the end of the Yüan Dynasty Chang Ch'êng and Yang Mao, both pupils of Yang Hui of Hsi-t'ang, were famous for their carved red ware. But very often the vermilion lacquering of their ware is thin and not strong and is apt to flake off. Carved red lacquer is greatly favoured by peoples of Japan and the Liu Chiu Islands.

[A] 'Carved Red Lacquer. At the present time, craftsmen of Ta-li Fu in Yünnan are skilled in making this type of lacquer but many of their products are imitated by others. These objects are often found in noble homes in Nanking. There are two kinds, vermilion red and darker red (or vermilion red all over and with black marks). Fine specimens are extremely expensive; but there are many imitations that call for careful scrutiny.

[O] 'Built Up Carved Red Lacquer [Tui-hung]. Imitation carved red lacquer is made by building up putty and covering it with a coat of red vermilion lacquer. Hence the name "built up" red lacquer. The designs are confined to sword-guards and hemp flowers. They are not worth much; they are also called "red-coated".'

[O] Several examples of the work of Chang Ch'êng and Yang Mao exist, the respective signature being incised in small characters, of thin construction, on a black lacquered base. None of their work is precisely dated, and we only know that they worked at Hsi T'ang, Chekiang Province, in the second half of the Yüan Dynasty and that they carved red lacquer well. So well indeed that they became famous, and so famous that in the early fifteenth century they were summoned to the Chinese court by the Emperor Yung-lo. It is said that they were both dead by the time the invitation arrived, and it was Chang Tê-kang, the son of Chang Ch'êng, already a lacquerer in his own right, who went in their place. The emperor was so pleased with his work that he appointed him to the office of works—Ying Shan-so—as assistant in charge of making carved red lacquer furniture for the newly constructed palaces. It is interesting to note that every piece produced in this Imperial workshop was required to receive thirty-six coats of lacquer.

A recently divulged source of information on lacquer of the late fourteenth century records a gift to the consort of the Japanese shogun in 1403–4 by the Emperor Yung-lo. The gift comprised fifty-eight pieces of carved red lacquer— amongst other treasures—and the types included tables, bowls, plates, round and octagonal boxes, each piece being decorated with one of the designs now so familiar to all interested students. The date of the gift is significant, for this complex repertoire must have been anticipated by several decades of development. Additional evidence is supplied by the catalogue of the shogun's collection *Kundai-Kan sayu Cho-ki* made by Noami towards the end of the fourteenth century which refers to both plain and deeply carved lacquer.

From the early fifteenth century onwards, the majority of lacquer was carved, the surface being built up layer by layer until a uniform thickness was achieved. When it was dry the design was then carved out of the lacquer to expose one or more of the layers. Red was the most popular colour, black came next, while yellow and green were used only for supplementary ornamentation. When black was used for the base colour, it would be covered by several layers of red through which would be carved the ornament, leaving the original layer as a background. This method is known as 'cut colour', and layers of yellow and green could also be incorporated in the build-up structure. The core of the vessel was usually made of pine wood, of which thin strips were glued together and carefully finished, so that both inside and outside were perfectly smooth. Ramie, tin, or pewter, were also used. In the Hsüan-tê period, the red colour was brighter and fresher than that of Yung-lo, and the black base was of a more vibrant tone. The six-character mark of the respective reign-period, when it was used, is also significantly different, those of Yung-lo being scratched on in poor calligraphy, while in the later epoch they were carefully cut with a knife and filled in with gold. An interesting point is that a number of pieces have the Hsüan-tê mark inscribed over that of Yung-lo, with the obvious intention of concealing the earlier reign-mark. A reasonable explanation for this has been that the lacquer produced late in the fourteenth century or during the reign of Yung-lo was superior to that of Hsüan-tê and that Imperial demands for equality of manufacture resulted in this deception.

Fifteenth-century lacquer is found decorated with floral and landscape designs, dragons and other animals, the phoenix and other birds; all deeply carved with skilful, yet spontaneous strokes. The floral patterns usually have a plain yellow surface, while the landscapes are created against diaper grounds which illustrate by different motifs the respective zone of decoration, sky, earth or water.

Mother-of-pearl inlay on lacquer is another technique requiring as much, if not more, precision. Our earliest precisely dated piece is of the Ch'êng-hua period (1465–87) and so too late for the *Ko Ku Yao Lun*. But since this technique has been in existence since T'ang times, the relevant passages from this authoritative work are being quoted: 'Mother-of-Pearl Inlay. Those made in the past or for the Sung Imperial Court were in solid lacquer. Some of them have copper thread inlays. They are very good. Those made recently at Chi-chou in Chiang-hsi are mostly made of putty, pig's blood, and *t'ung* oil. They are not solid wares, being easy to make and liable to damage.

[A] 'In the Yüan Dynasty, rich families ordered this type of ware, but left the manufacturers to take their own time in their making. The products are in very solid lacquer, and the designs with human figures on them are delightful to the beholder.

'The materials used in present-day Lu-ling hsien of Chi-an Fu in Chiang-hsi products are mostly lime, pig's blood, and mixed with *t'ung* oil. They are brittle. Some makers even use arrowroot (in place of putty), which makes the objects even worse. Fine specimens are made only at the (buyers') homes under supervision if they are to be solid and durable.

'Nowadays in old houses in the town of Chi-an Fu, there are beds, chairs, and screens inlaid with mother-of-pearl in designs with human figures. The work is beautifully finished and quite delightful to behold. Fruit boxes, message plaques, and [Chin] Tartar chairs recently made to the order of important families are almost as good as the ancient articles, because they have been made under the buyers' supervision.

'Early in the Hung-wu period [1368–98], Shên Wan-san's home in Su-chou was searched and his property confiscated. Among the belongings taken to the offices of the Six Departments of the Palace i.e. in suspensa sub judice there were benches, chairs, and tables of either mother-of-pearl inlaid lacquer or carved red lacquer. They are very fine specimens, and are still there. [Shên, an extremely rich man, flourished at the end of the Yüan and the beginning of the Ming Dynasty. The founder of the Ming Dynasty, T'ai-tsu, wished to enlarge his palaces, and so

206

confiscated Shen's property.]'

Although the *Ko Ku Yao Lun* does not mention T'ang mother-of-pearl, we have evidence of its existence from the treasures in the Shoso-in Repository. Among the many superb examples that have survived are musical instruments, mirrors, and miscellaneous articles of furniture.

Leaving behind the eighth century, we return to our next precisely dated piece which is a beautiful example of Ch'êng-hua (1465–87) mother-of-pearl lacquer.

161. **1487** BOX of upright rectangular shape. Black lacquer decorated with mother-of-pearl inlay in shades of rosy pink suffused with green. The design of a grapevine with two geese is carried out in these colours highlighted with pearly white. The reverse shows two chickens under a clump of flowering shrubs with hovering butterflies. The inscription on the base is also inlaid with mother-of-pearl and is dated to the 'Twenty-third year [1487] of Ch'êng-hua.' Height 4 in (10.2 cm) *Sir John Figgess*

Throughout the fifteenth century, it is evident that the production of carved red lacquer continued much in the same style as was current in the time of Yung-lo. But before the century closes we witness an entirely fresh approach to the old technique. The new manner is exemplified in the delicately carved decoration of the next piece. It is another most important document in our chronology of inscribed lacquer, for it bridges the gap between the strongly carved lacquer of the early fifteenth century and the more detailed pieces which were to be produced in such large numbers in the middle Ming period.

162. **1489** DISH of delicately carved red lacquer on a yellow ground. Decorated inside with a palace by a lake surrounded by waves and rocks; over the door-way of the palace is inscribed 'Second year [1489] of Hung-chih', and on the door-pillars 'P'ing Liang' and the carver's name 'Wang Ho'. The base is decorated in black on a yellow ground with an inscription in relief reproducing part of the well-known poem on the Lan Ting Pavilion by Huang Hsi-chih (321–79). Diameter 7.9 in (20.1 cm) *Formerly David Collection*

The succeeding reign of Chêng-tê provides only negative documentation and so fifty years must elapse before our next piece which is of the Chia-ching period (1522–66), another example of the attractive mother-of-pearl technique.

163. **1537** Round BOX of black lacquer inlaid with mother-of-pearl on the top with a horseman and attendants approaching a pavilion, the rounded sides with lobed panels of figures in landscapes set in a hexagonal diaper ground. Similar panels on the lower part containing birds on flowering branches. On one of the posts of the pavilion is an inscription reading: 'Made in the fifteenth year [1537] of Chia-ching.' Diameter 11 in (27.9 cm) *The late Sir Harry Garner*

The next precisely dated piece is in the entirely different technique of painting a design on the lacquered surface. Few examples have survived because they are thinner in structure and therefore more fragile than the carved lacquers.

164. **1557** Square DISH of red lacquer painted in green, black, and gold in the centre with a bird on a fruiting peach branch, surrounded on the sides with phoenix among clouds between diaper corners in black and gold; flowers and scrolls in similar style and colour on the back. In red lacquer on the brown base is an inscription reading: 'Made for the Dragon Hall in the thirty-fifth year [1557] of Chia-ching.' Above this are good wish characters. Width 8.5 in (21.6 cm) *Formerly David Collection*

From now on, although the designs followed those of the previous century, a progressive decline in the quality of the carving becomes apparent. During the sixteenth century two styles of carving emerged, one in which the design was finished with sharply incised edges, while the other had softly rounded contours. The plain yellow ground was generally discarded in favour of a brocade backdrop. Several fine examples of precisely dated lacquer of the sixteenth century exist, however, and are recorded below.

165. **1573** Rectangular STAND or TABLE on four claw feet. Black lacquer decorated with various cloud formations in *guri* style showing red layers. An inscription in red on the black base reads: 'Bought at the Hall of the Five Jade Happinesses in the first year [1573] of Wan-li.' Length 24 in (61 cm) *Gruber, Tokyo (page 209)*

166. **1592** Circular DISH of multi-coloured lacquer with seven bands of colour, red, dark green, buff-yellow, orange, red, dark green, buff-yellow in succession, carved in the centre with a five-clawed dragon and phoenix with a flaming pearl, in clouds and above waves and rocks, with narrow panels of emblems around. On the rim a border of four panels with birds on flowering branches separated by flower sprays. An inscription on the base reads: 'Made in the nineteenth year [1592] of Wan-li.' Diameter 8.8 in (22.4 cm) *The late Sir Harry Garner*

167. **1595** Circular COVERED BOX of carved red lacquer, the top decorated with an audience scene showing the emperor seated in front of a screen on a terrace, flanked by two attendants and with a man kneeling at his feet, the background with cloud diaper in dark green and yellow. The sides are carved with two borders, each with four dragons in pursuit of the flaming pearl. On the base is an inscription reading: 'Made in the twenty-second year [1595] of Wan-li.' Diameter 9 in (22.9 cm) *Baroness Heeckeren van Walie-Tetrode*

168. **1595** DISH of carved red lacquer decorated in green and brown with a five-clawed dragon pursuing a pearl amid waves, mountains and shrubbery; the rim with panels of symbols and flowers, inside and on the back. On the base is an inscription reading: 'Made in the twenty-second year [1595] of Wan-li.' Diameter 8.5 in (21.6 cm) *Art Institute, Chicago, Gift of Mr and Mrs Philip Pinsof*

169. **1595** Circular COVERED BOX of carved red lacquer, decorated on the top with two dragons amidst clouds, waves and rocks, the sides with lobed compartments containing the flowers of the four seasons between fungus scrolls. On the base is an inscription reading: 'Made in the twenty-second year [1595] of Wan-li.' Diameter 8 in (20.3 cm) *City Museum and Art Gallery, Hong Kong*

170a, b. **1595** CABINET of upright square form, of carved red lacquer, decorated with dragons among waves pursuing pearls within lobed octagonal medallions surrounded by a squared frame, the intervening space filled with floral scrolls. The interior is composed of ten drawers, each decorated with dragons and waves. There is an inscription on the base reading: 'Made in the twenty-second year [1595] of Wan-li of the Great Ming Dynasty.' Height 15 in (38.1 cm) *Cleveland Museum of Art, Norman O. Stone and Ella A. Stone Memorial Fund*

171. **1595** Rectangular COVERED BOX with shaped edges, and carved in red, green, brown and black lacquer with a dragon in clouds above waves supporting the *shou* character over its head and surrounded at each corner by cloud scrolls. The sides have floral panels with a plum blossom at each corner. There is an inscription on the base reading: 'Made in the twenty-second year [1595] of Wan-li of the Great Ming Dynasty.' Length 12.7 in (32.3 cm) *Royal Scottish Museum, Edinburgh*

172. **1595** Circular DISH of red lacquer decorated in yellow, dark green and gold with a full-faced dragon among clouds, waves and rocks on a diaper ground; floral border on the rim. There is an inscription on the base reading: 'Made in the twenty-second year [1595] of Wan-li of the Great Ming Dynasty.' Diameter 7.5 in (19 cm) *City Museum and Art Gallery, Hong Kong*

173. **1595** Circular DISH of red lacquer decorated in yellow, dark green and gold with a dragon in profile among clouds, waves and rocks on a diaper ground; floral border on the rim. There is an inscription on the base reading: 'Made in the twenty-second year [1595] of Wan-li of the Great Ming Dynasty.' Diameter 7.5 in (19 cm) *City Museum and Art Gallery, Hong Kong*

Incised, painted and inlaid lacquer became very popular in the Ming Dynasty, especially during the reign of Wan-li. The first step was to incise the design on the lacquer ground, then to inlay the engraved lines with the desired colour, after which the surface was polished and given its final gilding and painting. The following pieces are excellent examples of this skilled technique.

174. **1601** Inlaid lacquer BOX decorated with two dragons pursuing the pearl above waves and rocks on the lid; scrolling flowers and leaves embellish the sides of the cover and the base. There is an inscription on the base reading: 'Made in the twenty-eighth year [1601] of Wan-li of the Great Ming Dynasty.' Length 13 in (33 cm) *Sir John Addis*

175. **1602** Cylindrical BRUSH POT of red lacquer decorated with inlaid and painted designs in various colours with incised gold outlines. On the sides are four quatrefoil panels decorated with dragons in clouds above rocks and waves. Between the former is a column twisted to represent a *shou* character and above their heads are two swastika; the surrounding area is decorated with symbols of the same motif on a diaper ground. There is an inscription on the base reading: 'Made in the twenty-ninth year [1602] of Wan-li of the Great Ming Dynasty.' Height 9 in (22.9 cm) *Royal Scottish Museum, Edinburgh*

176. **1605** Square lacquer BOX AND COVER with shaped edges, decorated in red and dark green on a brown ground with gilt outlines. The design on the lid with its diaper background is of two dragons flying among clouds above a rocky landscape; they are disputing the flaming pearl which contains the *shou* character. Panels of lotus decorate the sides of the box, while on the base is an inscription reading: 'Made in the thirty-first year [1605] of Wan-li of the Great Ming Dynasty.' Length 7.8 in (19.8 cm) *Royal Scottish Museum, Edinburgh*

Two more precisely dated examples of the mother-of-pearl technique are the following artistically decorated boxes.

177. **1608** Rectangular black lacquer BOX inlaid with mother-of-pearl. Decorated on the lid with a realistic scene of palace life; landscape and figures on the sides. On the base is an inscription in the same medium reading: 'Made in the thirty-fourth year [1608] of Wan-li', and further embellished with the seal of 'Chao Erh-yu'. Length 23 in (58.4 cm) *Museum of Fine Arts, Boston*

178. **1609** Square black lacquer BOX with basketry panels. Inlaid with mother-of-pearl and gold and decorated with a landscape scene of Taoist figures with their respective attributes. On the base is an inscription in red lacquer reading: 'Commissioned to be made for sale in the thirty-fifth year [1609] of Wan-li.' Width 5.4 in (13.8 cm) *Cleveland Museum of Art, Purchase, Edward L. Whittemore Fund*

179. **1610** Rectangular lacquer BOX AND COVER with incurving corners, decorated in red on a black ground. The design on the lid is of two dragons disputing the flaming pearl above a rocky landscape; cloud bands and floral scrolls decorate the sides and the incurving corners. On the base is an inscription reading: 'Made in the thirty-sixth year [1610] of Wan-li of the Great Ming Dynasty.' Length 17.5 in (44.5 cm) *Asian Art Museum of San Francisco, Avery Brundage Collection*

180. **1610** Rectangular BOX with a hinged lid and woven bamboo panels; the edges and corner pieces surmounted by metal bands. The top is decorated with a garden scene, a lake with overhanging trees and flying birds. On the base is an inscription reading: 'Made in the spring month of the thirty-sixth year [1610] of Wan-li.' Length 10 in (26 cm) *William Rockhill Nelson Gallery of Art, Atkins Museum of Fine Arts, Kansas City*

181. **1620** Circular BOX with basketry panels and handle. Painted in different colours and gilding on a red ground on the top with birds on a camellia branch and along the edges with floral scrolls. On the base is an inscription reading: 'Made in the forty-sixth year [1620] of Wan-li on an auspicious morning in an autumn month for the overseas residence of Wang. Wang Chai, I-shan, of Wai-yang [from abroad] marked'; and inside the lid: 'I-shan recorded'. Diameter 18 in (45.7 cm) *British Museum*

Three years later, in the reign of T'ien-ch'i, a remarkable object of painted lacquer was made by the Jesuit Fathers, Manuel Diaz the younger and Nicolo Longobardi. As the earliest known Chinese globe, it can be held to rank with Father Matteo Ricci's map of 1602 as one of the two most important relics of early European cartography in China. It is from the Imperial Palace in Peking and may have been intended as a present for the Emperor T'ien-ch'i, or at least commissioned by him, since he himself was a great carpenter and lacquerer.

182a, b. **1623** GLOBE, painted in lacquer on wood. Diameter 23 in (58.4 cm) *British Museum*

The globe is made on a scale of 1:21 million, and thus large enough to convey a detailed picture of world geography. In their long explanation, the Fathers set out their views of the universe founded on Ptolemaic theory, for even in Europe this theory was only slowly being superseded by the theories of Copernicus, Tycho Brahe, and Galileo. There follows the theory of the five zones on latitude, equatorial, tropical and polar, and a description of the five continents, Asia, Europe, the Americas, Africa, and Magellanica (as the southern continent was called). The continents are distinguished on the globe by means of different colours. As they all lie to the west, or, of course, to the east of any given point, a discussion on the relativity of compass directions is then set out. This idea was further complicated for the Jesuits by the traditional Chinese concepts of Yin and Yang. It seems that strong opposition to the Jesuits' ideas must have come from the association in the Chinese mind of Yang with hot and south, and of Yin with cold and north. Europeans probably found it difficult to understand the force of these opposites in daily life and in every ritual observance. To accept the idea that 'south can also be cold' must have demanded a great intellectual readjustment, even for the scholar converts.

The inscription continues with a description of the mounting, which sets the globe on a vertical axis, in the Ptolemaic system.

The authors complete their inscription with a religious reference, followed by the date and their signature. 'So we can deduce the origin [of heaven and earth] in the King of Creation. How respectfully we should apply ourselves to this study! T'ien-ch'i third month, third year [1623] the European [naturalized] officials Yang Ma-no/Lung Hua-min.' The Chinese names are based on European forms. The *ya* sound of Diaz is enough to suggest the common surname Yang, and Ma-no is a representation of Manuel.

14

WOOD

WOOD-CARVING IS PERHAPS THE MOST IMPORTANT of all the minor arts in China, for the variety of grain and colour, allied with such diversity of contour, natural and applied, allow the imaginative craftsman unlimited scope for his talents. At its magnificent best it can be fully appreciated in the field of architecture, for which the wood-carver has a natural affinity, and this is readily apparent when the building was entirely of wood. Even at a later date, when stone and brick filled in the walls of a building, the stability of the structure still depended on a wooden framework and the decoration of the interior was again entrusted to the versatile carver. For Buddhist and Taoist temples the woodwork was sculptured with sacred scenes and figures encompassed by floral scrolls and intermingled with conventional emblems distinguishing the two religions. For Imperial buildings, the floral scrolls enclose panels of dragons and phoenixes in clouds, interspersed with other mythological creatures among swirling waves. For ordinary use, the principal motif would usually be figure scenes from history and romance, separated by panels of birds and animals, butterflies and insects, all featured against a floral background.

For a comprehensive list of rare woods and some interesting observations, we again turn to the *Ko Ku Yao Lun*, and quote the following excerpts from this illuminating manual: 'Ch'i-ch'ih Wood [known also as *tzŭ-yüan-yang* (brown mandarin duck)]. This comes from the Western Barbarian Regions. The markings are coloured half dark brown (with "crab-claw" markings) and half black, like ebony. When in the shape of chicken claws, the wood is expensive. The Western Barbarians used it to make camel nose-rings, for it does not get stained by grease. I have only seen sword handles made of it, but nothing larger.

'Amianthus. This comes from the Mountains in Tsê and Lu Prefectures (in Shansi). Its colour is green and white, and it is as hard and as heavy as stone. If one wraps it in paper and dips it into naphtha, and then sets it alight, it will not be reduced to ashes. It is often used to make sword handles.

'Tartar Birch Bark. This is produced in the North. It is yellow in colour with a pinkish hue and with spots as large as grains of rice or beans. It absorbs grease and is hard to come by. It is best used for the manufacture of sword sheaths. [A] Nevertheless, people today use it to make or to decorate bows, which are called "Tartar Birch Bows". It is also used in the manufacture of shoe soles.

[O] 'Red Sandalwood. This is produced on Hainan Island, and in Kuangsi and Hu-kuang (Hunan). It is hard and red when new, but becomes brown in colour when old. It has "crab claw" markings. The colour of the new wood can be washed out in water which can be used for dyeing other objects. This is best suited for the making of hair-pins. [A] Genuine red sandalwood, when rubbed against a white wall, leaves a red mark. Other dark coloured woods do not do this. Yellow sandalwood is very fragrant, and people of to-day often use it to make belts.

[O] 'Tiger-stripe Wood. This is produced on Hainan [Island] and is so called because of its stripes.

'Ebony. This wood comes from the Southern Barbarian Regions and is the hardest of all kinds of wood. Old ebony is pure black and brittle, while new ebony shows veins [of a different shade].

'Gnarly Wood. This comes either from Liao-tung or Shansi. The gnarls in birch wood have fine and delightful markings, but is normally to be found only in small pieces. The gnarls in cypress wood are large with coarse patterning. *Ying* is the gnarl of a tree. To the north of the Great Wall, wood of the willow tree often has many gnarls. It is a hard wood, with delightful markings. It is good for making saddles.

'Rosewood. This [kind of wood] comes from the Southern Barbarian Regions. It is maroon in colour like laka wood, and also scented. Its markings sometimes look like ghost faces, and are quite pleasing. When they are large in size and light in colour, the wood is less valuable.

[A] 'People of Kuangtung often use it to make tea cups or wine cups.

[O] 'Dice Cedar. This is produced in the Western Barbarian Region near Lake Ma [in the lower reaches of the Chin-sha River between Szechuan and Yunnan]. Its grain is always twisted. When it forms a pattern of landscapes or of human figures, the price of this wood is very high. The wood is hard to come by, even in Szechuan. It is also known as "scented dice cedar".

'Fir. This is produced in Szechuan and Kuangsi. It is white in colour with yellowish and reddish veins. It has a delicate fragrance. Some say that camphor of the Southern Barbarian Regions is produced from fir trees. Fir wood with fine patterns like those of a pheasant, is hard to come by. It is delightful, even if its markings are coarse, but the commonest type has no markings except for straight veins.

'Tree-fern. This is white with large and yellow veins. It is beautiful and is commonly known as Japanese tree-fern. Most [specimens] of this kind of wood are, however, not marked. There is another variety, slightly harder and with straight and fine veins, which is known as leather tree-fern. [A] The tree-fern comes from Hu-kang and from Yang-shan and An-wen in Chiangsi, which is known as grass fern.

[O] 'Coconut Cup. This is produced in Annam, and in Kuangtung and Kuangsi. It is to be found shaped like a gourd and thick, and solid, and in a brownish black colour. Its flesh is edible. [The nut] can be cut with a saw and then either painted or set in silver to make wine cups, wine pots, individual plates, wine ewers, and water ladles.

'Nutmeg. This is produced in Annam and on Hainan [Island] and Liu-leng, and has delightful, deep patterns on its surface. It is very hard and solid, which is why it is called Diamond Nut. Nutmeg rosaries are warming [to wear] in the winter months. Some of them are the size of loquats, others paulownia fruit, or of hazel nuts.

'Bamboo Sticks. Square bamboo comes from Szechuan and the Fei-lai Peak of Hangchou. There are spines at each joint, so the inhabitants of Szechuan call them "thorny bamboo".

'Hsiang bamboos are to be found in Kuangsi [Province]. They have light coloured spots which have haloes with a dark brown dot in the centre, rather similar to the spots on the leaf of a reed. They are best for the manufacture of flutes. [According to tradition, when the great Shun died at Ts'ang-wu, his consorts wept bitterly. Their tears fell on bamboos to become spots. These bamboos are also known as "consorts" bamboos of the Hsiang River].

'"Cloud bamboos" come from Kuangsi [Province]. They have large red spots on them and also have haloes.

'"Cymbal bamboos" are to be found in Szechuan. These are slender with very big points, like [pairs of] cymbals; hence the name.

'"Child bamboos" come from Szechuan [Province]. Their [roots] are about a foot long, like the intestine of a dog or a pig.

'Palm bamboos are to be found in Szechuan and Kuangsi [Province]. Their leaves resemble palm leaves, but their stems are those of bamboos, very hard and solid. They are also known as "peach bamboos". All varieties of the bamboo are suitable for the manufacture of walking-sticks. Variegated rattan is to be found in Kuangsi [Province]. The slender variety with black spots is suitable for the making of walking sticks, the thicker kind being quite common.

[A] 'Iron-strong Wood. This is produced in Kuangtung [Province], being pure black and very hard and heavy. The inhabitants of Tung-wan generally use it for building houses.

'Betel-nut Wood. Betel nut is produced in Yü-lin Chou in Kuangsi [Province]. Its trees are like palm trees being about seventy to eighty feet high. Their leaves can be made into fans, which produce a [soft] breeze, yet do not cause illness. The better kind of these nuts have pointed kernels. When eaten with lime, they give a black coating to the teeth. From this fact there has sprung the custom of engraving designs on black teeth.

'Human-face Wood. Human-face wood is to be found at Yü-lin Chou. It flowers in the spring and bears fruit in summer. The fruit ripens in the autumn and looks like two human faces, one on each side. Hence it is called "human-face wood".

'Fragrant Cedar. This is to be found in Szechuan or in Hu-kuang [Province]. It is yellow in colour and fragrant, and this is how it gets its name. It makes the best shop-sign boards. A different variety, brownish black in colour. Both are very costly. But white cedar is poor [in quality].'

The earliest examples of ornamented wood display a series of diapered patterns in low relief. The decorative feature began with simple parallel lines, to which others were gradually added; first at right angles to form a square, and then at different angles to form a variety of designs. A stage later involved the use of the eight trigrams, the swastika, and the key-fret motif. These were then augmented by the introduction of circular and curved patterns. When such basic elements of design are reinforced with the familiar floral scrolls, and the wave and cloud formations, one has the essential ingredients for an infinite variety of decorative schemes. Plant and animal life were another artistic addition to the repertoire, especially in the popular theme of the squirrels and the vine. Landscape and figures, two of the most elaborate subjects for the wood-carver, were also introduced. The former perpetuated the traditional style developed in the T'ang and Sung Dynasties, where rocks and ancient trees complemented the grandeur of the towering mountains and cascading rivers. The figure subjects generally portrayed scenes of palace life and famous personages of the past. When the landscape elements were combined with these historical anecdotes, they represented dramatic scenes of vital significance.

In pursuit of a creative idea, the wood-carver shows the important role his imagination has to play in determining the most artistic way in which to utilize the particular wood at hand. Consideration is first given to the natural growth of the basic material, for which the main source of inspiration comes from nature itself. Appreciation of the plain surface is just as important, since the finished article should display a complete picture from every side and from every angle.

Lattice work, a characteristic feature of ornamented wood, is used for dividing rooms, for doorways and for internal decoration. It is used most advantageously to enclose the area between the floor and roof in temples and garden pavilions, for the effect of light penetrating the open spaces emphasizes the beauty of the design.

The art of the wood-carver is seen at its most ingenious when applied to the objects for the scholar's writing table, which traditionally, by allusion to classic literature, have been the means of expressing his artistic and literary pursuits. These objects took the form of wrist-rests, brush-rests, brush-pots, water containers, and flower vases. They were sometimes fashioned in boxwood, mulberry, sycamore or olive, but usually in bamboo, that favourite and most versatile medium, for the smooth and straight jointed hollow stem and the knotted and distorted roots can both be worked in a variety of ways to achieve the ultimate in graceful contours.

The cylindrical brush-pots are made from a cross section of the stem, cut so that the natural partition at the knot between the two joints forms the base of the receptacle. The decoration can be carved in high and low relief or in openwork, can be composed of floral and fruiting sprays or dragons, phoenixes and other birds, encircling the cylinder; a more ambitious design portrays scenes from ancient history and mythology. The typical wrist-rest is a section of one side of a joint, cut longitudinally so that the hand of the writer may be guided by the straight edge while his wrist is supported by the convexity. The wrist-rest is usually decorated with a lightly incised design, often accompanied by an inscription, or the latter, with perhaps a signature and seals, can appear as the only decorative element. The shape is a cherished survival from ancient times, and prior to the T'ang Dynasty such slips of bamboo were used for writing and strung together into books. Bamboo frequently makes the framework of fans, and like many other woods was used for carving quaint little objects of a purely decorative character such as animals in a naturalistic setting and sprays of fruit and flowers.

China is rich and abundant in flora, and the wild and cultivated varieties supply favourite motives for the carver. Like the lotus, sacred to Buddhism, some flowers are selected for their religious associations. The Taoists take as their sacred plant the manifold floral emblems of longevity, pride of place going to the peach, whose fruit, ripening but once in three thousand years, confers on mortals the coveted gift of immortality. Other frequently-used emblems are the branching fungus and the 'Three Friends'—the pine, the bamboo, and the prunus—the first two because they flourish in winter and the third because it blossoms from the leafless stalks in extreme old age.

The wood-carver also found the dried gourd a good decorative medium. Sometimes the surface was covered with incised designs, in other instances the soft young gourd is forced tightly into a patterned mould so that as it grows and expands the design is impressed on to its surface. A favourite use for these decorative gourds was the housing of crickets which the Chinese admired for their good vocal qualities. In the T'ang Dynasty, this quiet pastime changed when it was discovered that the songsters could be trained to fight, and so provide an alternative form of amusement. From the Sung period, the cult of the cricket became so popular that it was the subject of several treatises. These were devoted to precise details for the care and treatment of the many species then known to exist, and to descriptions of cricket cages of outstanding artistic merit which had been made for celebrated personalities. Many of these had perforated lids of jade, coral or ivory. These moulded gourds were used just as effectively for brush-holders, water containers, bowls and flower vases. Some of them were lacquered inside, and this plain surface was in turn often decorated with a design or an inscription in thinly applied gold.

For carving and incense, gharu wood and sandalwood are most in demand, and both were of the scented variety. They have been imported into China since the tenth century when a heavy import tax was levied on them, the customary procedure on all similar goods from abroad.

Gharu wood was held in the highest esteem, and the best came from Cambodia, according to Chau Ju-kua, that renowned twelfth-century traveller. A pair of small cups, fashioned from this wood are in two private collections. They are of irregular form and carved round the sides with a landscape scene of trees, mountains, rocks, paths, houses, and figures. On one cup is incised a small circular seal above the foot reading 'Chan Ch'eng', and on the other a square seal of similar size reading 'Chan Ch'eng Shang'. These seals are of the two Ch'eng brothers who worked in the time of the Emperor Sung Kao-tsung (1127–82), for whom they are said to have designed a bird cage with bamboo perches engraved with birds and flowers as fine as silken thread. Their work was considered miraculous, both for the creative genius of the design and the masterly manner of its execution. The cups are 4.5 in (11.5 cm) tall. Gharu wood or *chen-hsiang (aquilaria agallocha)* is so called because it sinks when immersed in water.

Sandalwood smoulders so well that it is considered the best for incense. It has been used for carving Buddhistic figures since early times, and is still considered the best medium for making their rosary beads, numbering one hundred and eight large and eighteen small. Traditionally, the latter are carved to represent the Eighteen Lohan. The best sandalwood comes from Cambodia, Annam and India. Fan sticks were also fashioned from this scented wood, which according to Chau Ju-kua was brought to China in the tenth century.

Buddhist statuary of the Chin, Sung and Yüan periods has already been discussed in connection with stone sculpture (see pages 173–80). The following are two carved wood examples.

Since there is nothing of the impressionistic art of the Sung Dynasty about the first figure (Plate 183), it seems that sculpture was the medium least affected by change and continued as before in a spirit that is reminiscent of the rather voluptuous figures of late T'ang.

The date of the next figure is of particular significance for it gives a positive attribution to a type of sculpture that had formerly been labelled T'ang or Ming 'renaissance' of T'ang (Plate 184). The distinguishing characteristics appear to be the slightly oval face with square jaw, and the stranded hair which now encircles the ears and covers the shoulders. The linear movements are accentuated by a winged V-shaped hemline and graceful drapery folds, which are clearly a revival of an earlier style. These statues originally formed part of a group of three or more deities flanking a central Buddha image, and are as colourful and as grand in scale as those impressive figures of the former T'ang Dynasty.

During the Ming Dynasty (1368–1644) both simple and elaborate pieces of carved wood were made in great quantities for the palace and for the scholar's writing table. It is regrettable that so few of the carver's names have been recorded, and that even fewer precisely dated pieces are known. Sometimes an object was inscribed with a poem, and infrequently with the name of the maker, whose identity was often

honey yellow to deep mahogany, with many spotted varieties to relieve the monochrome shades. On some pieces an attractive decorative theme is achieved by leaving the skin on and then darkening the design with pigment; sometimes burning metal tools are used to engrave the ornament. The skin being lighter in colour than the wood, the design can very effectively be left in reserve to show up against the darker background. The selection of the bamboo to be carved must be made very carefully. There are many varieties to choose from, and the deciding factor really lies simply in the grain of the wood, which as it must be completely smooth to the touch is known as 'jade bamboo'. Other grades render the task of carving very difficult, or impossible. This preliminary task is only the more obvious hurdle, and the subtle technique involved in the creation of a masterpiece remains the prerogative of the carver himself.

It is evident that by the beginning of the T'ang Dynasty bamboo carving had achieved a high degree of artistic merit. This should put the inception of the technique some decades earlier. Certainly the degree of excellence was maintained during the Sung Dynasty, and was to become an even more specialized technique when the Ming Dynasty began its reign of nearly three hundred years.

The three most famous of the Ming bamboo carvers, appearing in contemporary literature, were undoubtedly Chiang Hsi-huang, P'u Chung-ch'ien, and Chu San-sung, who signed his works 'San Sung'. The last named was the famous son of a distinguished father, Chu Hsiao-sung (Chu Hao), and a member of the Chia-ting School, which specialized in bas-relief carving. Chu San-sung became famous for his bamboo brush-pots, all of them decorated with elaborate figure subjects in sculptural relief and executed with a fine attention to detail. Chiang Hsi-huang, whose paraphernalia for the scholar's study excelled all others, specialized in arm-rests and in brush-holders which he decorated with landscape scenes. He is said to have originated the idea of 'cameo carving'. In this technique, the uppermost skin of the bamboo serves as the design layer, with the smooth inner layer acting as the background, thus creating a design in two relief layers. Very often the bamboo was carved while still green, so that very exacting details could be carved from the skin and left in low relief. Later, through various processes of drying and staining, the background is darkened, which makes the design areas appear lighter in colour, and because they were carved at a young age they often assume delightful spring-like shades of pale greenish-blue. Chiang Hsi-huang also specialized in carving ivory, although very few examples exist. One of these rare pieces, in the form of an ink-cake stand, is decorated in slight relief with an old man seated in a boat fishing beneath a pine tree; overhanging rocks and mountains in the distance, are testimony to his skill in this field. None of his pieces are dated, and only bear his signature 'Hsi-huang'. P'u Chung-ch'ien was equally skilled in the creation of bamboo masterpieces by turning the twisted root and gnarled joint into elegant trinkets. One of his most delightful achievements is a paper-clip of carved bamboo cleverly executed from a single piece of the wood to form a scholar seated by a rock under a pine tree. The object is not dated, and only bears his signature 'Chung-ch'ien'.

There are some nine other Ming bamboo carvers whose names have been recorded. They each specialized in a particular object, or group of objects, and these included the making of flutes, the framework of fans, the cutting of seals, and all the small decorative objects so much admired by the Chinese *cognoscente*. The last, but by no means the least accomplishments of these craftsmen, were the paraphernalia for the scholar's writing table; the cylindrical containers to hold the brushes used in writing or painting, the water-droppers to wet the ink-stone, the arm-rests to give freedom of movement to the writing hand, and the ornamental flower vases to hold one single perfect blossom.

V

Ivory and Horn

15

IVORY

ACCORDING TO THE *Ko Ku Yao Lun*, 'Ivory comes from the Western and Southern Barbarian Countries, as well as from Kuangsi [Province] and from Annam. Tusks to be found in the Southern Barbarian Regions are long and thick whereas those found in Kuangsi [Province] and in Annam are short and thin. When the elephant tusk is newly cut, if it is of the finest quality it is pink in section. [A] Ivory from Yunnan can be made into combs. But good (combs) should be cut vertically; for those cut horizontally are very brittle.'

The elephant has been indigenous to China since Shang times. Ivory was one of the commodities required by the court at Anyang, thus necessitating expeditions to find sources of supply which often led into regions far from the capital. The royal tombs of this period are surviving testimony to the skill of the artisans, for alongside the magnificent ceremonial bronze vessels are to be found wrought ivory work, musical instruments, and sculptured marble.

Gradually the spread of human population had driven the elephant south of the Yellow River to the densely wooded banks of the Yangtze Valley. From here they had again to retreat and by the second century B.C. the breed had become virtually extinct in China except in the provinces of Kuangtung and Yunnan. Although it is said that the elephant was used for domestic purposes in ancient times, there is no reliable evidence for this fact or for the animal being employed in the field of battle. Yet it was already generally known that by the second century B.C. it was so employed in other countries. This fact substantiated by Chang Ch'ien, a minister under Emperor Wu Ti, who became famous as an explorer when he returned to China in 126 B.C. from a memorable visit to Western countries, including India, where he found this versatile pachyderm used as a means of transporting troops in times of crisis.

The provinces of Kuangtung and Yunnan continued to be a source of supply until the beginning of the T'ang Dynasty. Then demand far exceeded domestic output and it became one of the chief imports from Africa and India, according to a

T'ang pharmacopoeia, which also comments on the value of ivory as an inlay of furniture. Support for this statement is to be found in the Shoso-in Repository, which provides a living memorial to the glories of this age when ivory was used to fashion the complete article as well as an instrument of inlay. Such pieces were among the personal possessions of the late Emperor-Abdicant, Shomu-tenno, which, as we have seen, were presented by his widow, Komio, to the Great Buddha after his death in 756. The day of the gift was 22 July, and was intended for the dedication of an image to the Great Buddha, a project for which he had long and earnestly laboured. In the northern section of this famous shrine is to be found our earliest precisely dated piece, a most important object which anticipates the event by almost three years.

186. **753** IVORY TAG inscribed in gold 'The Shinkio Sutra constantly carried by the Empress-Abdicant (Gensho) when the Court was at Heijo (Nara)', and on the reverse the date 'Twenty-ninth day, third month, fifth year [6 May 753] of Tempio-shoho. Prepared for the celebration of the Great Buddha of the Todaiji', though the sutra itself is missing. Length 7.5 in (19 cm) *Shoso-in, Nara, Japan*

There are several other ivory objects, including sixteen daggers variously embellished, and six-foot rules engraved on both sides with designs of birds and animals.

For the talented craftsman, ivory, with its close-grained texture and resilient surface, is the ideal substance for the most intricately carved designs, of which the following is an admirable specimen, having great appeal to a sensitive and refined taste—it appears to be the only precisely dated example from the Sung Dynasty.

187. **968** Elegant FIGURE of a high-ranking official, standing serene, wearing a long-sleeved gown and a winged hat. Darkening by age and incense smoke may have deprived the original of some of its inherent characteristics, but on the other hand, they seem to have endowed him with the sombre appeal appropriate to his exalted position. On the back of the figure is a carefully incised inscription reading: 'First year [968] of K'ai-po', and below it, 'Respectfully designed by Tsung Yüan-hsieh', an official of the Imperial court in the last quarter of the tenth century. Height 6.5 in (16.5 cm) *Formerly David Collection*

This figure is one of the few surviving pieces which has acquired by natural causes a chameleon-like change from ivory-white to smoky-black, an effect which cannot be achieved by artificial methods. The tusk probably entered China through Canton, the chief port for overseas luxuries, including ivory, according to the Arab merchant, Suleyman, writing in the middle of the ninth century. In the Sung Annals for around the year 995, ivory was still one of the chief imported articles, like medicine, pearls and rhinoceros horn, which were traded for Chinese gold, silver and porcelain.

Maritime trade, which had been steadily increasing throughout the T'ang

Dynasty, surpassed all records in the twelfth century, when Hangchou was the Southern Sung capital and Ch'üan-chou the chief port. Although herds of wild elephants still roamed the forests of Kuangtung and Yunnan, ivory, which had by now become a government monopoly, continued to be one of the most regularly imported articles. This situation continued under the Mongols, who found the material so attractive that they established in 1263 a Bureau for Carvings in Ivory and Rhinoceros Horn, where more than one hundred and forty workmen were employed in the making of furniture and furnishings for the Imperial household. Ch'üan-chou, which was still an active port for overseas trade, also became an important ship-building yard and a centre for Moslem worship, many of the mosques retaining some of the distinctive features of their land of origin. Marco Polo, who was in China from 1275–92, relates how 'Five thousand elephants of the Great Khan were exhibited in procession at the New Year, covered with gay saddle cloths and carrying plate and furniture on their backs.'

The Chinese have, since ancient times, inlaid ivory with turquoise, and at various later periods they have enamelled it artificially, or embellished it with lacquer and gilding. A much more attractive result is obtained from frequent handling, for this produces the warm tints and suffused glow that transforms it into a soft seductive material, an effect that cannot otherwise be achieved. It is a most delightful piece produced by such natural causes that represents our next precisely dated example.

188. **1400** CUP for drinking, of oval pear-shaped form and of a mellow honey tone, with attractively delineated crackle darkened by age and habitual fondling. One end is fitted with a silver ring and handle in the form of a finely etched prunus flower. The carefully written inscription at the mouth of the vessel reads: 'Made by Pei-kung in the second year [1400] of Chien-wên.' Length 4.5 in (11.4 cm) *Museum of Fine Arts, Boston, Gift of Eugene and Paul Bernat*

From early Ming times direct trade was established between China and Africa, mainly as a result of the energetic Admiral Cheng Ho, a eunuch in the emperor's service. In 1405 he set forth on his first voyage in command of a fleet of junks that lay at anchor in Soochou creek. His native province was Yunnan, and as a Muslim he was ideally suited to lead these expeditions, since Islam was the state religion of most ports of call on his itinerary. He returned triumphant with surprising information on navigation and foreign customs, with many fascinating curiosities, and with much tribute from native rulers.

It is virtually impossible to distinguish the differences that exist after the tusk is cut and carved, between the Asiatic and the African varieties, so that place of origin cannot be used as indicative of date, and other methods must be found for correct attribution.

There are numerous ivory figures, seals and other objects attributable to the Ming Dynasty, which was a period of the highest technical skill in all the minor arts. Signatures are virtually unknown and precisely dated pieces quite scarce. Two seals from the time of Cheng Ho have been traced, and two other objects from the sixteenth century.

189. **1418** Square SEAL with handle in the form of a lion seated on a ground of fungus scrolls, and with an inscription on one side reading: 'Dedicated to Hui-ling at the first moon, twenty-second day, sixteenth year [1418] of Yung-lo.' Height 3.3 in (8.5 cm) *British Museum*

190. **1427** Square SEAL with handle in the form of a Buddhist 'wheel of the law', and with a

dedicatory inscription reading: 'Presented to the Lama Ch'ao-pa Tsang-pu in the second year [1427] of Hsüan-tê.' The face is carved to impress four characters reading: 'The seal of Yang-shan-tsung.' Height 2.7 in (6.9 cm) *Mr and Mrs R. H. Palmer*

The seal was presumably intended for a Tibetan ecclesiastic on a visit to China, and the characters, which mean literally 'expounding religion', may well have been the name by which he came to be known there. Perhaps the seal was made in anticipation of a proposed visit by the ecclesiastic in 1427, but destiny decided he should not receive his auspicious gift.

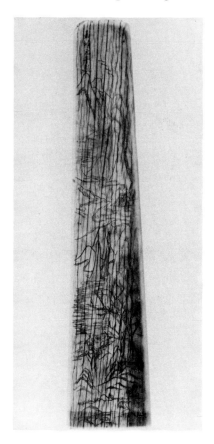

191. **1522** TABLET, probably used as a wrist rest, engraved on one side with a crane standing on a rock, surrounded by waves and a flying bat with a streamer of two cash; the reverse with a mountainous landscape, trees, and pagodas; fine pale brown patination. An inscription above the landscape reads: 'Made in the first year [1522] of Chia-ching.' The court tablet is the insignia of office held before the breast at court while having an audience with the emperor. Height 8.7 in (22.1 cm) *Mrs Walport*

192. **1576** BOX AND COVER in the form of a Chinese lute, supported at one end by two flat circular projections and at the other by two indented corner feet. Below these are five tiny nodules around which the strings of the instrument were threaded to connect them with the five tiny circular holes on the lid of the box. On the base is an inscription reading: 'Made in the fourth year [1576] of Wan-li.' Length 8.2 in (20.8 cm) *Formerly David Collection*

16

HORN

For the Chinese, the rhinoceros horn possessed magical properties; it detected poison, it prolonged life, it cured many ailments, and it was an aphrodisiac. It was also one of the ingredients used in the composition of certain inks. From the fifth century we learn that the Chinese extolled its virtues, and for that reason it rated high on their list of imported articles, a custom that still prevailed in the middle of the ninth century, according to Suleyman, the Arab merchant who visited Canton at this time. Mas'udi, a traveller from Baghdad, writing almost a hundred years later, reports that the same conditions existed, while in the thirteenth century Chau Ju-kua, commissioner for foreign trade in Ch'üan Chou, adds the territories of Annam, Java and Sumatra to that of India as the chief areas for the exportation of horn to China. In addition, he mentions the Berbera Coast of Africa as the supplier of the largest horns, but whether this attribute was a virtue, apart from the greater area of decorative surface it provided, is a matter of speculation.

The one-horned as well as the two-horned variety of rhinoceros is recorded as having existed in China. A splendid model of the latter is one of the outstanding Shang Dynasty (c. 1550–c. 1030 B.C.) bronze treasures in the Avery Brundage Collection; the former appears in the *Po ku t'u lu* in the shape of a Shang Dynasty bronze kettle. The northern climate apparently did not suit the animal, which seems to have disappeared after the Chou Dynasty (c. 1030–256 B.C.). They fared better in the south, for as early as the second century of our era they were considered worthy tribute gifts.

According to the *Ko Ku Yao Lun*: 'Rhinoceros horn comes from both the Southern and the Western Barbarian Regions as well as from Yunnan. Those which are long, thick, transparent, dappled with delightful designs are expensive. But the long, slender, light and unpleasantly dappled pieces, are only good for medicinal use. There is a variety with a grain like fish roe, generally known as "millet spots", each of which has an eye like a "millet eye" and so called. This kind of horn is known as mountain rhinoceros horn. Rhinoceros horn pieces should be smooth and mellow; the "millet spots" or other designs that are in the horn should be pleasing to the eye. Its colour should be either lac black or chestnut-kernel yellow: and the horn should be translucent from end to end. It should show clearly "clouds" on the top and "raindrops" at the bottom. Such are the criteria for fine pieces. The most valuable horns have in them designs resembling definite objects, extending from the bottom of a piece to the top. Two other varieties are also valuable—the double-dappled (yellow on black and black on yellow) and the plain dappled (yellow on black). The inverted dapple (yellow spots barred with black) is a less valuable variety. An even less valuable kind has a darker yellow colour dappled with spots like wild pepper seeds. The pure black variety is the cheapest, good enough merely for making chessmen or similar objects.'

'The rhinoceros horn pieces on girdles are often made of ordinary horn with a thin layer of rhinoceros horn stuck on top. This can be ascertained by examining whether the patterns on the upper surface correspond with those on the lower. One can also find them by looking for their seams where the layers are stuck together. In some cases, the natural patterns are imperfect when they are dyed black with certain chemicals. In that way, there should be no "clouds" at the top nor "raindrops" at the bottom, and where black and yellow diffuse into each other, it becomes dull and pure black. When the "millet spots" are not perfectly circular, it means that the dapples are not in their centres by nature. So the horn is not in its natural state. All these points should be carefully noted.'

'Rhinoceros horn pieces should be beautifully carved and carefully shaped. They should be frequently handled and examined, but should not be exposed to the sun lest they become dry.'

This last passage is a further indication by the Chinese of their high regard for rhinoceros horn. This can be augmented by the large number of vessels and ornamental paraphernalia created out of this mass of agglutinated hair, which forms the composition of the horn. The original yellowish grey colour can be transformed into shades varying from mellow honey blond to deep golden brown, according to the amount of staining and polishing the surface receives. When the desired effect is achieved the horn is used to fashion dishes and bowls, a multiplicity of drinking vessels, brush holders, wrist rests, and book covers for the writing table, while for the dressing table, cosmetic boxes, combs and hairpins are but a few of the articles for which this attractive material has been so successfully employed since T'ang times.

To find evidence for our earliest visual documentation of horn we must again turn to the Shoso-in Repository. Among many treasured objects were four pairs of sword hilts, four knives, either with horn hilts or horn sheaths, a horn foot-rule, four horn sceptres, one inset with glass and crystal balls in gold, the handle carved with the word 'Todaiji' in red, and the following item which is for our present purpose the most important object in the storehouse.

193. **811** Shallow horn DISH described as a medicine vessel and inscribed in ink: 'Examined on the seventeenth day of the ninth month of the second year [7 October 811] of Konin.' The shape of the vessel is similar to one of the Ch'ang-sha lacquer dishes, but without the ears. Length 17.4 in (44.2 cm) *Shoso-in, Nara, Japan*

Very few precisely dated examples of horn exist, although there are a number of pieces which bear the mark of a reign-period; from the Sung Dynasty, for example, that of Hsüan-ho (1119–26). From the Yüan Dynasty, again no precisely dated pieces are known, despite the establishment of a workshop which produced various household articles of rhinoceros horn for the royal court. This was a speciality of the manufactory, and their creations included girdle ornaments, belts, beads, curtain weights and furniture made either entirely of horn or with horn inlaid to form part of a decorative scheme.

It is the same story with the early Ming period, and although a boat-shaped cup bearing the six-character reign-mark of Hsüan-tê (1426–35) is known, it is not until late in the sixteenth century that a precisely dated specimen is available. There are other pieces that bear a reign-mark, but without a cyclical year their attribution is rather too indefinite to be of real help in the present treatise. The two following pieces are of the Wan-li period (1573–1619) and are precisely dated.

194. **1580** CUP with dragon handle, key fret border round the lip; the body ornamented with an archaistic bronze design in slight relief. On the base is inscribed a four-character mark reading: 'Eighth year [1580] of Wan-li' above a seal. Diameter 5.7 in (14.5 cm) *Formerly Madame Wannieck Collection, Paris*

Dated to the same year is a cup in the Museum voor Land en Volkenkunde, Rotterdam.

195. **1599** FIGURE OF KUAN-YIN pouring balm from her vase on an attendant, whose hands are clasped in adoration. The piece is inscribed on the base: 'Joyfully offered by the disciple Mi Wan-chung to the Chin Kang Tung [a Buddhist Shrine] of Chiu Hua Shan on the twelfth day of the third month of the twenty-sixth year [1599] of Wan-li.' Mi Wan-chung was a well-known painter of the late Ming period, who died in 1628. Length 6.5 in (16.5 cm) *Fogg Art Museum, Harvard (Bequest of Mrs J. N. Brown)*

In Europe during the sixteenth and seventeenth centuries, rhinoceros horn seems to have been almost as popular as blue and white and *blanc-de-chine*, for it is represented in the majority of the famous royal collections of the time. Some of the earliest examples were brought together by the Habsburgs and are now in the Kunsthistorisches Museum in Vienna. Other collections are to be found in the Pitti Palace, Florence, where several of the cups have received a European silver-gilt fitting attached to the mouth-rim and to the base of the foot. In England some fine specimens are to be found in the Tradescant Collection, presented to the University of Oxford by Elias Ashmole in 1683, and in the collection formed by Sir Hans

Sloane and bequeathed by him to the British Museum in 1753. In the Sloane Collection there is also a drawing by Dürer based on a sketch of the live rhinoceros which was sent in 1515 as a gift to King Manuel of Portugal by Muzaffar, king of Cambay. In the following year this same rhinoceros was despatched as a present to Pope Leo X, but the vessel carrying the animal encountered a storm and all aboard were lost at sea.

Chronological Table

T'ANG		618–906

FIVE DYNASTIES	Later Liang	907–922	
	Later T'ang (Turkic)	923–936	
	Later Chin (Turkic)	936–948	907–960
	Later Han (Turkic)	946–950	
	Later Chou	951–960	

Liao (Khitan Tartars)		907–1125
Hsi-hsia (Tangut Tibetan)		990–1227

SUNG	Northern Sung	960–1126	
	Southern Sung	1127–1279	960–1279

Chin (Jurchen Tartars)		1115–1234
YÜAN (Mongols)		1260–1368
MING		1368–1644

Hung-wu	1368–1398
Chien-wên	1399–1402
Yung-lo	1403–1424
Hung-hsi	1425
Hsüan-tê	1426–1435
Chêng-t'ung	1436–1449
Ching-t'ai	1450–1457
T'ien-shun	1457–1464
Ch'êng-hua	1465–1487
Hung-chih	1488–1505
Chêng-tê	1506–1521
Chia-ching	1522–1566
Lung-ch'ing	1567–1572
Wan-li	1573–1619
T'ai-ch'ang	1620
T'ien-ch'i	1621–1627
Ch'ung-chêng	1628–1644

Select Bibliography

Ayers, John. *The Baur Collection of Chinese Ceramics*, Geneva, 1969–74.

Bary, Theodore de, editor. *Sources of Chinese Tradition*, Columbia University Press, New York, 1960.

Brankston, A. D. *Early Ming Wares of Ching-tê-chên*, Peking, 1938.

Bushell, Stephen W. *Oriental Ceramic Art*, New York, 1897.

Bushell, Stephen W. *Description of Chinese Pottery and Porcelain; Being a Translation of the T'ao Shuo*, Oxford, 1910.

Bushell, Stephen W. *Chinese Art*, London, 1914.

Couling, Samuel. *The Encyclopaedia Sinica*, Shanghai, 1917.

David, Sir Percival. 'A Commentary on Ju Ware', *Transactions of the Oriental Ceramic Society*, 1936–7.

David, Sir Percival. *Chinese Connoisseurship; The Ko Ku Yao Lun; The Essential Criteria of Antiquities*, London, 1971.

Donnelly, P. J. *Blanc de Chine*, London, 1969.

Dubosc, Jean-Pierre. *Exhibition of Chinese Art*, Palazzo Ducale, Venice, 1954.

Garner, Sir Harry. *Oriental Blue and White*, London, 1954; third ed., London, 1970.

Garner, Sir Harry. *Chinese and Japanese Cloisonné Enamels*, London, 1962; second ed., London, 1970.

Garner Collection, Chinese and Associated Lacquer from the, British Museum, 1973.

Giles, Herbert A. *A Glossary of Reference*, Shanghai, 1900.

Gompertz, G. St. G. M. *Chinese Celadon Wares*, London, 1958; second ed., London, 1980.

Goodrich, L. Carrington. *A Short History of the Chinese People*, London, 1948.

Gray, Basil. 'Art Under the Mongol Dynasties of China and Persia', *Oriental Art*, I, 1955.

Gray, Basil. *Early Chinese Pottery and Porcelain*, London, 1953.

Grousset, René. *Chinese Art and Culture*, London, 1959.

Gyllensvard, Bo. *Chinese Gold and Silver in the Carl Kempe Collection*, Stockholm, 1953.

Gyllensvard, Bo. *Chinese Ceramics in the Carl Kempe Collection*, Stockholm, 1964.

Gyllensvard, B., and Pope, John A. *Chinese Art from the Collection of H.M. Gustaf VI Adolf of Sweden*, New York, 1966.

Hobson, R. L. *Chinese Pottery and Porcelain*, New York, 1915.

Hobson, R. L. *The Wares of the Ming Dynasty*, London, 1923.

Hobson, R. L. *The Art of the Chinese Potter from the Han Dynasty to the End of the Ming*, London, 1923.

Hobson, R. L. *The George Eumorfopoulos Collection, A Catalogue of the Chinese, Corean, and Persian Pottery and Porcelain*, London, 1925–8.

Hobson, R. L. *Chinese Ceramics in Private Collections*, London, 1931.

Hobson, R. L. *Chinese Pottery and Porcelain in the Collection of Sir Percival David, Bt.*, London, 1934.

Hobson, R. L., *Handbook of the Pottery and Porcelain of the Far East in the Department of Oriental Antiquities and Ethnography*, British Museum, 1937.

Honey, William B. *The Ceramic Art of China and other Countries of the Far East*, London, 1945.

Jenyns, Soame. *Ming Pottery and Porcelain*, London, 1953.

Jenyns, Soame, and Watson, W. *Chinese Art: the Minor Arts*, London, 1963.

Lane, Arthur. 'The Gaignières-Fonthill Vase; A Chinese Porcelain of About 1300', *Burlington Magazine*, CIII, April 1961.

Lee, Sherman E. *A History of Far Eastern Art*, New York, 1964.

Lee, Sherman E. and Ho Wai-kam. *Chinese Art Under the Mongols; The Yüan Dynasty (1279–1368)*, Cleveland Museum of Art, 1968.

Lefebvre, d'Argencé, René-Yvon. *Chinese Ceramics in the Avery Brundage Collection*, San Francisco, 1967.

Lefebvre, d'Argencé, René-Yvon. *Chinese Treasures from the Avery Brundage Collection* (exhibition catalogue, New York, 1968).

London, Arts Council Gallery. *Loan Exhibition of Chinese Blue and White Porcelains, 14th to 19th Centuries*, 16 Dec. 1953–23 Jan. 1954.

London, Arts Council Gallery. *Loan Exhibition of the Arts of the Ming Dynasty*, 15 Nov.–14 Dec. 1957.

London, Arts Council Gallery. *Loan Exhibition of the Arts of the Sung Dynasty*, 16 June–23 July 1960.

London, Arts Council Gallery. *The Seligman Collection of Oriental Art*, 7 May–7 June 1966.

London, Royal Academy of Arts. *The Chinese Exhibition; A Commemorative Catalogue of the International Exhibition of Chinese Art*, Nov. 1935–March 1936, London 1935.

Los Angeles, County Museum of Art. *The Arts of the T'ang Dynasty*, 8 Jan.–17 Feb. 1957.

Low-Beer, Fritz. 'Chinese Lacquer of the Early 15th Century', *Bulletin of the Museum of Far Eastern Antiquities*, No. 22, Stockholm 1950.

Low-Beer, Fritz. 'Chinese Lacquer of the Middle and Late Ming Period', *Bulletin of the Museum of Far Eastern Antiquities*, No. 24, Stockholm 1952.

Mayers, William Frederich. *The Chinese Reader's Manual*, Shanghai, 1924.

Olschki, Leonardo. *Guillaume Boucher, A French Artist at the Court of the Khans*, Baltimore, 1946.

Paris, Musée de l'Orangerie. *Arts de la Chine ancienne*, Exhibition, Paris, 1937.

Peking. *New Archaeology Finds in China*, Peking, 1972.

Peking. *The Genius of China*, Exhibition of archaeological finds of the People's Republic of China held at the Royal Academy, London, Sept. 1973–Jan. 1974.

Percival David Foundation of Chinese Art. Illustrated Catalogues of Sections 1, 3, 4, 5, 6, and 7, London, 1953–71.

Pope, John A. *Fourteenth Century Blue and White in the Topkapu Sarayi Müzeei, Istanbul*, Washington, 1952.

Sickman, Laurence. 'Chinese Silver of the Yüan Dynasty', *Archives of the Chinese Art Society of America*, XI (1957).

Sickman, Laurence. 'A Ch'ing-pai Porcelain Figure Bearing a Date', *Archives of the Chinese Art Society of America*, XV (1961).

Speiser, Werner. *China, Spirit and Society*, London, 1960.

Sullivan, Michael. *The Arts of China*, London, 1967.

Sullivan, Michael. *Chinese Art. Recent Discoveries*, London, 1973.

Transactions of the Oriental Ceramic Society. 'The Arts of the Ming Dynasty', XXX, 1957.

Transactions of the Oriental Ceramic Society. 'The Arts of the Sung Dynasty', XXXII, 1960.

Tregear, M. *Guide to the Chinese Ceramics in the Department of Eastern Art*, Ashmolean Museum, Oxford, 1966.

Tsui Chi. *A Short History of Chinese Civilization*, New York, 1943.

Washington, D.C., National Gallery of Art. *Chinese Art Treasures, a Selected Group of Objects from the Chinese National Museum and the Chinese Central Museum*, Taichung, Taiwan. Exhibition held 1961–2, in Washington, New York, Boston, Chicago, and San Francisco. Lausanne, 1961.

Watson, William. *China before the Han Dynasty*, London, 1961.

Watson, William. *Style in the Arts of China*, London, 1974.

Index